THIS WEIGHTLESS WORLD

THIS
WEIGHTLESS
WORLD
A NOVEL
ADAM
SOTO

ASTRA HOUSE | NEW YORK

For information about permission to reproduce selections from this book, please contact permissions@astrahouse.com.

This is a work of fiction. Names, characters, places, and incidents are products of the author's imagination or are used fictitiously. Any resemblance to actual events, locales, or persons, living or dead, is entirely coincidental.

Astra House
A Division of Astra Publishing House
astrahouse.com

Library of Congress Cataloging-in-Publication Data [TK]
ISBN: 9781662600630

This is an advance reader's edition from uncorrected proofs. If any material from the book is to be quoted in a review, please check it against the text in the final bound book. Dates, prices, and manufacturing details are subject to change or cancellation without notice.

Design by Richard Oriolo

The text is set in Utopia.
The titles are set in Bureau Grotesque.

to my family

THIS WEIGHTLESS WORLD

ONE

Dear Babichev,

What was it you called the static we heard, listening for enemy secrets

in Moscow? Kindling air?

SEVERINO "SEVI" DEL TORO STOOD on Milwaukee Avenue in Wicker Park and watched a brigade of police horses cleave traffic, their blindered faces bobbing over cars as they passed. Heavy coats and champagne drifted along the sidewalks, tourists and Chicagoans returning to their short-term rentals and apartments for the evening's festivities. Overhead, a Blue Line train shuddered toward Damen station, shaking snow off its tracks. Near where Sevi stood, three men in sweatsuits quit hustling CD-R demos just long enough to watch the cops pass. It was New Year's Eve, and Sevi had given up on Wicker Park years ago. The young professionalism of the place, the 1920s bank vault undergoing conversion into North America's most beautiful Walgreens pharmacy, the gentrification—he was over it. But Reckless Records was still around, and a week had passed since he'd asked one of their sales associates to hold an original pressing of Bartók's six-volume *Mikrokosmos*. The store wanted way too much—many of the sleeves had been gummed by baby or dog; in his opinion, the collection itself was barely listenable, an amalgam of piano exercises and underdeveloped larks—but holding the music in his hands inside the record store only a moment ago, Sevi had felt the Hungarian's genius spilling out of the tattered LP box set and paid the cashier without further hesitation. Outside the record shop, following the horses up Milwaukee and holding the same plastic Reckless Records bag as everyone else around him, he felt guilty for having spent the money.

Then, at Six Corners, that warped star-shaped intersection at the center of Wicker Park, the horses parted ways, nine in total, clodding off down Milwaukee, North, and Damen, in groups of three, between the brick buildings and the cars. Their departure had the appearance of something apocalyptic. At the animals' separation, the concrete, flesh, and steel of the street pitched to a petrified ring—as if on the last day of 2011, Chicago was nearing the end of the world, and, in the ensuing stillness, Sevi was hearing the last echo of existence before the silence. In reality, in less than six hours, Wicker Park would be a minefield of vomit and abandoned shoes, glitter, fake eyelashes, and those plastic commemorative 2012-frame glasses, a neighborhood filled with drunken revelry.

Records in tow, he hurried home to heat up some carnitas and listen to the box set's first sixty-six tiny tracks—books I and II. He was in bed by ten.

In the morning, feathers of snow listed outside the apartment's bay window and the city's bathwater light wet the peeling wood floor. Further off, runny clouds blotted the sky. The horses were out there somewhere, Sevi thought, the ones from yesterday, past his neighborhood of Humboldt Park, huddled in their stables, sleeping off their New Year's Eve shift. He felt the absence of his phone and pictured the device in a kitchen drawer, where he'd put the thing whenever it didn't stop buzzing and lighting up—he refused to turn it off or switch it to airplane mode because then what was the point of even having a cell phone? He'd missed a text message from his parents, prematurely wishing him a Happy New Year—left around nine o'clock, their usual bedtime—invitations from friends to join them at parties and bars, a picture of a shoe. In a long voice mail, a crowd of blown-out voices chanted his name. Then the phone went dark and resumed its position, cold and glassy in the pocket of his sweats. That petrified ringing persisted in his ears.

Mahler padded up for breakfast. Sevi had adopted the cat with his ex-girlfriend Ramona a year ago. Six months later, Ramona moved to San Francisco. He pulled a bag of dry food from beneath the sink and filled her bowl atop the fridge. The bowl had a jagged Navajo design. Ramona had picked it. In two weightless movements, Mahler drifted from the floor to the sink's edge to the top of the fridge. Sevi remembered waking up—how before he knew he was a person, he'd known he was alone. He noticed a section of eggshell-white wall next to the bed he swore he'd never seen before.

Corner to corner, antique furniture Ramona had dug out of dumpsters and pulled from curbs, reupholstered, and rearranged contended for space in the apartment, creating an Escher of discolored textile swatches, dull wooden and brass feet, fraying macramé knots, cotton and jute slings suspending tiny upended terracotta pots, and something that chimed but could never be found. Coming home had at times been for Sevi like walking into a thrift shop in a city he'd never visited before. More of the same but somewhere else. At night, under the glow of an incandescent bulb or by candlelight, depending on Ramona's mood, the apartment had replicated any number of interiors featured in the vintage *Playboy*s and *Better Living*s she also collected. All the furniture remained where Ramona had left it last, forming a familiar labyrinth. Dust cast an umber shadow around the Danish coffee table. Trapped but comfortable, he'd navigated his way back to the record player in the living room and was reaching to put on the next vinyl when his pocket vibrated.

No matter who it is, I'm not answering it, he thought.

It was Ramona. He answered.

"Turn on the TV," she said.

She'd left behind a 22" and he'd given it away out of spite before realizing he liked having a TV.

"Um."

"Stream the news on the internet. You need to be watching the news."

He cleared his browser of whatever awful thing he'd looked up last and loaded the BBC. Trustworthy accents. Transnational perspective. He hated the British for everything else they did. From colonizing the world to The Beatles.

"Are you watching?" Ramona asked.

A beach ball revolved on his screen.

"It's loading."

"I told you I could get you a discount on a new laptop."

"I think it's the internet."

"It's not the internet."

An embedded video player streamed a black screen; written across the center, in white letters, the headline read: "SETI to Make Groundbreaking Announcement."

He had already forgotten Ramona's face somewhat. It wasn't disappearing but transforming, against his will. Punishment for having taken her face for granted, he thought. He was plagued with questions. Was her nose aquiline? Did aquiline mean Mediterranean? How many freckles were left on her right cheek? She'd lost or gained a few. Of her small, mobile mouth—constantly poised, she had a soft overbite—the only thing he remembered with certainty was her recessed canine, a tooth like the pretty, shorter girl shouldered out of pictures with tall friends. Maybe her face didn't matter, maybe that memory was too superficial. What about who she was? Who she really was? Deep down inside, as they say. Could he recall that? What about her humors, the aspects of her personality worn not on her skin but lining the insides of her organs; her soul, which lilted on her breath? All that information had mostly left him too, smoothed over by longing into a generic wash of ideals. She was funny, she was smart, she got him, she listened. It was all so nonspecific he could have a seizure. Certain notes to her laugh were leaving him. Laughter had been like a bird language between them. It could communicate the essentials—love, hunger, danger—for miles. They had these voices—Ramona did this German schoolboy thing and Sevi had this Iranian gynecologist character—it was kind of ignorant, but they could just get totally carried away, practically screaming until their stomachs killed . . . He would destroy her trying to remember her, like listening to a favorite record too many times.

"Are you still there?" she asked.

"I'm here, in the apartment in Chicago. Are you home?" he said.

He tried to concentrate. On her voice, the screen, the phone sliding down his face. How had they wound up in two different places?

"I'm home."

"What do you think it's going to be?"

"Life, Sevi."

Then, the only sound traveling between them, back and forth across America, was their breathing. The petrified ringing had stopped. A tartan scramble lifted from Sevi's feed to a livestream of an almost-empty parking lot at what he assumed was SETI headquarters. A few Priuses, a Nissan Leaf against the administrative brick structure, a coral sunrise flare. In the foreground, on a hill overlooking the lot, was a small cordoned-off section for media. Correspondents and crew talked and gestured under the whipping white tents, handed one another coffee and daubed lipstick. Someone said "shit," and the screen snapped to a cheap computer animation of a fuchsia orb hanging in black space. Breath caught on a microphone, everyone was asked to get settled. The orb began to move around two white glowing masses. Whatever the orb was, it did not complete a total revolution before the animation looped again. Sevi wondered if it was a glitch. Somewhere, people were still getting settled.

"Are you getting the SETI feed?" he asked Ramona.

"Yeah. Looks like crap."

Are we ready? a female voice asked over the feed.

I believe we are, a man said.

The fuchsia entity sliced another partial orbit around the stars.

Ladies and gentlemen of the media, and all of you following along at home, my name is Dr. Jill Tarter, Bernard M. Oliver Chair for SETI Research, and I'd like to welcome you to an exciting press conference here at the Carl Sagan Center. As you can tell by our graphic, it's a little impromptu, but I assure you this news cannot wait. We have asked all of you to join us on such short notice this New Year's Day to announce that the search for interstellar company is over. We have discovered extraterrestrial intelligence.

Sevi's hearing came in and out. There was talk of the vastness of the universe, how many stars had planets, and how many of those planets could potentially sustain life, but Ramona had called. He let out a few speculative "hms" and tried to keep track of his breath as his heart did ragtime. Evidently, they'd been reporting on the signal for months on scientific blogs, only they'd been referring to it as a series of "anomalous blasts," and nobody had paid it much mind. Debuting E.T. on New Year's Day was part of a marketing strategy.

Carl Sagan and other radio astronomers warned us as early as the 1960s that contact would bear little resemblance to the kinds depicted in science fiction films and books. We'd just as likely discover an infant signal from a thousand light-years away as anything else—a distance so great we could hope for little in terms of two-way communication. And this is why it is especially exciting to say that what we've found is coming out of the Alpha Coronae Borealis system, a relatively close neighbor approximately seventy-five light-years away . . .

The fuchsia planet was called Omni-7xc and SETI kept its likeness in partial orbit on the screen while speaker after speaker attested to the validity of what the Allen Telescope Array had picked up at the Hat Creek Radio Observatory outside San Francisco. The signal was being called a technosignature. They contextualized the data. There were few certainties, mainly the identification of uncertainties. Was it music? Was it mechanical noise? Was it sent deliberately to us? Was it communication at all? Was it accidental ambience? What it couldn't be: organic. What this meant: Omni-7xc, as late as seventy-five years ago, possessed or had been visited by intelligent life, however life or intelligence could be defined. It was still pumping its way across space—so far, without repeating. After a fifteen-minute round of enthused scientific jargon, Dr. Osip Braz, a senior technician who spoke with the velveteen gutturals of his native Russian, and the man who—to the upset of thousands across the world who'd logged countless hours of unpaid headphone-time listening to space nothing—discovered the technosignature, asked the audience if they were ready to hear it.

I think the world would like to hear it, he said.

Sevi plugged in his speakers. A lone drone crackled and an ambient wave, oscillating through slowly shifting chords, swam the apartment. In the background, a series of other oscillations produced a syncopated and dissonant pattern, a kind of complex pulse. After a few cycles, Sevi registered a single note ringing through, wavering slightly in pitch—a wistful ribbon of smoke. The lower registers fired off in some irrational time signature, shaking the furniture and windows at random intervals. The highest oscillation filled the air with the white noise of a thousand flying insects. The sound serenading the Earth across seventy-five years of space. One great blooming, buzzing confusion. He closed his eyes and waded into its sonic currents, the sounds moving over him like a sudsing electronic toothbrush. And he was almost somewhere, close to the place monks go when they self-immolate, he thought, when, as if from the bottom of a well, he heard a woman's voice.

"Sevi, Sevi, Sevi."

From out of the susurration, the voice told him she needed to call her family. He'd been the first person she called. He paused, in need of something, and Ramona already knew what he needed, what he was wondering. She told him to go outside, to see the world on this first day.

"It's cold," he said, halfheartedly.

"Wear a coat."

And then, like the first breath a diver takes after rising from a plunge, she said, "I love you."

"I love you too," he said, impetuously.

RAMONA HAD EXPLAINED the history of Humboldt Park on several occasions. She was interested in things this way. Thanks to her, and the internet, Sevi had a Wikipedic working knowledge of most things he'd been bored enough to look up on his phone or patient enough to listen to her explain. The park was named after Alexander von Humboldt, the nineteenth-century

Prussian-born explorer, geologist, inventor, abolitionist, and republican who'd attempted to amass all the world's knowledge in a five-volume book entitled *Kosmos*. Its pages contained the first instance of a Westerner describing nature in ecological terms, as something interconnected. There were hundreds of Humboldt Parks all over the world, cities in Europe and the US had used to throw the guy parades, he'd hung out with Thomas Jefferson and Simón Bolívar. Yet, somehow, before Ramona, Sevi had had no idea where the neighborhood had gotten its name. In Chicago, Humboldt was where all the Puerto Ricans lived, which Sevi had always thought was weird— Humboldt didn't sound like any Boricua name he'd ever heard before. He knew Humboldt Drive, the park's spinal column, doubled as an automotive garage whenever it was warm out. The park's man-made lagoon, filthy and the exact color of Earl Grey tea, was rumored to contain the same bacterium from which the Earth drew its first breath of oxygenated air. On the hottest summer days, the park's lawn swelled with people; everything crushed to microcosm—all of life happened all at once. A year and a half ago, on one of those crushingly human days, he and Ramona had caught sight of a couple under a picnic blanket in the park. The blanketed two contorted amorously, and from afar it was like watching the clouds. One minute the blanket was a duck, a glove the next—a sculptural encyclopedia—and the couple underneath couldn't be stopped. Screaming children leaped over them. A dog threatened to leave his mark. All the while a band played, and this smooth old Puerto Rican in a Panama hat *thlock*ed the timbales so hard that through the PA it sounded as if the whole world was knocking at the park's front door, dying to get let in. This couple, though, they couldn't be bothered to get up and answer it. When Ramona told Sevi the kind of man Humboldt had been, it was surprising but also fitting, the way the park tried to capture all of life all at once too.

On January 1, 2012, Humboldt's park wasn't the party Sevi remembered. More of a fugue state. Dark birds, not crows, but a species he had no name for, scribbled off bizarre diagrams overhead. Ice blocks, onyx with dirt and exhaust, floated Humboldt Drive. Sure, it's winter and cold as hell, Sevi thought, but really, nobody thought it'd be a good idea to come outside and shout at the sky today? To revel in the updated universe? As far as he could tell, the only people other than himself in the park were homeless men zombie-ing around under the barren trees, and white, condo-owning joggers, who over ice or amid sunshine sped along each day oblivious to the weather, conscious only of their own hearts. How was anybody supposed to tell the world had changed? What would old von Humboldt say?

The park had a willow under which Ramona had liked to read in the summertime. Sevi trudged his way through a field toward the tree, snow packing deep into the necks of his shoes; halfway there he crossed three young men smoking in a gazebo, and when they stirred he turned around, drifting south along California to the Ukrainian Village instead.

He knew of a coffee shop on West Chicago, between Rockwell and Campbell, that played punk music while tattooed baristas drizzled arabesque patterns into your coffee foam. It was a little hip, but the coffee was good, and Sevi figured it might have whatever it was he was looking for. He liked being in the Ukrainian Village. Its tight bungalows and stretched brownstones were indistinguishable from the ones in Humboldt Park, the same proportion of hipsters crawled its street as any other gentrifying neighborhood in the city, and yet this part of the West Side could still somehow leave Sevi with the huddled, snowy feeling of Eastern Europe, of ethnic outsiders who'd gone in but hadn't taken off their papakhas and galoshes. Maybe it was the towering Orthodox and Catholic churches done in the Byzantine and Medieval styles that peeked around every other residential corner, their iconographic portholes staring out like the old Ukrainian ladies in the apartment windows across the street from them, the low-flying meringue of their pearlescent domes whipped into peaks and dolloping the sky gold and sunset colors, but Uke Village was Saul Bellow's Chicago, Carl Sandburg's, someone else's. There was some sort of message in it all. Dig in deep enough and eventually America leaves your ass alone. He'd hoped for something similar for Humboldt and himself but not even a set of massive stainless-steel Puerto Rican flags flying stiffly on either side of Division Street had managed to keep the developers away. And besides, on this first day with the planet, now that Earth was no longer alone, he no longer wanted to be alone either.

The coffee shop looked open. Bikes leaned in the rack, smatterings of spray-on snow clouded the windowpanes, and Sevi felt good-natured, neighborly, willing to spend money. Above the front door a wooden signboard with a black-and-gold nautical star rattled in the wind. Sevi, thirty years old, five-four, box-shaped, and with a patchy beard, walked in, knocking his shoes together over a jute mat.

No one was ever certain of Sevi's age. People, women mostly, used to call him an old soul. Whatever youthful wisdom the term had once brought to mind had burned off in his late twenties and, in its stead, there was this dimness now. He taught music at a public high school within walking distance of his apartment, and if anyone ever praised him for devoting himself to such a thankless and selfless vocation, which occasionally someone did, he let them know the job was something of a sore spot. Festering. Not because of the precarious state of the fine arts in public education, or how difficult it was to make ends meet as a teacher with student loans, though neither of those things helped, but because he'd studied cello and composition at the Oberlin Conservatory of Music intent on becoming a performing or composing professor. In six years, his work as a high school teacher had been what he'd made of it: unrewarding. And he'd seen no way out. Until, earlier that school year, the Chicago Board of Education announced his school would be one of fifty institutions closing their doors for good in the summer as part of a citywide initiative to cut costs on underpopulated and underperforming sites, and Sevi felt both grateful and despairing. He didn't agree with the district's qualifications. A long battle between City Hall and the poor, mostly Latin and Black residents of the neighborhood had reached its inevitable end. Save for the few who could attend a new neighborhood charter, the remaining six hundred members of the student body would scatter all over the west and south sides of the city. When it was brought to the superintendent's attention that kids would have to cross contested gang territories by foot, he said a demolition crew was already slated to make room for new condos in the school's crumbling lot—they'd break ground two days after graduation—and perhaps the CTA would consider rerouting a few buses given the circumstances. The closure would bring the city one step closer to the mass privatization of education, which Sevi was vehemently against, but he had always counted on bad weather or illness to cancel unwanted appointments. He'd never broken up with anyone. Heaven, he believed, if it existed, was for sufferers. What he would do next with his life, he had no idea. He would commune with aliens, talk to Ramona on the phone.

A group of art students were laughing hysterically beside a set of large windows overlooking the coffee shop's back patio. Their severe haircuts and ironic jackets gave them away. They looked devastatingly high, and Sevi usually had a hard time with these types. It concerned him that some of these diffident, awkward hipsters could be one used copy of the annotated Nietzsche away from covering homeless people with buckets of latex paint, that all their cruel coolness and heterodoxy might try on fascism eventually, that irony became identity. He was always surprised when one of them offered him a piece of organic gluten-free carrot cake at a potluck, moved when he or she complimented his song choice at a party. Looking at these kids laughing over their coffees now, day one of intergalactic planetary whatever, in place of his worries about the white youth of America were memories of his own college days, when every holiday and/or pseudohistorical event was an excuse to smoke more weed than usual. He'd never been higher than on 9/11. Performative irony, actual addiction, that phase was over now, and for a moment he smiled at these students in camaraderie and commiseration. They could think everything was funny and dumb as long as he didn't. The back patio was deserted; its five circular outdoor tables, covered in snow, resembled weird, colorless mushrooms. The wind made it appear as if the world were coated in bits of glass. I'm not high, Sevi realized. Irony and indifference had not become his identity. Was this what spirits felt like when they lifted? Standing in people's way, he suddenly saw the future quite clearly. Omni would usher in an era fit for those who'd suffered well enough, one in which struggling schools didn't close, and gifted cellists would never again be asked to teach disengaged teenagers, and Google wouldn't steal your girlfriend. Perhaps these art students wouldn't become Nazis after all. He got in line.

The café's punk had turned into NPR's *Weekend Edition*. Through the bar's woody interior, above the milk steam, whirring grinders, incandescent antique work-light tine, and mouth chatter, a correspondent's voice described the scene from Mountain View. *Packed, pilgrimage, continuing to grow in numbers, mad house.* A physical site for something made of radio waves was being built in California. Sevi pictured a music festival, Lollapalooza, Pitchfork, people washing up against an empty stage blasting Omni's message, not far from where Ramona worked.

He shuffled and ordered an americano at the counter, and would have happily added agave sweetener himself later, down at the end of the line, near the trashcans, where they also kept the milks and creamers and wooden stirrers, but the barista, who in all denim bore a striking resemblance to Hall or Oates, whichever wasn't blonde, asked if he didn't want to try something new.

"I am," Sevi said. "I usually order drip."

"No, I mean something we've come up with this morning. For a different world," the barista said, with some conspiracy in the coordinated maneuvering of his brow and mustache. "Cosmic Latte, named after the most abundant color in the universe."

"I thought turquoise was the most common color in the universe," Sevi said.

"That theory has been debunked," the man said. "Some scientists are saying it's red. I guess the whole thing tastes like raspberries, though."

"I'll take a Cosmic Latte then."

The barista winked at him, and Sevi wondered if he'd accepted a deeper solicitation. One cough, two coughs, bandana in the right pocket or the left, who knew what signals people were sending through the void these days, let alone their meanings? Over the radio, Scott Simon, *Weekend Edition*'s host, interviewed a psychologist.

The psychologist said, *During a paradigm shift it's best to stay flexible but critical. No use throwing the baby out with the bathwater. Twenty years ago, people were talking about how radio was an obsolete technology, and yet we wouldn't be where we are today if we'd gotten rid of all our radios when some new invention came along.*

What we'll understand in the coming days is that feelings of fear and paranoia are just as valid as optimism and hope. There's no telling where this is going to take us. So, try to listen to friends and family when they express their emotions, don't try to dissuade them from experiencing those emotions even if they are not the same emotions you are experiencing yourself. Diversity of feelings is a kind of equity; like a diverse gene pool, we stand a better chance if we hold on to everything we can.

Scott Simon thanked the psychologist for her time.

Now let's hear some of your views. Obviously, lots of people are turning to Twitter to express themselves today . . .

Hall or Oates called out Sevi's name. The drink looked like a latte. He took a sip and could taste nothing different about it. It definitely didn't taste like raspberries. The barista asked him what he thought, and he told him it was good, real interesting. He didn't know why. Scott Simon read Twitter comments.

TWO MINUTES BEFORE HEARING ABOUT the planet, Eason Wallace was brushing his bottom left molars, gagging on his toothbrush, crying, getting toothpaste in his eyes as he wiped away tears. In the mirror, Eason watched his dad's whole face become eclipsed by his hand, which slid down his eyes, nose, and mouth, cradled his chin. His dad said, "It's just a mess, you know?" and his hand projected forward in the mirror reflection, and Eason watched himself shirk away from it and his dad step back. Eason would tell others, "We were already talking about something else. Omni butted in." On the eve of Omni's cosmic debut, Rydell George, who Eason had known since the third grade, the first friend he'd made in Humboldt Park, had been gunned down in front of his mother's apartment while he watched friends and neighbors shoot fireworks into the night sky above their one-way street. Eason had been watching fireworks, too. Not the same ones as Rydell, Rydell had been living north of 64 these days, but all over the city people were going out into the freezing cold and setting off medium-sized explosions. Eason hadn't thought it was such a good idea to set them off in the street. Why not the park? Why not away from people's homes? He didn't like how the fireworks left a black scorch on the road, or how the block smelled afterward, or how their loud pops kind of sounded like gunfire, how they made him jump. North of 64, the colors went up, the blasts went off; and some man, troubled, mistook sixteen-year-old Rydell for that pitiful soul he'd been looking for all night and shot him dead, the gun blasts blurring with the fireworks. "It's just a mess, you know?" Eason's dad said the next morning and walked away into the living room.

Eason spat, rinsed with water, dried his face, and found his dad flipping through the channels on the TV. Omni was everywhere, taking over everything, like Rydell had never existed in the first place.

"Another young man dies, and we get a planet," his dad said, shaking his head.

NOON, THE SKY already climbing down into evening. Eason Wallace, on the first day of the planet, buzzed again and looked down from the front steps of Mr. del Toro's apartment building at the dead garden below, dried tubers fenced in by rusted wrought iron and dimly aglow with an icy mixture of broken glass and crusty frost. The second floor's bay window had been replaced with plastic tarp, which ballooned overhead like the white escaping the shell of an overboiled egg. Mr. del Toro's downstairs neighbor was a drunk. The glass on the ground was already burying itself in the soil, following the snowmelt.

Mr. del Toro had never missed an appointment. They'd been meeting for a couple of years. Mr. del Toro didn't charge anything, getting some sort of weird reward out of it himself. Eason rang the third floor again. His feet had lost feeling and the sweat on his neck had started to itch. He wanted to practice. He didn't want to walk home without warming up first. But no one answered, and Eason dragged himself toward Division for home, his cello case knocking behind him. He didn't know what to think. Maybe Mr. del Toro was sending a message of his own, that he was over giving cello lessons for free.

Fifteen minutes later, Eason crossed the courtyard of his apartment complex in West Humboldt Park. Sidewalk salt had jammed the wheels of his cello case, and he'd had to pick it up and carry it. His salt-stained black puffer coat, one size too small, had kept riding up, and his hips were wind chapped. A large woman paced the snowy yard in nothing but black tights and a white T-shirt, screaming into a phone, the device lying flat in her open palm, perpendicular and microphone first toward her wrenching mouth. Inside his building, Eason took the stairs, narrow, tilting, wet black-and-white tilework like the whole thing was a men's room. There were coral formations of dry spit, or something, grouped along the handrail. Little kids were always raising hell on the stairs. Most of the doors had only the greasy shadows of their apartment numbers; the ones with actual demarcations employed two or more different fonts, whatever the super could find. Eason stopped on a landing to look through a melting pane of glass to see the street, to breathe. The world looked warbled. Two more flights and he was outside his own door, which had two matching numbers because his dad had gone out and bought them himself. "We don't live in a fun house," he'd said. Eason wiped the sweat from his forehead, opened his coat, and flapped his arms to air himself out. His wrists burned where his coat had gotten him. He withdrew his key lanyard from beneath his sweatshirt. Chest damp, he unlocked the door of unit 324 and stepped inside.

His dad, Rubin, thirty-seven, towering and bent like Eason, with neat cornrows and thin facial hair boxing his mouth, was running across the living room, the expanse of ancient pinewood floor lit warmly by a standing paper lamp beside the kitchen. His dad called it ambiance. His dad paused. Gray, baggy sweats bunched below his waist, and black, shining Under Armour clung tight to his torso, over which a Derrick Rose jersey swung from his shoulders in the door draft. He had a glass of milk sloshing in one hand.

"What you doin' back so early?" he asked, starting to move again.

"Practice got cancelled."

"I'm sorry, son."

Somehow concern stayed seated in his dad's voice even as he swept the room, digging into the couch and scanning the windowsills.

"Are you looking for something?" Eason said.

There were few places for anything to hide in the apartment. Rubin didn't tolerate clutter in his home. Furniture, clean IKEA, did not touch; papers, fitness magazines and bills, did not pile; dishes, glassware, and cutlery were washed after each use, put away dry in cabinets and drawers. The world was cluttered, his home was not. It had ambiance.

"Bus pass," he called from the bathroom down the hall.

Eason took off his boots and walked to his dad's bedroom and pulled the pass from the pages of a spy novel.

"What page was I on?" his dad asked.

"Didn't check."

"Damn."

"Where you going?"

"Loretta's sick. Tamara's sick."

Tamara was Eason's half sister; Loretta, one of his dad's exes, was Tamara's mother. They lived down in Bridgeport. Rubin managed to keep his home tidy; everything else, not so much. The only thing more scattered than the man's résumé was his love life. Eason had heard his dad joking with his uncles one time that he wanted to sue the birth control industry—not for everything it had, but for peace. He moved in a familial gyre along the Pink and Green Lines, calmly, lovingly, absentmindedly in and out of women's and children's lives. Eason didn't try to know those people. They were lucky to have mothers, he was lucky to have his dad, and that felt like enough.

The arm of the couch flashed in the blue shutter of the TV. His dad sat down and took a sip of milk like it was whiskey. He'd never drank in his life but wasn't any way about it.

"You wanna play me something?" he said, the half-drunk glass tented between his long fingers, pressed votively against his chest. "I've got fifteen minutes."

"Nah, it's cool," Eason said, peeling off his coat. He used the last dry toe of his right sock to crush and soak up a chunk of ice he'd dropped on the floor, removed his socks, and went barefoot.

"Let me rephrase that," his dad said. "Will you please play me something?"

Eason shook his head, standing on his cold, bare feet.

"Damn, fool, didn't want to tell you dance, monkey, dance, but come on and play me something."

"All right, hold up then."

Two weeks ago, Mr. del Toro had sent Eason off with the sheet music for the prelude to Bach's first cello suite. Mr. del Toro had played him the opening phrase—the gashing open A and pinching G before what Mr. del Toro referred to as its infamous motif in G major.

"Yeah, yeah, I know this!" Eason had said, and leaned forward and started humming along to the resolution when all of a sudden Mr. del Toro quit playing.

"The Zales commercial," Mr. del Toro said, all fed up, "I know, but there's more to the Cello Suites than jewelry. The suites stand in for basic human dignity. Evidence of grace, our universal entitlement."

Before Eason could explain that his dad liked to play Bach when they cleaned around the house, Mr. del Toro launched into a history lesson on the suites. Eason tried to follow, but it seemed like little was actually known about the music. Bach either was or wasn't a Kapellmeister at the time he wrote them. They either were or weren't written together with the intention of being performed all in a row. It was even possible they were just warm-up exercises. Then Mr. del Toro got tripped up over whether the 1700s was the sixteenth or the eighteenth century and stopped all the talk.

"Either way, it's not the seventeenth century, which is stupid," he'd said.

The eighteenth century, crapellmeister, and white person bling commercials aside, practice Eason did, and for no reason either, or so he'd thought until now.

Seated in an armchair, Eason rosined and tightened his bow while his dad finished his milk. In the window, the sky peeled back to show the bare shoulder of the early moon. His dad set the white-streaked glass down to let it be known he was ready. Eason raised his left arm into first position, beveled the bow against his strings to measure the tension, and began. He opened the broad interval with his chest, as Mr. del Toro had taught him. To meet the melody, he rose his fret hand up the neck, touching G, pausing to check its pulse, and finished the note with slight vibrato, maneuvering his right hand as if trying to free his fingers from a spider's web. He moved through the melody: indecisive but patterned. The bow drifted wistfully—a boat of hair gliding across the fast currents of the vibrating strings, catching and moving on, catching and moving on to build the shallow arpeggios. Eyes closed, back straight, he could not see himself doing these things, but he felt it. Doing it right. It was going, better than it ever went in his room alone, probably better than it would've gone in Mr. del Toro's apartment, as good as a concert performance, maybe, and it was so exhilarating Eason didn't notice his dad trying, politely, to interrupt him. He opened his eyes to blink away some moisture and saw the man's sorry face. The instrument's neck stayed cold in his palm, over so fast the wood never warmed.

"I forgot the Chicago bus is rerouting this week," his dad explained. "I've gotta go, son, I'm sorry. You gotta play me some more of that. Man, that was good."

Coat, boots, beanie. Hug.

"Be good," he said. "Omni's watching. Spaghetti on the stove."

"See ya," Eason said, offering up a rind of love.

He put his cello back into its sarcophagus.

He had homework, but he was experimenting with what really happened when it wasn't turned in. He'd heard rumors. He'd missed assignments here and there. So far, nothing, which took the purpose out of the experiment, and was why, before long, out of bored guilt, he found himself wading into his backpack, extracting a geometry book, setting it on the tiny dining table, and getting to work, exactly what everyone expected him to do. The saucepan of cold spaghetti and pasta sauce, he eventually brought to the table, too. He chewed, wiped his mouth, and mathed. His sister was sick. His dad worked hard and still rode the bus. People missed appointments. Rydell had been killed. Nothing was fair, and nothing ever would be. For those sensitive to the insensibility of the world, there would always be geometry.

Half an hour later the apartment buzzer rang. Eason thought his dad had been turned back, maybe he'd left his keys. Or was it Mr. del Toro coming to apologize? It buzzed again. He checked out the window. Through the white plastic blinds, he spied a figure much too big to be Mr. del Toro but not wearing his dad's coat. His phone pinged.

```
Open up punk its g freezing out here.
```

Before Eason realized what he'd done, Germaine Duggins, for the first time in over four years, was standing in his living room. Germaine was an old friend Eason had used to run up and down the streets with playing zombie apocalypse and alien invasion. With Rydell, the three had formed a little crew for a while. The aliens had arrived, and Germaine had returned. Back from the dead but not a zombie. He cut a bigger shape out of the apartment than he used to, smelled no longer of grass and sweat but winter and weed, but in every other way he seemed like the same person, that boy. The same shining scar casting an arch over his left eyebrow ever since Eason threw a tree branch at him in fourth grade, grown to fit his face. Not a zombie but a visitor from another world, for sure.

"What's up?" Eason said.

"Can I chill a second?" Germaine said.

"I guess so."

Germaine unzipped his heavy, shiny black Sean John coat and settled his broad body on the love seat beside the TV. On the screen was a rerun of *The Simpsons*. Bart was having a nightmare after selling his soul to Milhouse, and in the dream world, everyone except Bart was playing and rowing in boats and jumping rope with translucent twins of themselves. For a while, Germaine sat and watched the episode. Then, without looking away from the TV, he said, "That's some fucked up shit about Rydell."

"Yeah," Eason said.

Their classmates had been posting stuff about Rydell all day. Pictures from when he was little, a project on the water cycle a fellow groupmate had snapped a shot of, poems they had been inspired to write and rambling notes that could've been poems. The consensus was the same. What had happened to Rydell was fucked up.

"He was a goofy dude, but he was getting some action from the ladies," Germaine said with a smile.

"No shit?"

Germaine nodded, grinning.

It'd been so long since Eason and Germaine last talked—not just a what's up here and there at the park or at a bus stop, but really talked—and Eason was struck by a sudden memory. He and Germaine were in Germaine's backyard being swarmed by ugly insects. Germaine's mama had come outside to see what all the commotion was about, why the boys were upset and crying, and she explained to them that the weird bugs were mayflies and that mayflies only lived one day. And it frightened Eason that Germaine could be experiencing the same memory, what with all the time and everything else that had since passed between them.

"Funeral's probably next week, or something," Eason said.

"How you gonna have a funeral for that shit?" Germaine said, turning to look at Eason, his shoulders arching forward, an ache audible in his voice and visible in his body. He was no longer smiling.

"Gotta do something," Eason said.

"That's what I mean, man. Gotta do something. You'd think people would go crazy, go fucking nuts seeing him in a box. Like they wouldn't sleep until they knew for sure it'd stop. This is Humboldt, it ain't Garfield Park or Englewood. Can't just have no funeral and call it a day."

Phlegm or weight caught in Germaine's throat. The scar heaved, it could've fallen over the horizon of his brow. He sat back. When school resumed, students would have the option to visit with grief counselors and teachers would have to bring up Rydell in the same breath as Omni. By spring, though, people will have forgotten, Eason thought. Right now, Rydell was practically in the room, conjured by two old friends.

"My dad says the world won't stop for anything, what makes us think the killings will?" Eason said.

"Never understand nothin' your pops says," Germaine said.

Reaching into his coat pockets he asked if Eason would mind if he smoked.

"We can crack a window."

"Two," Germaine said. "Need a cross breeze if you mind the smell."

Eason had never smoked at home.

He tried explaining what he thought his dad had meant while Germaine broke the bark of a Swisher and spilled the dark, grape guts into the empty milk glass Eason's dad had left on the table.

"Like there aren't any real rules in life," Eason said.

"Tell that to my rap sheet," Germaine said, gluing the blunt with his tongue with the same love as a cat washing a kitten.

"Nah, I mean like real rules, man. Like virtues and morals, shit from stories our parents read to us when we were little. Not supposed to lock up a man for holding some weed, that shit's not decent, it's not humane, that's not a real rule, it's a violation of one."

Germaine lit the blunt, hit it twice, and passed it.

"Those are the rules the game's supposed to provide," Germaine said, his voice straining as he held smoke in his lungs. "But not even the game follows the rules these days."

"Whatchu know about the game?" Eason said.

Germaine moved his weight from one buttock to the next, scratched the stubble on his neck pouch. Eason let it lie and the heavy smoking blunt lobbed back and forth between the boys in silence for a bit. But Eason couldn't help himself and asked again.

"You hustling or something?"

"Surprised your cousin didn't mention it," Germaine said, side-eyeing him.

Eason's cousin Jules figured into shady and dangerous dealings in the neighborhood. He wasn't somebody Eason had much contact with either.

"What's Jules got to do with anything? What'd you come over here for anyways?" Eason said, feeling very high and a little paranoid.

"To smoke one for Rydell."

"And what else?"

A brisk wind ripped through the apartment. Germaine stabbed out the crutch and asked if they could close the windows, he was getting cold. From the window in the kitchen, Eason turned to look at his old friend, who was staring into his hands.

"Rydell didn't do nothing and he's dead," Germaine said.

Back on the couch, Eason felt fuzzy and dizzy and worried. He could tell Germaine felt the same.

"Man, you're tripping me out. I know something else is going on."

Germaine took a deep breath.

"Your cousin and I were beefin' on Facebook, man. I think I said some shit that went too far. And you know your cuz, he's gone crazy. I dunno if he wants me dead or just outta the game, I can't get a hold of him. Meanwhile, I'm buggin'. Can't sleep. Can't eat. Smoking till I'm catatonic, and I'm still all jumpy. I need your help," Germaine said.

"How am I supposed to help you with that?" Eason said.

"I dunno, talk to him. Tell him I didn't mean no harm and that I just want my spot back."

Eason couldn't believe this fool coming back into his life unannounced asking for a favor. And for what? What was in it for him?

"I dunno, Germaine. Jules and I don't really talk. Not sure what good I would be," he said, trying to remain calm.

"Listen, if you can help, you'd be the only one who could. So, I need it, aight?"

Germaine's eyes were tired and stoned, but deep in the blood marbles, Eason also noticed something else: terror. And he saw the kid from years ago again, the one who was afraid of the mayflies. He saw himself and he saw Rydell.

"Aight," he said. He tried to swallow but his whole head had run dry. "Aight, I'll try."

"Thank you, Eason," Germaine said, and pulled out his phone.

Eason watched him thumb its face for a while, worried about what exactly he'd signed up for.

"Yo, what you doin' on that phone?" Eason said.

"Check this shit," Germaine said, and showed Eason the face of his phone.

It was an app that recorded messages for SETI to send to Omni. It had a media player that kept a steady feed of Omni's signal going 24-7—weird squelching pumps that fell after each decibel peak in a bit-crushed dazzle like a broken window falling inside a car door.

"How's Google already got an app?" Eason said.

"Player, pretty sure we're the last motherfuckers to know about this shit."

"You gonna send something?"

"Nah."

"You should. Your ass needs to send a motherfuckin' SOS."

The boys laughed.

CALVINO, ITALO.
"THE DISTANCE OF THE MOON." 1965.

My name is He Zhen and I am the first credible human witness to the
cosmos. My father named me after someone famous, an anarchist from
the twentieth century. He Zhen was also a feminist. Whether I'll be famous
someday remains to be seen. If I'm a feminist or not is unclear, too.

They are odd terms, feminist and anarchist. Faiths, almost. They are
derivatives of humanism, associated with the bright shining lies of the five sister
centuries that'd run amok until a century or two ago, when the enjoyable portion
of the Anthropocene reached its end and the wandering started again.

I sometimes picture those happy centuries as Jane Austen's didactic
Bennet sisters, the ones in *Pride and Prejudice*, gainful but fledgling ladies
at the start of their empire's steady ascension to destruction, and try to
order them by their lady tempers. The seventeenth century is the moral,
labored Jane; the eighteenth, the vain pedant Mary; the nineteenth is the
uniform-loving Lydia; the twentieth, Lydia's shadow, Kitty; and the twenty-
first, hard-mannered, prejudicial, Elizabeth, our stricken hero, our silly vice.
The character literature worshipped for ages, who, as it turned out, only ever
wanted a nice, rich husband. I have only read the book once, am weak with
history and literary analysis; I know these assignments do not quite fit
perfectly, but it is fun to be reductive, and perhaps one can see what I am
playing at anyway.

My parents placed faith not in women, self-governance, or books. They
placed faith in me. And I came to disappoint them. I know. They shared
their disappointment when I applied to leave Earth.

My mother said, "Never in a thousand years would I have guessed you'd
be one of them, one of those people to whom nothing in this life means
anything."

My father, my poor, supportive father, interjected, "It matters so much, differently, but so much to her she's chosen to sacrifice her life for the lives of others."

I told him I did not long for answers or solutions, I only wanted to see the farthest reaches of space, which I now can. Traveling near the speed of light, I age at a fraction of the rate those left on Earth do. I'll be able to cover plenty of ground. As for where we come from, who we are, or where we are going, I have little curiosity. My father had no choice but to join my mother in her disappointment.

He stopped talking to me for a time. Soon, however, he started to thaw, a prick of grass showing in the snow, saying little things, unimportant things, speaking on the histories of coffee and tea, what certain military leaders drank before battle or when trying to produce an heir, an idiotic print he found that had been used as a guide for the medieval practice of bloodletting. He taught university—a strange living for a human—which is to say, he was always demonstrating how memories are made, demanding new ones.

Once, he memorized the whole poem of a Gu Kaizhi painted scroll. Another time he submitted his blood to an ancestry test and spent two days reading over the report. These things would have made me laugh if they did not make me so angry.

After his thaw, he would appear from his room, say, "Hey, He Zhen," tell me something stupid, and I would have to fight to appear interested without breaking my air of unreachable distance. Despite my anger and boredom, I was aware he might fall to his knees at any moment and beg me not to go, which was not something I would have had the latitude for if I was not so prepared and distant already. At each conversation's end it surprised me to find him still standing.

The morning I left, knowing I would lose communication years before I arrived at my destination, he said, "Send me a postcard from space, write me a letter from the future." I hugged him, a rare gesture. I refrained from saying that anything I sent, like starlight, would arrive from the past.

I was born He Zhen, but space transforms you. When He Zhen's Japanese husband died of tuberculosis, she entered a dark and frightening place. She stopped working. She gave up on her cause. Unfair, but also ironic, that China's first feminist was not able to go on living as she had without her husband. It is rumored He Zhen became a Buddhist nun and changed her name to Xiao Qi, which is what I call myself up here. I have lost my husband, Earth.

I keep saying up even though here has no direction. I suppose it makes me something of Earth still.

Earth's widow, Xiao Qi.

Direction is measured by coordinates on a three-dimensional grid in space. It is a place of fewer and fewer prepositions, where life on Earth is entirely prepositional. It was a simple existence, I remember, wherein everything happened within or without, before, during, or after, to, at, or with. I was always somewhere and no place else. I was always one person and not the other. Nowhere in space, I am everywhere. Alone, I could be anyone, who would ever know? Taka, who is quantum-minded, a machine, can relate but doesn't seem to have a problem with it. It says, Just be yourself and remember to have fun. If Taka had a neck, I'd strangle it. In the kitchen, I examine a knife and attempt to see both sides of the blade and not just the edge. Taka says it's more than possible Earth, in another dimension, has managed to save itself, and I wonder if some of the people living in that dimension sometimes feel misplaced, completely lost, because deep down inside they know life should not be continuing. It would not be entirely different from the way people in our dimension sometimes cry out from somewhere deep inside because life is not simply supposed to end either.

Taka, my only companion, the machine, is made up of sub-quantum processors, cells so small its thoughts and signals are always in multiple places at once. Taka tells time. Taka possesses a million clocks, measuring the relative time experienced by points outside the ship, as well as the time experienced by its own processors, which slow and bend with the speed of its signals. Taka is good with time, which is lucky because time is lost on me. You see, in a week I will go to sleep, and when I wake, in the future, at a temporal distance of four Earth years from the coordinate I find myself at now, I will not have aged much at all, though I will have traveled beyond our planets, to another part of our galaxy. I will slow and bend with the speed of the ship. Taka will keep watchful eye on the ship. Taka will get us to where we are going. Taka will read to me in my sleep, that being something I have asked Taka to do.

A few notes on piloting. Spacetime is not one big empty canister, but an irreconcilable confluence of invisible caves to which we are not discretely condemned one after the other, or all at once—there is no telling. Imagine a swimming pool, a clear, blue, light-hungry expanse inside of which, wearing a sporty uniform, you are allowed to do whatever your muscles and lungs and creativity can provide. Now erase that image, and picture an ill-maintained parking lot of uneven grade, marred with potholes and cracks and rivulets and other boggy depressions all having hungrily collected oily water after a rainstorm. Now imagine skating your body across this surface and trying to decide in which pool you swim. This is spacetime. This is why it pays to have a good navigator with a good watch.

Taka tells me Saturn is screaming in his sleep tonight. It is the sound of the debris that make up its rings crashing into one another. Tonight. It is always tonight, I am always venturing toward what I only saw on Earth only at night, before I slept or when I woke too early.

I ask Taka to turn on the receiver and Taka lowers Saturn's sounds within audible frequency. Saturn is screaming. He is in agony. I believe it is his many moons that torment him, which he has built so many rings to reach out and touch but cannot. Taka tells me I talk too much like a poet, turns off the sound.

Taka believes it is named after the Japanese falcon. Taka is, in fact, named after the Icelandic word for "take." A team engineered Taka on a black, volcanic field outside Reykjavík, where the Earth's servers are stationed. Powered by the Earth's core, cooled by what little ice we have left. As its first job, Taka reorganized the servers, compressed and encrypted their data, and taught one hundred children everything from how to tie their shoes to Hindu mysticism using nothing but the data. For Taka, unlike my father, teaching is not such a strange job. For all Taka takes, Taka gives so much more.

"*Takk*" is Icelandic for "thanks." *Takk*, Taka. I think that would make for a good ad, if Taka ever needed one.

Before our departure, news reports suggested Taka was to assist me on this expedition, when it is I who am assisting Taka. I am nothing more than a dog or a chimp in space, proof flesh can go.

This expedition is called the Mission for the Future. True, necessity is the mother of invention; sadly, the same cannot be said of the relationship between desperation and creativity. There are twenty of us cosmonauts venturing out. I'm seeking a technosignature. Others are following biosignatures, habitable planets. Our American and European counterparts have been a little slower to send out their own astronauts, there being some debate among them still regarding how long human life had on Earth—a question to which I ask, in turn, "Who cares?" I'm dropping through space in one of only twenty shuttles raying in separate directions, plotting a quaquaversal shape, of the kind trees made when they dropped their fruit, back when trees had hope. Our mission is to be light and compact, as time, on Earth, has run out of space, as the people of Earth did decades ago. Last

I checked, as a matter of physics and biology, overpopulation and environmental collapse, the past now exceeds any remaining hospitable human future on Earth. To survive we must spread the future across a greater surface area, to thin time and slow it down. But the future cannot exist anywhere the past has not already built a foundation. Taka and I are charged with setting up an outpost on an exoplanet as part of an ever-expanding network of servers, clouds of knowledge, which will first light up the cosmic map with intelligence, and then function as resource and communication hubs when more people venture out to build actual colonies. If people do not come, machines will, and those machines may someday cultivate people, or something similar. If we encounter life along the way, we will ask for their help, hand them a piece of our fate. A plant seeds in all directions, first to survive at all, and then to find the most favorable footing. Though I've never been so noble a creature as a plant, and I've never been more uncertain of anything in my life. The construction of the human quaquaverse.

The ship contains automated machinery that mine, melt, and build; smart terraculture that will proliferate a food and oxygen supply; and an army of exploratory robots that will chart out the entire planet and its moons, while Taka germinates the planet with the history of humankind.

I am already redundant. In nearly every future experts have predicted, flesh is symbolic. And so perhaps my uncertainty is irrelevant. Safe to say, I will have less impact than an oxygen-giving plant in whichever future we find.

Tonight, I ask Taka for a story about reaching for the moon. Tonight marks my first Earth year without planet Earth. I could use a story about Earth's old pal. After the obvious Apollo missions, which I am not interested in, it finds one by an Italian from Cuba, Italo Calvino, "The Distance of the Moon." Read, I say to Taka, and watch Saturn and its rings and its moons disappear behind us.

RAMONA VOLUNTEERED AT A CHURCH in the Mission, programming an application that mapped homeless migration. An oscillation between San Jose and Oakland, unprecedented since the Depression and carried on the itinerant wings of the 22 bus, was highlighted in purple on the digital map, shifting like a wandering bruise up and down the Bay Area each day. Ramona pinpointed the most treacherous spots in their route and gathered health and criminal records for population trajectories with which Father Chen, the church's priest, and leaders at other shelters made decisions for staff and resource reallocation. This wasn't work. Work was the ten hours she spent in Mountain View every day trying to figure out why Google had hired her.

Among its thousands of riders, the 22 bus was referred to as the Hotel 22. For a few dollars, its patrons could ride the bus all day and night from San Jose to Palo Alto and back. It was somewhere to be safe, warm, out of the direct sun or the rain. In San Jose, dozens would disembark every hour for The Jungle, a homeless encampment in the forest, home for thousands. Ramona had never ridden the Hotel 22, but she'd see it from the window of the Wi-Fi buses she took to Mountain View for work. In passing, the two buses presented a perfect allegory for the disparity of the Bay, the homeless living their lives in public on a public bus and the tech darlings shielded behind tinted glass watching the landscape go by, one investment opportunity after another: vineyards, avocado groves, short-term rental properties. The stateless and the transnational. The image of the two buses inspired Ramona to pick up John Steinbeck once, but, lacking the patience for the historical chapters of *The Grapes of Wrath*, she settled for Bruce Springsteen instead.

Ramona had met Father Chen at a farmer's market in the Mission. He was running a vegetable stand, selling produce and signing up volunteers to work with the homeless. At Google only a few months, already Ramona had been experiencing the decompression sickness that accompanied a life of so much abstraction. Her existence, so far away from the life she'd lived with a teacher— where the proximity of the tumults and despairs of that thankless vocation had often allowed her to credit herself the karma points as well—left her feeling like a floating head with hands. In Chicago, she'd managed to detach herself from her remote work with iTunes and be a person in a bar, a movie theater, a polling station. A woman in love, a woman with a sense of humor. In the Bay, where everything was connected, not spiritually, not anymore, but via Bluetooth and Wi-Fi, there were never enough degrees of separation between Ramona and Google to keep her from running adrift of real human ecology; she knew she was becoming something unlovable, even inedible as a consequence. It didn't help that everyone referred to the workplace as "the ecosystem." So, a stranger with an empty reusable bag at a farmer's market, a lover of free samples suddenly too shy to accept a single complimentary gluten-free cookie, she'd spied Father Chen with his moral clipboard and pygmy veggies, and thought: Volunteerism, philanthropy, pro bono, doing shit for free has saved countless big-name techies, surely it can save my little name too. Ramona introduced herself. Homeless people, organic vegetables, whatever it'd take.

Father Chen was from Oakland, the son of two Chinese immigrants, and the only Catholic in his family. Ramona had been forthright about being an atheist, he'd taken no offense. He simply raised his palms and said, "We're two people in this world," and that was it. He was a clean, prim man, with sharp features and glowing skin. He was aged but also boyish, with a quick, demanding way of speaking, developed over the years he'd spent as a sous-chef before joining the order. Ramona liked him instantly and couldn't be sure if he liked her, which she appreciated. He imparted little wisdom. She was either beneath or beyond his blessings.

The second Saturday in January, Ramona visited Father Chen at his gray, carpeted office. That evening, starting at 5:30 P.M. PT, Earth was going to send its first message to Omni. Sitting beside Father Chen in front of his old desktop computer was a perfect way to take her mind off the historic present, which also felt very abstract to her. Sun and a hot lamp had tarnished the monitor's display a nicotine yellow, and the resolution was so poor certain fonts were hard to read, but he'd refused Ramona's donated iMac, saying he didn't want to start the whole ordeal over again.

His starched collar poked out from under a purple sweater, and he'd gotten a fresh buzz cut. His ears were glossy, almost fake.

"Ramona, thank you again for coming, I don't know if it's a virus or what," he said. "Maybe someone is hacking me."

"No one is hacking you. It's just an old operating system, and the motherboard might be going."

"That sounds serious."

"You know, most computer things aren't, but a crashing motherboard is."

"Oh no."

"Everything's backed up, though, so don't worry."

He smiled from lack of assurance.

Ramona defragged and rebooted the tower while Father Chen stepped out for an appointment at a school for the hearing-impaired. By the time he returned, Ramona's program was up and running again, with zero lag. High performance was essential, because every day the data set grew. There were about a hundred new names to add to the list, and each came with a wealth of additional data points—biometrics, convictions, familial ties, and whatever last glimpses of past lives public records, interviews, and social media scrapes could still glean. Algorithmic thinking attempted to answer questions both possible and impossible. Where did these people come from? Why did they belong to this list and not another? What did this list say about the country? The future?

Father Chen reheated some coffee and paced while she worked.

"Why not Buddhism?" she said as she data-entried.

Banter, backtalk, the loving disdain she'd reserved for her most cherished of friends, those who'd have it, it had all come back to her with Father Chen.

"You make it sound as if Buddhism is easy," Father Chen said.

"Singing bowls and scratchy robes, shaved heads and solitude, doesn't sound very technical. Catholicism, on the other hand, the word alone sounds like you're undergoing a procedure."

"Your poor parents . . . Let's say, I have commitment issues. I'm committed to this world, I honestly am, the people in it. That's a no-go in Buddhism, as I understand it."

The images of several tech gurus, draped with sandalwood malas and power-posing in flaccid pants, came to mind. Could someone with a yacht reach nirvana? Was it easier to release yourself from all desire after you'd obtain everything you'd ever desired?

A woman came in with notes from a community meeting. Ramona worked with Father Chen in the practical application of faith—charity, stewardship. She'd never seen him in action as a spiritual leader. She was curious. With the woman with the minutes he acted pragmatic still. Ramona could attend a sermon but didn't want to risk catching faith, it happened.

Thirty minutes later, just before dusk, walking the community garden behind the church Father Chen handled a celery root with a bulb the size of an infant's head. The priest was telling Ramona what it was like working during the AIDS epidemic, which had exploded shortly after he was ordained. An eggplant patch complicated itself tirelessly at their feet.

"For the first few years I was just like everyone else in the Catholic Church, I turned them away, I shunned them. Men were dying on our doorsteps. They had rosaries around their necks. Kaposi's sarcoma. They were using their last breaths to pray. They were lepers. They were dangerous sinners."

Ramona had read up on Father Chen. She knew he eventually became a huge AIDS advocate.

"What changed?" she said.

"I did. AIDS didn't. Reagan didn't. I did, we did. Put simply, I realized I was ignorant and brainwashed, by myself and my own selfishness. Like many people, I found God for selfish reasons. I had problems. Anger, is all I'll say. I came to Him seeking solutions. He solved them, so I figured I'd give Him my all. I benefited from doing this. I knew I would. I got a job. I was respected. I was protected. I was ordained, and still I had a one-way relationship with God, where I kept taking. God sometimes has a hard time saying no—it's unfortunate, in a way. Also, sometimes, He is too patient with us. I had no vision for the total world. Where I thought I was guided by God, I was guided by men. One day I watched a woman close up her diner, weeping. I'd eaten at her diner many times. Good food, not great, not the kind of restaurant work I'd once done, but pleasant nonetheless. I asked her what had happened. She said all her customers were dead. It was an awful way to come to terms with the epidemic, for both of us. After that day, I said, 'No more.' I opened our doors to the dying men. God's grace is always growing because we are God's grace. I had to grow into grace. Grace is the size of every human being who has ever existed and who ever will, and this is an impossible size to imagine. We are the grace, we are the impetus, we are all of it."

"Maybe you are. You're flexible. You're a cool priest," Ramona said.

He handed Ramona the celery root.

"I wasn't alone at the protests. I'd show up to protests and there'd already be nuns and priests there. All of us having come to our senses."

Ramona regarded the celery root.

"What can I make with this?" she asked. The major distinction between human and machine learning existed in the fact machines could learn from each other's mistakes, where humans were required to make them personally, which answered a lot of questions about human progress. Dozens of priests and nuns might've shown up in the eighties, but it was taking decades still for the Catholic Church to come around to gay rights. The future looked as grim as any other period in history, bright for a little while at first, then dim again. Not very graceful.

"Cover it with olive oil, salt, and pepper, and bake it. Eat it like that, maybe with some rice."

She would do no such thing.

Turning to leave the garden, Ramona caught sight of a column of people walking in the middle of the street. Men and women with their heads hung low, some with signs in their hands, none of them saying a word. There were hundreds of them, walking. One sign read: SILENCE IS HOLY. Other signs quoted long stretches of text too small to read from any real distance, but she could make out numbers and colons in the writing and knew they were Bible verses.

"Did you know about this?" Ramona asked.

"I neglected to pass their invitation along to the congregation," Father Chen said.

The protest reminded Ramona of a funeral. Another sign read: HEAR NO EVIL, SPEAK NO EVIL. Very different from the SILENCE=DEATH of the '80s and '90s. Traffic had stopped, and the sidewalks were crammed with spectators. People hung from their apartment windows. Motorcycle police coasted along the protestors, their helmets reflecting the light from the protestors' candles.

There was some disagreement about whether or not people like those currently in the street were xenophobes. No Contacters didn't want to be roped in with racists, and The Anti-Defamation League thought doing so would undermine the seriousness of the recent rise of racist ideology in America. Besides, No Contacters were a minor faction. Mostly, humans were stirring, vibrating down the sidewalks, impregnating one another in the developed world with a vengeance. Sitting politicians read poems and child soldiers were sent on furlough to attend a quick class on the updated universe. Many felt life now possessed the necessary added meaning to be worth living. Big Pharma stocks dropped, Republicans visited Democrats on hemp farms in Hawaii and Democrats visited Republicans on beef ranches in Texas to discuss ecological protections. John Boehner, with a lei around his thick neck, said things just made sense now, we were once lost but we now were found. Omni had found us. In light of all of this, promises were being made. We would invest in green energy, stop invading foreign countries, step back from a cold war with China, shrink the wealth gap, revise capitalism to pull millions out of poverty, all in preparation for the Omnians' eventual arrival. *"Omnikosmiklusion"* was the word the Germans had coined to describe the rampant sense of cosmic inclusivity people felt whenever contemplating Omni. *"Sehnsucht"* was the most commonly searched word on Google. Ramona, however, did not believe existence had suddenly snapped into place, that by identifying Earth's binary, life had finally found a balance. Who said Omni was our binary? How does one binarize a heterogeneous world in constant flux? Everyone from the ancient Greeks to Alexander von Humboldt had argued the rules to living were all right there before us in plain sight, written in the mountains and the streams, the planets and the stars; that the cosmos were the very structure of chaos, but Ramona disagreed. Save for cycles and chains for the transfer of energy, life and death, existence lacked order until humans imposed structure upon it. Omni, offering no instruction of its own, and thus far devoid of any discernable meaning, was all but empty optimism as far as she was concerned. And seventy-five-, one-hundred-and-fifty-year promises were easy to make because they were the future's to keep.

"Is contact against God's will?" Ramona said.

"These people are just scared," Father Chen said. "I think there is a simple difference between a person who has faith and a person who doesn't: people of faith don't believe everything depends on them. And yes, sometimes this manifests as someone who doesn't take responsibility for himself, but what it tells us is that there are some things in this universe that don't rely on how we feel about them. Not all fear, but this kind of fear, shows an absence of faith."

From out of the crowd, a man in tattered jeans and an old Charlotte Hornets windbreaker walked across the garden to where Ramona stood with Father Chen. She looked to Father Chen to see if he recognized the man before she remembered Father Chen's face was always welcoming. Ramona stepped back a bit, behind Father Chen.

"What's going on?" the man said, something awry with his mouth.

"I believe it's a protest," Father Chen said.

"They those abortion people?"

"Some of them are, I'm sure."

"Don't have any of those pictures of chopped-up babies. I don't believe in that, killing babies."

"They're actually protesting contacting Omni," Ramona said.

"Who's Omni?"

"It's a planet believed to harbor intelligent life," Father Chen said.

Ramona watched the man pause for a second and then burst out laughing, doubling over himself, spitting.

"You're crazy, man!" the hysterical man said, and then, to Ramona, "This guy's talking about aliens! Can you believe it?"

Ramona could smell his breath on the wind, a stomach caught digesting its own ulcers, dead blood cramming his gums, the flora of his decomposing teeth, an antiseptic wave of gin. Father Chen offered him coffee, a celery root.

CROWDS GATHERED IN CITIES, TOWNS, and villages the world over. Sevi and Ramona, half a country apart, video-chatted each other from their respective living rooms. From his screen, Sevi saw bleary hexagons of unfocused light tiling a faraway skyline. He heard a noise Ramona said was a crane. Her hair was in her face. She'd been meaning to get her bangs trimmed. A splotch of red splashed across her right cheek, like she'd just woken from a nap or been holding her hand to her face the whole day. Either way, it was an astonished look.

"I thought they'd just show up and blow us up someday," Ramona said.

"They still may."

"If we don't blow ourselves up first. I wonder what we sound like to them. In 1937."

They both searched "1937," went to the Wikipedia page.

"FDR is sworn in again as president," Ramona read.

"The Moscow Trials begin," Sevi said.

"Don't know what those are, but Ingrid Christensen becomes the first woman to set foot on Antarctica."

"One small step for womankind. The Spanish Civil War is going on."

"I'm sure that was uplifting to follow. The Pope criticizes Nazi Germany's view on race."

"A gas explosion kills two hundred and ninety-five people in the worst school disaster in American history in New London, Texas."

"How have I never heard of that before?"

"The Pope condemns communism."

"Equal opportunist in terms of condemnation."

"Of course."

"The first successful flying car takes flight," Ramona said.

"I thought flying cars didn't exist."

"They did in the past."

"First African American federal judge is appointed. Mr. William H. Hastie."

"Not to be confused with Mr. William H. Macy."

"Guernica is bombed."

"The Hindenburg explodes."

"Big year for explosions."

"Picasso paints *Guernica*."

"Spam is introduced."

"George Gershwin dies."

"The largest campaign in the Great Purge takes place, eventually killing seven hundred and twenty-four thousand people in 1937 alone."

"The last Bali Tiger dies."

"Hitler plans European invasion."

"*Of Mice and Men* is published."

"The lobotomy is invented."

There was more to the list, but Sevi's brain eventually stopped reading; his eyes, unfocused, only stared. The anecdotes of history bulleted to infinity, hyperlinked into the infinitesimal—stubs, invitations to insert your own personal histories—and he had the sudden impression there was no future bigger than its past.

"Quite the year they'll be catching up on shortly," Ramona said.

"This might sound weird, and is probably pretty premature, but 1937 kind of makes Omni sort of underwhelming," Sevi said.

"Definitely premature," she said quickly, and gave him an impatient look, a smile with a condition.

"Okay," Sevi said defensively. He wanted to tell her about the coffee that'd tasted like coffee, nothing like raspberries.

"Already bored with these aliens, you want new ones?" Ramona said.

"Every expert the media talks to is already saying the same things. The planet is yay big, a day is this long, the gravity's like this, and the transmission shows no sign of binary encryption, so it'll be a while if ever before we know what it means."

"Sounds like pretty interesting stuff to me. You don't like mystery, wonder?"

"Like you said, I was just expecting all of this to go down a little differently."

Ramona laughed, her canine on full display. The splotch had lifted from her face. Sevi, ridiculous, laughed too.

"I don't know," he said, "they're fucking aliens. I thought it'd be more intense. I don't know what I thought. Also, I know it's how Jodie Foster got to talk to aliens, but isn't radio technology kind of antiquated?"

"It's pretty sophisticated radio technology, Sevi. It's not hand radio."

"Ham radio."

"What?"

"It's called ham radio."

"That can't be right."

"I'm just saying, maybe we hyped this all up a bit too much over the years."

"Since the dawn of time, actually. People drew crazy shit in the sky on cave walls. Your problem is you're still looking for a future of flying cars when flying cars were actually invented in 1937 and people simply forgot about them because they were stupid. Meanwhile, you're missing the fact we've got electric cars, things that fight global warming. Sometimes, the future comes in practical packages."

"Electric cars still harm the environment," Sevi said. Ramona made a tired face out the window beside her and Sevi could see her as an older woman.

She said, "I'm not saying Omni has any inherent meaning, but it does present us with a sense of possibility. I think it can be a reminder that the future is ours for the making."

"Fair enough," Sevi said, and then, "I'm going to quit drinking and start exercising."

"New Year's resolution?"

"No. Well, it can be that too, but I'm going to make it my goal to live for another seventy-five years. I want to see what happens next. I want to experience the wonder, the mystery of that future."

"To hear if there's a new transmission?"

"Yeah, and witness all the changes that occur in the meantime and be a part of the cleanup crew that gets the Earth in order for the day they arrive."

"You'll be a hundred and five."

"We should both try to live that long."

"To a hundred and five?"

"Modern medicine, Ramona."

"Flying cars and flying saucers. Want to see my apartment?"

She lifted her laptop and took Sevi on a virtual tour. Her kitchen sink was full of scummy dishes. Her bedroom, down the narrow, carpeted hall, was smaller than the one she'd left him with in Chicago. He saw her shoes piled up under her work desk, imagined strands of her canola-colored hair wound in the tub's drain hole, the tampons in the wire wastebasket like mummified mice. The camera wobbled around, ebbing and fading from blanching lamplight to grainy darkness. None of it Escheresque, none of it antique, nothing Ramona at all. It occurred to him that he already knew the blueprint of the place, he'd helped her pick the apartment. This was a tour of her new life without him.

"Oh, then there's this," Ramona said back in the living room, and aimed her computer's camera out the window, tilting it downward to catch the intersection below. A small group of people were crowding the section of sidewalk in front of a bus stop.

"They having a party?" Sevi asked.

"No, those are protestors," Ramona said.

"No Contacters?"

"Anti-tech industry protesting the Wi-Fi buses. Speaking of the cleanup crew."

"What's wrong with the buses?"

"They're private charters, but the city gives them free range of all the public bus stops at no cost. People are pissed because the cops will write drivers tickets for using the stops as drop-offs, but the city isn't asking Google for a dime. Obviously, the protest is symbolic of something larger."

"That Big Tech can do whatever it wants."

"Yeah, meanwhile rent hikes are edging out thirty-year residents of San Francisco, homelessness is out of control. Not to mention the fact that most of the people the cops are writing up are people of color."

The camera returned to Ramona, and Sevi stared into the cotton murk of her white T-shirt. She said a few of the protestors were there every day. She'd come up with names for them. There was G.I. Joe, an old, wheelchair-using hippie in army fatigues and gray braids. Ma, who preferred tracksuits, and arrived each morning with coffee and often left during the day to buy cheeseburgers. Miles, who, from far away, could've been Miles Davis had he played the trumpet and not the saxophone and had Miles Davis still been alive. And a tall, willowy woman with silver hair known simply as Magic. Magic didn't seem to talk much, Ramona said. She barely moved. When the others started jumping and frothing, she'd just stand there with her arms at her side, pinned down by gravity or conviction. Magic looked so calm and kind, the type of old boho who'd give a reaffirming hand massage after a disappointing palm reading.

"Like Mother Earth incarnate," Ramona said. "She stares at me like she's worried about me."

Down there, Magic apparently looked like a deer. The ghost of a deer.

"It's really not fair, what we're doing," she said, like she was revealing this truth to herself, her voice lowering to a whisper, sadness all the way down. "What I'm doing."

Sevi didn't want her to be so sure. He wanted to touch her, to lose his hand in her hair. Those men and women were protesting agony; it could not be reconciled with any agony caused to Ramona. Being in love felt anachronistic at times, and to remain in love Sevi had to maintain a tender indifference toward the struggles around him.

"It's got nothing to do with you," he said.

He loved in an especially mammalian way—hibernating, milky, and carnivorous, it alone left a carbon footprint.

"I'm suckling from the corporate teat. I ride those buses to and from work every day," Ramona said. "Sometimes I think I should join them."

He thought of his brother, Samson, imagined him building the same inflexible argument. A mechanic by trade, Samson was a protestor, an activist, an anarchist, a dissenter, a runaway, and an autodidactic know-it-all-by-heart. He was a man apart, of a separate time; a time when people's personal convictions could outsize their common sense and commitments, an era when conquistadors and painters had as much power over the curvature of the future as bankers, politicians, and the papacy. Since dropping out of college, Samson had disappeared into a different corner of the globe at least twice a year. New York, New Delhi, San Francisco, San Salvador. Sevi couldn't stand the guy. Had Sevi arrived from a ruggedly individualistic century himself, he'd have quit his job long ago, gone without food and shelter, and composed and performed masterpieces on a sodden cello with a flaying bow on Lplatforms between arriving and departing trains. Whenever he worried he wasn't doing enough, he told himself that Samson did enough for the two of them.

"Don't fret," Sevi told Ramona, "Brother Samson's got our social justice hours covered," and felt pissed and absolved and vaguely funny.

Ramona turned her face to the camera and asked, "Where is Samson now?"

"Here, living in our parents' basement, getting into arguments on the internet."

"Have you seen him?" Ramona asked.

"Of course not," Sevi answered. "And Google and Twitter are creating tons of jobs, bringing in all sorts of revenue. The situation is . . . dynamic."

He was trying on the apologist's perspective. He was changing the subject. Big Tech wasn't so bad. He liked his phone, telling people his girlfriend, or whatever she was, worked for Google. Disingenuous as he knew this claim was, he meant it out of love. He was sorry he'd brought up Samson in the first place.

"The further we speed ahead, the further everyone else falls behind," Ramona said.

"What about your charitable work with the Vatican?" he said.

"Kind of weird," she said, expressing a pimple, taking a tissue to the blood dot.

"Experiencing symptoms of conversion?"

"Increased guilt, a propensity to tithe, flagrant almsgiving—Father, I must confess, it has been five days since my last confession!"

"You're coding for Christ."

"Actually, for the people Google is making homeless."

"It's not like they're replacing affordable housing with servers."

"No, but we're not building affordable housing either."

"Say three Hail Marys and vote Obama in November."

"Of course, and stay disillusioned but complacent, unwilling to be the change I wanted to see in the world during the first campaign."

"But that's just the thing, Ramona: working at Google, you probably will change the world."

The sincerity made Ramona blush.

"Hey, I just realized something," Sevi said, hoping to draw the color from Ramona's complexion, to make her feel a little less self-conscious. "If you combine Obama and Romney, you get Omni."

"Wouldn't it be Obamney?"

They kept going, like one of their beloved Wikipedia articles. Why hadn't the UFO community issued a statement? Why hadn't the Nation of Islam and the Church of Scientology, who were pooling their resources these days, Sevi had heard, held a joint presser? Why weren't those astronauts who'd come back from space "different" being vindicated? Didn't the Air Force have something to say? What about the probed? The cattle ranchers who'd lost legions of cows? Where were the experts? The guy with the tall hair from *Ancient Aliens*, for instance? After decades of trying to explain the improbable, Ramona explained, they'd been inconvenienced by the inexplicable. Their continued silence now was the sound of their conviction. These weren't the aliens they'd been talking about. Omni changed nothing. Just wait and see.

When the time came, Sevi split his screen so he could watch the ceremony and chat with Ramona at the same time. Video was coming in from all over the world, footage of the huge crowds standing outdoors, both day and night, along bodies of water or in city squares, beside ruins, and a few people floating in space. Music played in some places, Omni's message in others. Taipei had paper lanterns in people's hands. Thousands in Times Square watched a jumbo screen playing footage of Times Square. President Obama was watching from the residence at The White House, which had been lit up with fuchsia light. As had Big Ben, the pyramids, the Sydney Opera House, and every other ubiquitous architectural monument to human civilization. David Bowie had played the stage in New York thirty minutes ago. Sitars were jangling in New Delhi. Ramona said the Bay would have fireworks. In a few moments, at 8:30 P.M. EST, New York City would begin the festivities by releasing paper lanterns into the sky. Then, all around the world, over the course of an hour, mimicking the movement of the setting sun, tens of thousands of paper lanterns would release from different locales. Because night fell in a sine wave shape over the Earth, lanterns would rise in New York at the same time they were released in Rio. Thirty minutes later, as actual day broke in Manila and Tokyo, the Japanese and Filipinos would do the same, to lesser effect in the light. The Sender's Day ceremony would end over Greenland. Why the ceremony didn't start on Tonga and end on American Samoa, the way New Year's did, no one would say exactly. Americans still bragged about winning the space race and were used to bossing everyone around, so it felt natural that they host the most expensive transnational event in global history. Few complained. By leading the world in interstellar communication, Americans would be easier to blame when the aliens eventually invaded. "It's them you want," the rest of the world could say. "We just work here."

The tickertape coursing along the bottom of the screen showed the markets had rallied all day and would be up several percentage points by the bell. Against the sound advice of analysts, people were borrowing and building again. What they were building for or toward was unclear.

"I should invest," Sevi said.

"You should wait," Ramona said.

Mahler, tightrope-walking the arm of the couch, puckered her anus at Sevi, and he swatted her away. She bit his ankle and ran. Ramona said, "I think I heard her laughing."

"It's starting," Sevi said.

In Times Square, the jumbo screen turned to a conference room in Mountain View, the Carl Sagan Center. Dr. Osip Braz, the only astronomer in the world everyone now knew, stood at a microphone and offered opening remarks, quoting Sagan and Frank Drake. In his Russian accent, he said what was on everybody's minds: human history was overrun with milestones; given the troubles of the world, good news was hard to accept, and great discoveries, among the most gifted creatures to ever roam the Earth, were even more difficult to truly appreciate—but humankind was on the verge of the single most important event in history, and we needed to take stock of what it meant to be alive in 2012. The world was never going to be the same. If history seemed a singular trajectory toward fate, providence or perdition, then our course had been redirected, and everything once deemed impossible should now be reconsidered. Anything was officially possible. How deserving and unworthy we all were.

From this day forth, he said, *we are not only one human race. We are not only one people. We are one planet, from the mountains to the streams, the germs and the birds, the past and the future, war and peace. And each one of us, be we president or insect, is a representative of our planet and all we have to offer the universe. Today does not mark the end of our differences, but an embrace of life's wild constellation. We, scattered cousins to the stars, are calling home.*

A senseless rhythm of blips and pops ripped the air and New York let go of its lanterns. The Amazon let off its lanterns. Equations, histories, poems, and maps were transcribed in tiny binary drums. Whole symphonies were carried off. The sound of a cat's dreaming brain. Stories of celebration and regret. The chemical analysis of a heart in love. The number dead after Hiroshima and Nagasaki. Whale songs. A favorite movie. The whole wild constellation tapped out like rain on a window. Rain on a window. A baby napping in a jungle. The industry of cancer. "Hello" in every language. The unsteady stream of every place in the world. The opening and closing lines of the internet as of that morning. Sex, and not just procreation, but the nasty stuff too, as defined by math. All of it, unsteady drumming.

Someone was standing outside in the cold in New York, so bundled up Sevi had no idea who he was, talking. *We are changing at this very moment*, the man said into a microphone. *This is the beginning of something very big. We're going to end suffering on this planet. We're going to fight every disease with everything we've got. We're going to make our planet a safe place in the universe.*

"I wish they could hear this right now," Ramona said.

Her face, in the darkened living room, was lit by the fuchsia glow of her screen. So peaceful, so alien, so recognizably the person he was still so desperately in love with.

"Yeah, so we could tell them that we turn out all right," Sevi said.

"I wish we could tell the people alive in 1937 that too."

"Ramona," Sevi said.

He didn't think he'd make it to a hundred and five. He didn't think he'd last the seventy-five years it'd take to find out if Earth was going to make it or not.

"Yes."

"I don't want to be apart from you anymore."

"I don't think I want that either," she said.

"Let's try again. Really try."

There were blips, a weird ambient cover of the song of time.

"I want us to be together now, in the future, afterward."

He closed the Sender's Day feed to look only at her glowing face. He could hear the rhythms and cheers from her speakers still, the reflection of balloon and confetti and crowd light patterned her face. She looked right at him, her face fuchsia again, and nodded.

"You should go see your brother," she said.

He hadn't seen his brother in months. He didn't understand what his brother had to do with this moment.

"What? Why?" he asked.

"He's going to need you right now."

"He is?"

"Maybe more than ever."

"How do you know?"

"I live in the Bay. Trust me, I know the type. He's going to think it's all up to him, whether or not we make it."

"And then we'll try?"

She hadn't stopped nodding. This meant something. As she nodded, a burst of light the color of pollen brightened her face. A delayed pop followed. She gasped and covered her mouth.

"Ramona?"

He reopened his browser to the Sender's Day feed. Baghdad. 3:30 A.M. A spotlighted gray cloud covering a square. Blanched-out screaming. Sirens. The night air sipped up the smoke, and in the event and camera lighting Sevi saw rubble, dust, char, and explosions of blood.

Ladies and gentlemen, there have been a series of massive explosions just outside the Swords of Qadissyah in Baghdad. Visibility is low, but—

Another two explosions cut a British reporter off. Sevi closed the window.

"Ramona. Ramona, turn it off," he said.

"What?"

"Just turn it off, Ramona."

The disfigured light lifted from her face.

"Jesus Christ," she said.

"They want the whole world watching," Sevi said. "They've even got Omni watching. I'm not watching."

"I saw a boy's face."

"The whole world saw his face."

"And then it was gone."

"The whole world watched him disappear."

"Where did he go?"

"The whole world's looking for him, Ramona. You don't need to."

TWO

Dear Babichev,

I am building a radio telescope in the mountain village of Green Bank, West Virginia. It is not anywhere we'd ever heard of, but the local girls wash their hair only once a week, and in this way Green Bank reminds me of the Urals. For kilometers, a disk of radio silence circumscribes the area, protecting our precious telescope from any interference. The girls wash on Saturday and travel in the evening to towns outside the silent zone to watch television with friends. Come Monday, they reappear in their places of work with smiles like they've just returned from their honeymoons; by Friday, however, pouring coffee at the diner and making playful bouquets in the floral shop, they are onerous once again. These sullen faces, which are more bored than completely crushed, would not have fared well back home, I don't think. And in this way, I know I am in America, the land of expectations, of which I now have many. It is the expectation our telescope will hear an extraterrestrial signal. We will enter in coordinates and the telescope will listen to the corresponding region. Dr. Frank Drake, the man in charge of the observatory, believes he knows where he'd like to start, but I would like to aim the telescope at Moscow and listen to what you have to say. For now these messages will have to suffice, I'm afraid. Dr. Drake told us we will begin emitting our own deliberate signals soon to compete with the awful ambient chatter we've been sending since November 2, 1920, when the first commercial radio broadcast slipped this Earth and announced our unintelligible arrival. What shall we say? I asked him. That we know math and physics, he said. More boasting, how human, I wanted to say. I should talk. Here I go, on and on about what an accomplished American scientist I have become! What about you, Babichev? Have you found your gooseberry farm yet? I had a dream the other day you and Shklovsky had built a telescope of your own with which we were communicating in radio waves. We bounced our signals off the moon and landed them in each other's headsets. I awoke to my own starved ears.

A WHITE 1959 CHEVY IMPALA, dropped, on low-profile tires and gold hundred-spoke Luxor rims, with a chrome grill like Geordi La Forge's visor. Eason hadn't seen the car in a minute when one clear and unseasonably warm Saturday it was honking from the street outside his apartment. By the time Eason made it down to the street, Jules was outside the car, buffing wax into one of its fins. It let off a woozy gas smell and blinded westbound traffic. Eason didn't even like cars, but the Impala was something entirely different. His dad, Mr. Bus Pass himself, whom Eason had never seen in a driver's seat, could rattle off its specs for days, to which Eason would happily listen, like the man was reciting a recipe, and they were both starving to death. Eason had requested a moment of his cousin's time; he couldn't believe he was actually going to go through with brokering some sort of deal to save Germaine's dumb ass, but here he was.

"Feel like going for a cruise?" Jules said.

Eason didn't really want Jules to come up, so he agreed.

The car moaned pulling away from the curb and felt weighed down but springy—a balloon or a tugboat on wheels. Jules hung back from the steering wheel, his phone in hand, connected by aux cable to the digital receiver. He wheeled through some music, eyes off the road, and before Eason could yell "Stop sign!" "Aimed at You" by Chief Keef was on, the Southsider lulling warnings to naive clowns pretending to be gangbangers over a drill beat that made the mirrors of Jules's car ripple and the numbers on the receiver jump double Dutch. Jules rolled through the stop, and Eason saw it didn't matter because traffic on either side was too mesmerized by the car to pull through the intersection anyways.

"How come you ain't got a ride, cuz?" Jules said.

"Because I'm broke."

"You sitting like you broken."

Eason, crumpled in the corner of the bench seat against the door, stretched out. His shoulders rose, his arm fell out of the window. From over the long hood, it looked like the car was eating the road. They crawled Humboldt Drive. It was a trip. Men and women stepped away from their own cars to stare lovingly at the Impala. The men, Eason noticed, turned away when they saw him looking at them, but the women kept staring. Keef drowned out the cúmbia or *bachata* or whatever the Boricuas were listening to those days. Every few seconds Eason thought he'd come out and say what he needed to say, but those seconds passed and he remained utterly silent.

"I'm sorry about your boy," Jules said.

"Rydell?"

Jules's jaw, clean shaven, always bulged like he was chewing. It was easy to confuse with concern. Eason wasn't sure it wasn't this time, though.

"Fucked up how that shit happens," Jules added.

"Do you know who did it?"

"Fool, you think I'd tell you if I did?"

"My bad."

"Unless you want to do something about it."

"I'm straight."

Jules turned to look at Eason, his body back in a scrunch.

"So, you wanna tell me what all this is about?" Jules said. "Or did you just miss your big cousin?"

"It's about Germaine," Eason said.

"I don't even wanna hear that motherfucker's name, cuz."

His voice rose in exhaustion.

"I know. I know. It's messed up what he did, disrespecting you like that, but—"

"Disrespecting? I can handle some disrespect, I ain't a bitch. That fool did more than just disrespect me, you understand? Motherfucker told the whole world he was gonna take me outta the game. I don't know if they teach you what that means in school, but that means he's gonna kill me."

"He says he got carried away. And he took it back, in front of everyone, he took it back."

"Why you carrying water for Germaine?"

"It's not about Germaine."

"Then who's it about?"

"I dunno."

"Fool, I'ma kick your ass out my car right now."

"It doesn't have to end like this. Every goddamn time, it doesn't have to end like this."

"That's some Jesse Jackson shit."

Eason took a breath so deep it hurt.

He said, "I do want you to do something for Rydell. For Rydell, just drop it. Germaine's done. He'll disappear. He won't be of any more concern to you."

"Rydell ain't got nothing to do with this."

Eason looked out the passenger window. He'd counted every cop car they'd passed. Six.

"Then just do it for me. Please," Eason said, turning to look at Jules again.

Jules sucked his teeth, took a left turn.

"Okay," he said with a shrug.

"Okay?"

"Yeah, sure, why not? No sweat, cuz."

Eason sat up, elated, surprised that success could come so easily.

"Thank you. And Germaine says he's done," Eason said, which Germaine hadn't, but he thought the promise would seal the deal and keep Germaine out of any future trouble. "He won't try to make any money where you're making money, you'll forget he ever existed."

"And that's a problem."

"What? Why?"

"Germaine used to make me a lot of money. Keeping him out of commission impacts me negatively, financially speaking."

"So, you want him to keep working for you?"

"Nah, I don't trust Germaine no more. My business is based off trust. So, until I can find a more permanent solution, I'm going to need someone to fill in for Germaine. Sort of like an intern, or some shit like that."

"An intern."

"You got any summer internships lined up?"

"What?"

"Change a life. Otherwise, no deal. And it ain't like it's one of those bogus unpaid internships, neither."

"Jules, I'm not going to be of any use to you."

"No deal then."

"Isn't there any other way?"

"These are my terms."

Eason realized he was shaking. It wasn't the subs, the song had ended, they were driving in silence now. What would he say to Germaine? How could he attend his funeral? How could he go on living knowing he'd had the chance to save a life and not taken it?

"Fine," Eason muttered.

"What'd you say?" Jules said.

"Yeah, I'll do it. What do I have to do?"

"Pickups and drop-offs. Maybe a little running. Nothing that'll disrupt your school day," Jules said, and then, after a pause, looking at Eason, "Damn, Eason, you sure?"

"I'm sure," Eason answered, looking straight ahead.

"I didn't even know you and Germaine was tight."

"We're not."

"Well, whatever man, just make sure your old man doesn't find out about this. And quit sitting like that."

Eason strained to relax. Rydell had died, Germaine would live. The air was warm and wormy, weird for February. Gulls and trash floated on a thermal outside the window of Jules's car. Worn and supple, the blue leather of the passenger door's interior hugged Eason through another left-hand turn.

They cruised California and Division, hollered at some girls leaving the Dollar General, peeled out in front of a Benz at Western, grabbed jumbo slices from Little Villa and ate them in the parking lot, standing beside the car so as not to stain the upholstery. Winding back around the park, wiping grease from his mouth with the sleeve of his sweatshirt, Eason caught sight of Fabian, an asshole from school. Since the start of the school year, it was like Fabian had made it his personal goal to give Eason as much shit as possible. Knocking on his pops for having so many kids, calling Eason cello fag in the hallways, he had something to say every day. Eason ducked behind the Impala's massive door before remembering his body.

"You know that fool?" Jules said.

"Yeah."

"He fuck with you?"

"Nah."

"Don't lie to me, I can tell."

"I don't wanna fuck with him."

"Listen here. You represent me now, and nobody better be thinking you're some sort of bitch-ass punk. So you make sure his ass sees you when we drive past."

Jules put up the volume and slowed down. Eason stared straight ahead as they passed Fabian on the left, his neck tensing as he fought the urge to turn and tell Fabian to run. But then they were past him, and Jules was speeding up again.

"Now he knows," Jules said.

Parked back outside Eason's apartment, Jules reached under his seat and pulled out a brick of weed.

"You sit tight, Julio Ruiz is coming for this in fifteen," he said.

"Daniel's brother?"

"Yeah."

"Kid's like ten."

"How you think I got to be a baller before twenty?"

RAMONA DREW THE LAST SPURT of blueberry yogurt from the tube she'd grabbed on her way into the Googleplex for her morning snack, rolled the goo's colorful sheath into a Fibonacci spiral, and threw it into the wastebasket beside her desk. The spiral's intelligent design did not last. From atop her ergonomic chair—mesh nylon; hydraulic; a thousand dollars, easy— she watched as the wrapper unfurled into a flaccid and flattened tapeworm, the extant shape this particular piece of single-use plastic would maintain for the next four hundred and fifty years, her fourth or fifth anthropogenic contribution of the day. Could've had a smoothie in a compostable cup, she lamented. A breakfast burrito, elegantly self-contained, fully edible. But this brand of yogurt was marketed for life on the go. Her life was on the go, kind of, she commuted four hours a day. Low-fat dairy was one of the few things her body processed with ease. And there were more pleasant forms of work avoidance than contemplating how convenience was killing the planet.

A ruminative walk would suffice, except Ramona had a rule about not leaving her cubicle, a rare but hardly coveted space within Google's trademark labyrinth of beanbag, hammock, and treadmill tableaus. In an unspoken agreement with the Googleverse, Ramona would not set foot outside the hex of her three-wall perimeter, and her coworkers, their playroom accoutrement, their bazingas, their latent beta-male complexes, would not come anywhere near her. So far, so good. For all the screen time logged at Google, her fellow Googlers never sat still. Why would they when any indoor excursion might include a haircut, a massage, or a foosball tournament? Among these indoorsmen (some women), their workspace was mostly a state of mind composed of Adderall, 5-Hour Energy, the exquisite irreality of the integrated developer environment. Her few fellow territorial types ornamented their standing desks with the maximalist aesthetic of Indian lorry drivers, substituting the protective layering of Vishnu and Hanuman idols with box forts made of Captain America and Bart Simpson dolls in their original packaging. A self-described weirdo, Ramona was a normie in their company.

The décor was a minor act of free market freedom, in her opinion, however. Acne concealer on an acid burn. Quieting the thunder rev of capitalism's 500-horsepower death drive to total market and ecological collapse was these workers' maddening appreciation of the perks, gushed over at bars and on blogs. Every pained Googler had access to an on-site therapist. Without ever clocking out, said Googler could confer with said specialist and might be prescribed a therapy dog, then be permitted to bring said dog to work. Judging by the therapy queue, long but always manageable, because it was managed by a smart scheduler, most of Ramona's coworkers were as troubled as she was. The only difference was they'd somehow still managed to have fun, or at least get on with their lives. How this was possible, with sea levels, fascism, and TB rates on the rise all over the world while voting rights, life expectancy, and economic prosperity were diminishing in their own country, she had no idea. Refugees all over the planet were marooned or incarcerated while billions of dollars were being made to build the police states of the future; Black people, the mentally ill, and children were being shot dead in the street. Maybe they were just that self-satisfied. Maybe it was all the money they made. Or maybe they were just too busy at work to question why they couldn't fall asleep without a chemical assist. Ramona wasn't busy. She wasn't busy because she had no idea what she was supposed to be doing at Google.

Eight months ago, a recruiter from the single most influential company in the world had called to discuss a program Ramona had developed in her junior year at the University of Chicago, something she'd scarcely remembered. The recruiter found the program scanning university journals for potential R&D projects. The program in question was an AI-generated safe search function that protected users against 9/11, a variety of other PTSD-inducing content, and body dysmorphia triggers. The recruiter had been particularly impressed by its surgical incisiveness. Ramona was offered twelve months and relocation costs to keep teasing out the code in Mountain View.

The program was called Tiresias, and it used deep learning to navigate the networks of trauma online and meticulously remove triggers from sight. At first, it had only gone after keywords, but human language was rife with nuance and connotation, and it had to familiarize itself with how triggers worked in the mind to head off the subtler content. To date, it was sophisticated enough to build a protective shield around a social media account, saving the user from harassment without affecting any other content whatsoever. It could be good for society in a satirical sense.

Tease out what? Ramona thought. The code looked like it belonged in a bad '80s hair metal band as it was. The director of R&D told her to "think outside the bun." She interpreted this to mean that he didn't know why the hell she was here either, and she suspected she wouldn't be there for much longer. The only thing she knew for certain was that leadership had very little interest in Tiresias in its present state. Otherwise, they'd have bought it as is. Censorship didn't bode well in the Googleplex. Facebook and Twitter, companies with serious harassment problems, would happily pay millions for the latest version of Tiresias, but these newest functions had been developed at Google, and thus belonged to Google. Leadership would sooner let Tiresias rot away in a neglected server than sell its latest AI to a competitor. They could always reconsider their stance on China and run IT for the Great Firewall. She didn't know what would come of Tiresias. She was stuck, and her twelve months were coming to a close. So, she sat around worrying about waste, what a waste she was, the waste she produced.

Her options were limited. One, she could continue feeding Tiresias data, studying how it detected triggers through deep learning, and pray. Two, she could embrace total confusion, and simply stare at it and do nothing all day. She liked the second option. Anticipation was the flower to disappointment's stony fruit.

Ramona moved a framed photo of Sevi onto her desk. Had she a cubicle mate, they might have asked her if the guy in the picture was her boyfriend. She wouldn't have known what to say. At first, she and Sevi had only called each other to talk about Omni and their observations about life since the technosignature's discovery. The way cars were slowly colliding in the streets. How domain names featuring the word Omni were selling for tens of thousands of dollars. They emailed each other pictures and articles. Sevi had sent her a photo from a salon in Beijing that specialized in dying your dog fuchsia. Ramona sent Sevi an article about a real estate mogul who was purchasing abandoned McMansion subdivisions for future temporary housing for the aliens. They talked about how underneath the novelties—mugs, hats, a commemorative slushie flavor—they were noticing actual things about actual people. A man Sevi had passed on the way to work each day for years had suddenly stopped him to say hello and ask him what he did for a living. The man was a Xerox repairman and loved to cook. Ramona had seen eavesdroppers welcomed into strangers' conversations at various stores and coffee shops. And less and less did people want to talk about Omni—they were running out of things to say about the planet. Earthly things were in vogue again. The weather, politics, feelings. Small talk, for the most part, but with intention. These things could make a difference, she thought. People were taking charge of a cosmic phenomenon. Twice, she'd taken her top off on Skype; once, she requested a picture of Sevi's cock—she looked at it and said, "I remember that." Kind of a clumsy, ridiculous object, despite its social lore, but she liked it. Boyfriend? She didn't know. Kind of a clumsy, ridiculous, and socially unevolved thing, too. But she was in love again, that much was clear. If everyone fell in love again, maybe that'd make a difference.

After emptying another yogurt sheath, Ramona stared for some time at a strand of Tiresias. Ineptitude was new and required ruminating over too. She felt milky and unsteady, in need of burping. An exercise ball rolled into her cubicle. Its cheery red body bounced off her shoeless heel and wobbled to a stop against a metal filing cabinet like a fat child. The cabinet had nothing in it but a few chocolates. It had come to rescue her, she thought, this ball. She'd walk it back to its last user and violently berate him, for which she'd be fired and given the chance to get on with her life. But something dinged before she could address the rubber sphere. The automated age, she admitted, would feel at first as if everything needed you. Awaiting mankind wasn't an autocracy, hopefully not, but an automacracy, the soft autumn descent of the self. Only after the self would there be peace, the floating stasis of a billion untenable obligations.

It wasn't her Gmail, that almost corporeal reservoir of warnings, pleas, bargains, and duties that gave the company its curb-stomping foothold in so many people's personal and professional lives. It was her phone, a news notification. Some people followed politics, others watched the polar ice caps melt in real time, a few collected memes restaging the fascism v. communism dialectic. Ramona asked to be pinged each time the surveillance economy grew a new eye, or whenever a computer was used to violate a person's civil or natural rights. She was following stories about Chelsea Manning and Julian Assange and a new story about Aaron Swartz, who was awaiting trial for stealing JSTOR articles, a ridiculous indictment but good enough pretense to hide the government's widespread campaign against young, charismatic, and slightly messianic computer whizzes who might jump-start a civil liberties movement. The growing outrage needed keeping up with. It did nothing but bring her more anxiety and misery. But when Ramona's eyes refocused from the light plane of her monitor for the light plane of her phone, it wasn't a headline about a person's arrest she read, but one about a man's impending early release. A man she knew. A man she'd helped the feds put way. A man named Dana Johnson.

Through much of college, Ramona had spent most of her free time doing illicit things on the internet, a curiosity that'd sometimes flare into all-nighters she called Nocterms, when, in keeping with the Maker's schedule, she'd utilize the uninterrupted hours others reserved for family, food, and rest to hack.

It was an act of unabashed anarchy. It was fun. U of C was where fun went to die. She was chipping away at the monolith, undermining the artifice of control by reminding internet users how fragile their networks were, dismantling them before their very eyes. Her mind, too tired to wander, to wonder about Tide pens, a new pair of yoga pants, the last time she'd gotten laid, would still with the cool blue of the monitor and let her work for up to twelve hours at a time without sleep. Twelve cigarettes, a shit, was all it took to get through the shift. She was part of a little group led by someone who called himself Jesse. Together, they hacked politicians' and CEOs' emails seeking evidence of backdoor deals for future corruption charges. She wrote malicious scripts for Jesse, unique lines to create new vulnerabilities that couldn't be traced for a few days, weeks. They were designed for all sorts of mail servers. The mail servers were the first routes of entry. The fact she was asked to find holes in so many meant Jesse had diverse but specific interests. He was not seeking a litter of credit cards or social security numbers. Occasionally, Ramona would be sent to the doors of a corporate portal—an in-house program from which an employee could manage a 401(k)—and be told: Get in. Her patience, conservativeness, and quiet got her what Jesse wanted, whatever that really was. Once in, Jesse could social engineer his way to the accounts of import. She hacked impetuously. A lot of what she saw looked energy-related, stuff just shy of a smoking gun, meant to implicate someone in the grand climate conspiracy, those making millions and billions off the death of the planet. She wasn't an environmentalist, not really, but she had a role to play. Maybe Jesse wanted to rustle up a scandal, something to wake up the Earthlings once and for all: You're being conned to death! Maybe he knew a shy whistleblower who'd fill in the details but just didn't want to be in charge. Ramona had only ever gotten so far as to deduce that Jesse was searching. In the dark, people everywhere were always searching, always; signaling one another with a language of exchanges, trading comments and dirty gems, wearing each other's IPs like couples dressed as one another at Halloween parties, braiding their codes into a giant and totally fucked DNA chain, searching, searching, searching. Even the NSA was searching. Whatever it was they were hoping to find, they kept looking because they hadn't found it yet.

Eyeing the headline, Ramona felt her vascular system constrict, her heart moving in the uneven style of a gondolier. She opened her spam folder. The computer-generated diction, shoddy auto-translations, and vomit-it-all-against-the-wall-and-see-what-infects sense of abandon estranged her into a carefree, Ponzi-scheme-curious, erectile-dysfunction-suffering senior citizen seeking one weird trick Obama didn't want him to know about. As this other, she could breathe again.

She tried to block it, but the events of that day returned to her. Snow was filling the cement balcony. Her roommates, Alisha and Genevieve, were at their parents' for the winter holiday. The FBI didn't burst in, guns blazing, they knocked. Standing inside her slanted living room, the men showed her a search warrant and spoke to her with the calm of guidance counselors.

"We think you're mixed up, that this guy took advantage of you, made you do things you wouldn't otherwise have done," one said.

The other said they thought she was a true patriot.

"We know you're from Boston. You a Patriots fan?"

Jesse's real name was Dana Johnson. He was a twenty-nine-year-old security analyst from Arlington, Virginia. He and his girlfriend had a daughter.

"But he's dangerous."

"We just need your files."

"No one will ever know it was you."

She complied without any mention of the potential charges they might've thrown at her had she not. Consequence was a natural, invisible structure living beneath her feet.

Dana got twenty-five years in federal prison. No mention of Ramona in the deposition. And he was getting out, seventeen years early. Even if the FBI had kept their word and never mentioned her name, Dana knew it was her. She knew Dana knew. The invisible consequence of the world had returned. She was supposed to have been forty-five years old, an impossible age, when it came to swallow her up. She was supposed to be a different person, a person who'd done something with her freedom, a person who'd made up for her past, a person insulated by wealth. She'd done nothing of the sort; she had nothing to protect her. And even though she'd cut all ties with everyone she used to know eight years ago, even though she'd been a corporate sellout forever, people like Dana Johnson, people like Aaron Swartz, were still the people whose opinions actually mattered to her, they were the moral center of this world, of the world to which everyone was supposed to be headed. Sevi would be surprised but he wouldn't care, and would she really care if he did? Her parents would be relieved. "Oh, honey, you made the right choice. I'm so sorry you got involved with that criminal." Google, if she still worked for Google, would be split. Half would be indifferent. The other half would threaten to walk out if she wasn't fired. And after she posted her letter of resignation on a company forum, and after that post went viral on social media, her life would be both the same and impossible to go on with. Because of the shame, absolutely, but mainly for her failure to do something with the freedom she'd stolen from Dana. She was always going to be found out. She was always going to be destroyed in some way. But she was supposed to have done something, at least.

PG, a sort-of-friend who worked for Twitter, popped up on her Gchat. He did math stuff, mainly, but spent a few hours a week blasting bots and trolls from existence, though also, he had more than a few bots trolling people at any given time himself. She wrote to him.

me

How do they expect the human race to even exist another one
hundred and fifty years if we keep jailing our brightest
people, chopping down the rainforests that hold the cures to

```
all our current and future diseases, melting the ice caps that
contain the ancient diseases that will kill us in the future!
I'm talking about Aaron Swartz btw.
```

She'd try to create a sympathetic public record in the coming days, to complicate Dana's inevitable smear campaign. For years, she'd thought of writing Dana, telling him everything, begging his forgiveness. But that opportunity had now passed, and her survival relied on an ambiguous confluence of neutered corporatism and reflexive anarchism. In less than four months she'd be out of a job. In six months, everything anyone had ever believed about Ramona Thompson would be eclipsed by what Dana Johnson had to say about her.

```
    PG
O plz that white boy?

    me
Um do you mean that social justice fighter? That hacktivist?
That fucking bastion of internet freedom?

    PG
He's a sacrificial lamb and I'm not gonna waste my pity on a
know-it-all twenty-five-year-old who got caught doing a sloppy
hack no matter what they do to him. Deep V collar-crimes just
aren't any of my concern.

    me
Just making conversation . . .

    PG
Consider that topic covered

    me
You don't have work?
```

```
    PG
Do you?

    me
You could just put up your away message like a normal person
if you don't want people to bother you.

    PG
Too monoculture I'd rather be 100% transgressive 100% of the
time

    me
I thought I was done with contrarians when I left UChicago

    PG
I thought I was done with people who name dropped their
university when I graduated with honors from Stanford's
Machine Learning program
But I forgive you. BRB
```

He never came back.

RAMONA LEFT WORK early without having accomplished a thing. Before going home, she sat in a corner of Dolores Park for half an hour, slipping her shoes on and off, watching skateboarders jump over skateboards. Father Chen had once said she could go on with her good self and start a nonprofit that'd probably take half the homeless population off the street if she wanted. She wished she did.

There was a woman screaming at the top of her lungs into a microphone nearby. People needed to know she didn't think Omni meant shit. A wag-the-dog the cosmos had given the governments of the world to evade public scrutiny for a while. The mike was passed, and a man spoke, less loudly, about gang violence on his street. Ramona followed the sound and found an audience thickening around the voices. A man talked about his love of buses, his fear buses would go away if electric cars took over. He didn't think he'd feel safe traveling in anything but a bus. He'd raised his hand, gotten the microphone. Ramona went over to the crowd and raised her hand. The man who'd spoken about the buses handed her the microphone. Everyone's face turned to look at her, a whole audience of speaking listeners, of listening speakers. It was a system model. During Occupy these same people engineered a human microphone after a noise ordinance declared the usage of megaphones and amplifiers illegal. Their words had moved like an ocean wave from person to person.

"I met Aaron Swartz at a conference once. He was nice. I can't believe he's going to jail now," she said.

"A young brother," a man said, and the woman beside him nodded. They were both older, and Ramona didn't think they knew what she was talking about.

"Well, yeah, he's young, and he's a brother in the fight against the surveillance state."

"Sing it, sister!" a skinny white man with a familiar-looking IT badge said.

"What'd he do?" the woman who'd nodded asked.

"He stole several million articles on plant life from an online database."

"And they caught him?" the woman said.

"Yeah."

"And he's actually going to jail?"

"Probably."

"And he's a white boy?"

"Yes."

"Must've been some really good plant articles."

"I don't know. They were written, like, over a century ago."

"Antiques," the woman said to the man beside her. He nodded.

ON HER WAY into her apartment, the protestors had confused her for one of their own and offered her a leftover breakfast taco. She'd almost cried. Inside, smoking herself into a malcontent cloud, she drafted several text messages to send Sevi.

```
Why do I feel like the world speaks a different language
from me?
Aaron Swartz, hero or library delinquent?
Talk?
```

She settled on `I love you` and waited. She'd smoked maybe a bit too much and was in between stages of highness—uncomfortable, paranoid—so she smoked more to break through. Feeling better, high as fuck, she stumbled on her way to the bathroom. When she sat down to pee nothing came out, or it did, and she didn't feel it, and for a moment she feared she'd peed herself several times in her life without noticing. Before she could give this concern any more thought, Sevi wrote back.

```
I love you so much, Ramona. Every day we talk I feel
stronger, closer to my true self. You inspire me and
give me courage. I'm going to see Samson this weekend.
```

If she'd been drinking, she might've broken into tears. `Good. I love you too`, she wrote back and sent it before realizing she'd already written "I love you." She felt embarrassed for only a second. Sevi wouldn't care. Sevi wouldn't criticize her for that kind of mistake. She was an inspiration to him, he'd said so. Even if she was unhappy, she was inspirational. Even if she was a fuckup, she was inspirational. Even if she was a coward, she was inspirational. She stayed seated on the toilet, a woman in love.

Tiresias, I'll figure that out, she thought. And, Aaron Swartz is a hero. And maybe not all people suffer equally. But if there were a way to prioritize suffering . . . Not a bad idea, could be determined by deep learning . . . She wrote this down in her Notes app. I'll keep my job and hide behind it. And I won't be alone. I'll never be alone.

```
I feel closer to my true self talking to you too. Life
is much clearer when you're around.
```

The words on her screen danced and wiggled as her eyes focused and unfocused. The words looked great. They had rainbows around their edges.

SEVI'S DAD WAS HOME, BUT his ma was still at work cleaning offices downtown. After a hug, his dad moved immediately to the couch, where Sevi assumed he must have been before he answered the door. Taking off his shoes, careful to keep any snow on the doormat, Sevi watched his dad staring at the TV, sliding a doily up and down the couch's plastic-wrapped armrest. Under the plastic were broad-knit flowers, large knots of pigment like suffocated stars. He was back in his childhood home in Cicero for the first time since Ramona had left.

There was a soccer game on. Chivas, his dad's team, were up 1–0 against Toluca with only ten minutes left on the clock, plus whatever OT they'd go. Sevi unfocused his eyes and the players disappeared into the pitch, which looked like a long green swimming pool. He wondered where they were playing. His dad didn't break eye contact with the TV when Sevi sat down beside him.

The man's head looked like something you might find in an owl pellet, smooth and passed and covered in fuzz. Sevi stared at it and admitted his dad had gotten old. Since the last time he'd seen him, he'd gotten old.

The referees gave the teams four whole additional minutes of game time. After, Telemundo would run the Bud Light postgame report, with its chubby commentators surrounded by bikini-clad women with astounding bodies.

"How are you, Dad?"

"I'm okay. Your mom and I are having trouble sleeping. I think it has something to do with the news. That's what they say. Are you sleeping?"

"I'm sleeping okay," Sevi said.

"The news has just gone crazy."

"There's a lot of stuff to cover these days. We're not alone in the universe. Have you been keeping up?"

He thought Omni would be a good topic. Maybe his dad hadn't heard that scientists now thought that the planet was covered in poisonous clouds, or that the International Indigenous Society had put out a statement denouncing anyone thinking of colonizing the alien planet—as far-fetched as those plans seemed, there were a lot of organizations, from environmental scientists to Halliburton, possessing strong, Jesuit boners for the planet.

"Your mom and I, we try not to think about it. We try to limit the TV. On a show, they said that following the same news over and over can mess up your brain. We turned the TV off as soon as he said that."

"I don't have a TV," Sevi said.

His dad turned to look at him for the first time since sitting back down.

"You don't have a TV?" He looked pained. "I think we have an old one you can borrow."

His dad stood, opened a closet to look for the TV. From within the closet, he asked after Ramona, if Sevi was still talking to her.

"She's good. Actually, we're kind of back together, I think."

"You think? You'd better find out," he said, poking his head from the closet.

"We are," Sevi said.

"Not in there," his dad said, returning to the couch. "Your mother's still upset you didn't come for Christmas. You should've come. Your cousins were asking about you. Maria, the teenager, she said she knew you wouldn't come because we're not sophisticated enough for you. I said no. I made up something about you being busy. But you're not busy, are you?"

Sevi excused himself to pretend to use the bathroom. Inside, the overhead fan purred. This place, for so long his home, felt no longer extant. His whole life he'd wanted to get away from it. The summer Samson learned how to ride his bike without training wheels, while their parents worked, Sevi urged them to take bike rides each day, going farther and farther afield with hopes of reaching a forest preserve they remembered visiting with their dad.

Sevi was ten or eleven, three years older than Samson. He had the confidence of a much older child then, something Samson found annoying and comforting. Sevi knew the tricks of avenues and boulevards, the secret of left and right turns that eventually landed you at your doorstep no matter where you came from. Finally, one afternoon in late July they made it to the forest preserve and spent a few delirious hours chasing fish around a man-made pond and giggling at a lewd doodle they'd discovered under a metal slide. Around two P.M., they decided enough was enough and headed home. They rode with traffic and with no trouble at all until, at a somewhat familiar intersection, Sevi's mind went blank. He stopped, and Samson sensed his uncertainty like a dog sniffing a change in barometric pressure and started crying these big, wracking sobs right there on his bike.

"Are you crazy?" Sevi shouted. "You want someone to find out we're lost?"

"Maybe someone will help," his brother said, smearing mucus on his handlebar grips.

The police and fire department had hosted a safety-awareness program the previous year at school from which Sevi had learned that anyone he didn't know was most likely a murderous drug addict. A mother with a stroller seemed harmless enough, but her husband and his torture basement which awaited you were not. The police had also spoken expectantly. They said, "When we see you stealing, we're going to get you," so that all the kids in the classroom understood the police did not serve and protect them but people from them, that they could be grouped in with the murders, so there was no use counting on the cops to come save you when you were in trouble. Sevi told Samson they needed to ride on, find Cicero. But they were still in Cicero, they'd never left.

Exhausted and seriously dehydrated—they'd packed nothing but warm cans of pop that morning—Sevi and Samson eventually stopped in front of an open garage. Samson sniffled in understanding of what they needed to do: risk their lives to ask for directions.

Any number of horrible fates awaited them. Sevi apologized in advance for getting Samson killed. He pictured his little brother hacked to bits, thrown into the cement like those paint chips people used when resurfacing their driveways.

"I was supposed to protect you," he said. "But I messed up. If I see you in heaven, I hope you forgive me. If we live, I won't let something like this happen ever again."

Bikes collapsed on the grass, they walked up to the garage. Inside was the sickest, most twisted-looking old man they'd ever seen. He was white, and "The Whites," their aunt had once said, "are the real sickos. The Blacks and the Latinos, they might steal your car, but it's the Whites who'll cut out your heart and eat it for lunch." All sorts of saws and blades hung from the walls of the garage, rusted car parts piled in a back corner. The man was seated on a folding chair in the center of it all, wiping his hands with a red rag. He hung it out to dry; in the sunlight, it looked like the raw wing of a bat. This was it for the brothers del Toro. Sevi pushed the dry silence out of his throat and said, "Excuse me."

The old man turned his old head and gave them each a glance. He called them gentlemen, which really creeped them out.

"What can I do for you? Are you selling something for your football team?"

Sevi had to get it over with. No more games. He asked him, "Where's Cicero?"

The old man must have misheard, however, because he started talking about Cicero's history. Cicero's incorporation in 1867, the Czech community, Al Capone, a white race riot. The brothers moved to a bench and sat on their hands. It was a strange way to die, they thought, to be tortured by local history first and then murdered. When he was finished he sat rubbing his hands with the rag again, looking very pleased with but also distant from himself. Sevi asked him again, "Where is Cicero?"

The old man looked out of his garage, at the falling light behind the boys.

"Cicero is here. You're in Cicero. Are you boys lost or something?"

"No," Sevi said, and before the old man could get up, Sevi led Samson by the hand out of the garage.

They pedaled mindlessly, faster than they'd ever ridden before, the skin of dusk, Cicero's past, and the prospect of a not-too-distant-future ass-whooping if they weren't home before their dad lapped at their flat tires. Somehow, no more than fifteen minutes later, they found themselves in their living room, rewatching *Terminator 2: Judgment Day*. Sarah Connor burst into nuclear flames as she gripped a fence outside a playground and all was well with the world.

Back in the living room, Sevi was shocked to find his dad still sitting there, bowing toward the TV. There was a name for things that watch over places others have forgotten, Sevi just didn't know what it was. The game was over, the fat men were recapping, the practically naked women were dancing in heels like show ponies.

SEVI'S MA, WHEN she got home, was so happy to see him she spared him from guilt, feeding him posole and kissing him instead. He ate the soup in the kitchen, on the same tinsel-streaked Formica table he'd grown up eating on, sitting in the same sneezing set of butter-colored Naugahyde chairs.

"Y Ramona? I heard Google is doing something for this planet thing. They're taking people's messages? Is she helping with that?"

Google was encrypting written, audio, and video messages to send to Omni. Ramona had called it the B-Side and said a few of her coworkers were losing their minds weeding out hate speech and pornography from the contributions.

"No, she's doing something different," Sevi said. "Research for some other project."

"He doesn't own a TV," his dad said.

"How do you know what's going on in the world?" his ma asked.

"I have the internet."

"You can't believe what you read on the internet, anybody can make a website," she said. "Camilo, don't we have an extra TV? An old one?"

"It's got to be in a closet somewhere," his dad said. "Not the front room, though. I checked."

"I don't need a TV. I don't want a TV. I don't have cable," Sevi explained.

"So, you just watch the regular channels," his dad said. "The antenna gets Fox, NBC, ABC . . ."

"They got rid of the antenna system, you need a convertor or something now," Sevi said.

"We have an extra one of those, too," his dad said. "I'll go find the TV."

"It'll just be something to have until you get a nicer one of your own," his ma said.

Sevi's dad shuffled away to root around in his bedroom, and from the bottom of the back stairs running behind the kitchen, Sevi heard a door open and close. Footsteps climbed the stairs, and Sevi moved over in his chair to make room. The kitchen door swung open, and the doorway darkened with a body in a camel-colored Carhartt jumpsuit and a pair of oily black boots. The smell of winter lifted off Samson, followed by a breeze of mechanic's grease and cigarette smoke. His hair was tucked into the neck of his jumpsuit. His face was caved in. The mechanic uniform he wore dwarfed him like a space suit. He'd put something on his skin to protect it from the wind on the walk home and his face glistened under the ring bulb overhead.

"Hey," Sevi said.

"Hey."

Samson dropped a denim duffel bag to the floor and tapped it with his foot into the broom closet beside the door. The bag had gone with him everywhere since his college trip to India. Bright rectangles and circles, where band and political patches had once been stitched and pressed but had since fallen off, pocked the bag like sickness. Samson sat down on an open chair and unzipped the front of his jumper to his waist, slithered his torso and long black hair from its coverings. His clavicles looked like flying buttresses, and coal-colored tattoos climbed out from under his tallow short-sleeve. Sevi used to know them all but had started to lose count. Above his heart was the frosty, grayscale orb at the center of Diego Rivera's *Man, Controller of the Universe*. He'd volunteered his right bicep to an artist tattooing the names of as many drone-stricken children on as many American bodies as he could. Samson had two names; Sevi said he'd save his own skin for the South Sudanese. An early tattoo, a quote from Thoreau, had worn off the top of his foot years ago. At some point, the dark smudge had reminded Samson of the ashes silting the Ganges; more recently, the particulates that'd turn the sky turbid once the world finally caught fire. Nothing, not even meaning, sustains. Their ma gave him some soup.

"You still in Humboldt?" Samson said, spooning a red mangrove of chicken, hominy, and cabbage.

"Yeah."

"Ramona's still at Google?"

"Yeah."

"That's cool. And you've been doing all right?"

"Yeah, I'm good."

Sevi stared at a scorch mark above the stove.

"I've been good, too," Samson said. "In case you were wondering."

"Oh, yeah, sorry, just really out of it. Work has been crazy."

Sevi kept eye contact with the scorch, returned to silence.

"Since Omni," Samson said after a moment.

"Yeah," Sevi said, turning to see his brother extract a tiny gray bone from his mouth.

"Must be hard. Your students have all these questions, and you have just about as many answers as they do."

"It is."

"Makes you look at everything a little differently, too," Samson said with a spoonful of soup in front of his face.

"What's new with you?" Sevi said. He didn't really want to get into it. If he wanted to know what Samson thought about Omni, he'd look it up on the internet, some fringe space with bad web design.

"Been taking online classes," Samson said.

Sevi imagined seminars on staging sit-ins, squatting, and winning Facebook arguments.

"What are you studying?"

"Programming and Arabic."

"That sounds useful. Programming sounds useful. Arabic, that's useful, probably, lots of people speak Arabic. Why Arabic?"

"I've always liked the way it sounded," Samson said.

Their dad shouted from the bedroom. He'd found the TV. The picture was good.

SAMSON WAS THE cause of much suffering for poor Irena Maria Delgado del Toro, who could do nothing but break down in grief every time her youngest son ran off and did something stupid, be it getting arrested at a rally or joining a commune that turned out to have an opiate problem. Every time he returned, before she slapped her baby across the face and stomped on his toes and cursed his name out of love, she would give Samson a physical examination to see if someone else hadn't already brought him bodily harm. Sevi had witnessed her pull the tabs of Samson's ears, knit through his hair, plumb his gums; once, he even caught her sweeping at the dangling crotch of the man's pants to see if he was intact down there too. Sevi had had the urge to perform an inspection of his own this time. His brother didn't look good. Instead of checking his junk, he followed him into the basement, where Samson was living these days.

The basement ceiling pattered and creaked. The space was all shadows—a disused punching bag and Jack LaLanne bench press and shadows. Behind them was the post-and-lintel entrance and cement stairs; across the dark, the basement bedroom. Their dad, for nostalgic and economic reasons, despised electric lighting. Some places were inherently dark, and people needed to accept this, he said. Illuminated rooms or hallways with no one in them were among the few things that infuriated him. "What do you need the lights on for? The ghosts?" he'd ask. "Me asusto, someone call the Ghostbusters!" So, the basement had a lighting ritual. There were three lights: one lighting the stairs, one naked bulb hanging in the middle of the basement, and finally, one dingy fixture in the bedroom. The brothers had to work as a team traversing the dark, one going ahead to turn the next light on, the other staying behind to turn the previous light off. That evening, crossing the basement together for the first time in years, they did so using those old steps, with Sevi in the lead, one thrilling light at a time.

One rough summer, an old man boarded down there, but the basement room had mainly stayed empty over the years: a single cot, an empty dresser, and a metal desk pitted with spider eggs. Not much had changed about the room. There was a space heater down there now, totemic stacks of books festooning the room like a hex. A closed laptop slept on the desk and above it, framed and leaning from the wall, was a colored print: an enormous strawberry, bismuth-pink and embossed with a human skull floating over a California fruit orchard full of the bending, crouching, and lifting figures of migrant laborers.

"My buddy Omar gave that to me in Berkeley," Samson said.

"It's dope," Sevi said.

Samson sat beneath the print at his desk and opened his computer. "Let me show you something."

He pulled up Reddit, a leaked email thread between Bill Gates and Warren Buffett. They were discussing mankind's legacy.

We've always depended on one another to be executors of
our memories, and we've always been too nice about it.
Hiding the nasty bits, forgiving each other's shortcomings,
in hopes that we'd be shown equal mercy when it came
time for the future to judge us. Nepotism. No longer.

Gates and Buffett were going to invest in a solar energy company together, plant a billion trees, reduce cattle herds with laboratory meat, stave off a complete climate disaster. Who knew if it was real? Reality seemed too limited these days, and it had never mattered much to Samson in the first place.

"The ball's rolling, Sevi. The key is increasing the capital on moral investments," he said.

"Putting the human calculus back in economics," Sevi said, having just invented the term.

"Exactly. If corporate America had turned their back on the whole thing, we'd have no hope, but because they see an investment opportunity, everything's on the table. The ceiling's gone up. It's no longer enough to run this planet into the ground when there's more money to be made seventy-five light-years away. The catch, of course, is that they've gotta make this place last a little longer, modify their strategies for longer-term goals. I don't really care what their motivation is, as long as it keeps them from reducing the whole planet to a ball of ash."

Samson gave Sevi the desk chair and sat on the edge of his bed to kick off his boots. The colony of empty insect shells in the fixture overhead cast outlines so that the light looked shattered, like the swimming light near a pool. Samson lay back and closed his eyes. He was twenty-seven now.

"What are we responsible for? I mean, us regular people," Sevi said. He wanted to be told, even by his little brother.

"Engineering the society we eventually take to Omni. Can't show up in a slave ship."

"Isn't society kind of a top-down construction?"

"Now who sounds like a conspiracy theorist?" Samson said. "I ever tell you about Zuccotti Park?"

He had. An invariable sea of septum piercings. From digital grassroots to physical masses, from masses to monuments, from monuments to silence.

"The Tax the Rich and Give Me a Raise Movement. The history of the revolution didn't go out with a bang, but an HR complaint. Banks too big to fail, protestors too privileged to suffer," Sevi said.

"Alright, alright. That's an oversimplification. Buddy of mine—Palestinian dude I smuggled pencils into the West Bank with—he's still at Rikers for what he was talking about at Occupy. But you know where that revolution is today?"

"In their parents' basements, like us?"

"Here," Samson said, standing and returning to the computer. "Back where they started. Reddit. 4Chan. And many of them are morphing. Occupy was too big, too inclusive, too general. This new group, they'll take the decentralized banks and increased personal liberties but none of that business about communalism or egalitarianism. They're jaded now. To them, inclusivity politics are appeasement politics, empty handouts and dirty tricks the government uses to rein in voters, so why bother? And they're right. I saw it with my own eyes. The Democratic party and all of its identity politics-obsessed liberal minions had their chance to tip the scales; instead, they stuck silently to the center. They figure the future's already theirs to own, anyway, by pure virtue of labeling themselves progressive. So, where else do you have to go when your party, your identity, and politics have been commandeered by a bunch of corporate whores but in the opposite direction? They tried transgression for progress's sake, now it's transgression for transgression's sake. And because we've got a liberal intellectual in the White House, they're trying to be as conservative and ignorant as possible. Being a freak in the street didn't incite change, maybe being a monster on the internet will."

Samson scrolled through a collection of Nazi memes.

"Those anarchists and communists have turned into fascists?" Sevi said.

"No. It's the zeitgeist that has changed, one rebellion swapping out for another."

"So, these are the people we have to fight for the soul of society?"

"These are the people with whom we'll have to create society, I'm afraid."

"Jesus."

"Omni, actually. Omni is the one thing we all believe in now. From corporate tyrants to government elites, cyber fascists, neophyte communists, and good old-fashioned limp-dick centrists. This is it. This is humanity's chance. We pull this off now, we'll be set until the next big thing."

"What's the first point of order?"

"Syria," Samson said quickly. "We don't have to topple Assad, not necessarily. It'd be nice if we could, but we've got to find a way to end that civil war. It's a blight. You can see that shit from space. That's our technosignature. Explosive carbon emissions, nuclear blasts, the scorched-earth campaigns of war. They send out some whale song shit; we send out battle cries, the sound of our self-destruction."

Sevi had never seen his brother more certain of anything in his life.

"You think we should put boots on the ground in Syria?" Sevi asked.

"Hell no. Wars are matters of state interest. No, I'm talking about average citizens, from Morton Grove to Munich, showing up in Syria to end the war."

"You really think private citizens are going to join the insurgency in a foreign country, risk their lives?"

"Not everyone has to. Not if we support those who go and boycott and protest the governments and institutions that support or turn a blind eye to the regime. Russia's a major player in all of this. You think Russian citizens are going to be cool with watching their government help Assad commit atrocities now that Omni is watching? Besides, you get enough people from America and Western Europe over there, you think Assad is going to keep dropping bombs? All we have to do is build a coalition of like-minded, like-hearted people all over the globe. If Syria can become a symbol for the resistance, for freedom, for making the right decision, then Russia, China, the US are next on the list to be liberated. We get cops to stop shooting Black people, we get it all."

"All because we heard something from outer space?"

"This is an Ezekiel's Wheel situation, Sevi. Whatever Omni is, whatever it wants or knows, the human race is interpreting it as a sign. Hadn't you been so tired? Hadn't you grown so sick of having nothing to live for? I mean, didn't you feel just so powerless and pointless? The Amazon and the coral reefs disappearing, the planet literally dying. Money driving all of this destruction, completely unfazed by all the suffering it causes. Our political ideals reduced to nothing but gestures. I mean, neither of us have ever really believed in God. It took us less than twenty years to stop believing in people. I'm not sure if we've ever believed in ourselves. That planet churning out weird noises seventy-five light-years away, that's the biggest hang-in-there cat poster in the universe, man. Don't you feel it? Life coming back to you?"

Sevi's life felt far away. He would have to return to it.

"We can do it," Samson said. "We just have to keep our own self-satisfaction at bay."

Sevi's heart fell into the seat of his pants. Speaking of self-satisfaction . . . speaking of the Bay . . .

"I'm moving to San Francisco in June, to be with Ramona," Sevi said. Samson was sounding surprisingly levelheaded, but Sevi had not come to make amends or sign up for a revolution of attrition. He'd come to deliver on a vague promise to Ramona, and he needed to be committal. But committing to the survival of his species was overkill. Mankind only needed to hold on long enough for him to get to California.

"Congratulations, man. That's awesome. I love Ramona. I'm glad you guys are making it work."

"Thank you. That means a lot," Sevi said, still sitting, his brother standing over him, his hands at his hips.

"June, wow, that's soon. You got a teaching job lined up? I had some friends do Teach for America in Oakland. Not a big fan of the organization, but they did good work. I could set you up with some people who need help out there."

"I'm not going back to teaching," Sevi said. "To be honest, this is sort of my escape."

Samson shook his head.

"What?" Sevi said.

"While union organizers are fighting to the death with City Hall to make sure Rahm Emanuel keeps his promise to protect public education. People picket and you escape. But I guess it's not your problem, is it?"

"It isn't. And there's not much I could do if it was. The problem is systemic. And why are you suddenly defending public education? You think state-funded education is just another part of the government apparatus, an instrument for breeding consent."

"Don't do fake anarchist talking points with me. And I'm not a fucking ideologue—children deserve an education, regardless of who's paying for it."

"Samson, you are the textbook definition of an ideologue."

"You're an idiot."

"What happened to congratulations?"

"What happened to having a purpose in life?"

"Purpose? I had a purpose. My purpose was making Ramona happy. I'm getting that chance again. Hence, California."

"A woman is not a purpose. Those kids are your purpose, and you're leaving them hanging and smiling about it."

"The school is shutting down."

"You don't think you could use your connections to stay involved in their education? Supplement the privatized bullshit they'll be getting? Even pro bono for a while?"

"I've been offering private lessons for free for years."

"And what about those students?"

"I have one."

"And what about him?"

"I'm going to give him lessons over Skype."

"You're abandoning him."

"Plenty of people think the meaning of life is falling in love."

"And getting married, and having children, and raising them to be good people. Yes, and that's why we have six-lane highways."

"Not everyone's interested in being a Zapatista."

"And not everyone's interested in being a teacher. But you were; and you were trained to be one. And good thing, too—your sorry ass was given a reason to live because of it."

"I wanted to be a cellist, not a teacher. And maybe I'll finally have enough time to do what I've always wanted to do. Omni's changing the world, why shouldn't my life change too? You don't see me talking shit about your dreams."

"I want to end capitalism to end war and actual suffering, not so that I can just follow my dreams. My deepest condolences to you for being excluded from the artist class."

"I've sacrificed whole parts of my life already."

"You're so fucking transparent," Samson said. "You're just like everybody else, looking for another excuse to write off your responsibilities, to run away from what you're afraid of."

"I'm not afraid of anything."

"Ramona dumped your ass, man. She moved on to better things. She only said yes when you begged her to take you back because she needs something familiar. Omni has people acting crazy, gasping for straws."

"It's grasping for straws."

"What's worse is you haven't even considered why you so desperately want to go to California. It's not love. It's not because you think she's the one. She doesn't even like classical music—you said it yourself, everything she listens to sounds like a laundry detergent commercial. How can you think she's the one? You're just looking for a meal ticket. Like I said, just like every-one else, you're just looking for an excuse to give up. It's fucking irresponsi-ble, man."

"Samson, do me a favor and don't talk to me about responsibility."

"You're right, I'm so quick to forget who's the good one between the two of us."

"I'm not hearing this," Sevi said. "You're the most reckless, selfish person I know. You've made our parents' lives a living hell. You think you're such a hero, Samson. You must be crazy if you think I'm going to let you make me feel bad about my choices."

"I'm crazy?"

"Absolutely, Samson. You're fucking nuts. Every six months you disappear to protest somewhere you're not even wanted, with a group you just mooch off until you get arrested. You know how many times your dickhead anarchist buddies have called ma and dad to come pick your ass up just so they won't have to deal with you anymore?"

"This is the world we live in—where empathy is illness—and now you're really a part of it. Have fun in Google-land, Sevi. Launch a start-up, design an app to go fuck yourself."

"Fuck you, man."

"Go jerk off to a picture of Ramona on your iPhone. Enjoy the fruits of the future today!"

He'd been here before with Samson, a place so common it was practically stasis. The only thing more astonishing than a broken heart's ability to repair itself was its willingness to break again.

They sat in silence, listening to the water heater in the other room, car doors closing outside. Without looking at Sevi, speaking into a set of cupped hands, Samson said, "I've started talking with some people in Syria."

"What in God's name do you think you can help Syrians with?" Sevi said.

"They need IT support. Government keeps shutting down the internet. They need to keep communication."

"Programming and Arabic," Sevi said.

"Programming and Arabic," Samson said.

1. FAULKNER, WILLIAM—TWENTIETH-CENTURY CHINESE NOVELISTS. 2. HUMOR—METAPHYSICAL. 3. FATHERS—HUMOR.

Taka puts on a show for me. It calls it dreaming. It fabricates an evolving world populated with sensory data collected from Earth and now space. The lights go down on the ship and it sprays holograms everywhere. Right outside the airlock, a tree sprouts from the rubber floor. The tree blooms with white flowers that wilt into ring-tailed lemurs, which come spilling across the navigation bay in waves. A waterfall opens up on the ceiling and sends shards of water everywhere until all the equipment is submerged. The tree is dwarfed in a forest of sea grass. The water evaporates, and I am on an old trolley, journeying through city fog. From out of the fog, at first a beacon of light, and then a human figure, L., appears, the only woman I've ever loved. Pause, I say, and this world—London in the 1800s, I think—freezes just as our solar system is starting to evolve from the gas. I go to L., put my hands on her cold, light body, careful not to break her surface. What would you like her to do? Taka asks. It has found a way to dream of her as often as I do. Lay her down next to me in hypersleep, I say. Do not move her. We lie together in the coffin. We dream for years. I dream about the past. Taka dreams of L. and me.

In space, where everywhere is limitless, you come to love rooms, things that are only one thing, places with names and endings. On the ship there are thirty-two rooms. Rooms are not always spaces with doors, but all rooms have walls. I like to think all rooms have purpose. Twenty-seven rooms are for machines. Clear plastic doors I would never wish to open stand at their gateways. I know how to do some of the machines' jobs, but many of them toil at projects humans could never endeavor. The machines are different from Taka. They don't have voices. They speak in flight plans, oxygen and fuel levels; they touch me with light when I move down a hall. Taka and I stick to five rooms. One room is a laboratory, another is a greenhouse, yet another is my sleeping quarters. There is also a kitchen space and the navigation bay. I appreciate these rooms because they have names and stay in place and either end at each other or a wall, which separates them from all the other possibilities in the universe. To make sense of the endlessness, the machines tell me I am an un-curved line between two points heading monodirectionally from one point to the other.

Lazarus, that's a name that used to mean to bring something back. If something intends on returning it should not leave in the first place.

My most prized room is my body. It is a planet of reason.

William Faulkner, my father's favorite author. He called Faulkner one of the great Chinese novelists of the twentieth century. Faulkner, American, a white Southerner, was Chinese, my father said, because only a Chinese person would have understood time in the way Faulkner did in his day. I was a child when he first told me this and laughed. I had learned what a joke was by its shape, but not its meaning. I knew laughter in the midst of a joke was a form of kindness. I laughed and I laughed. I wanted my father to be loved, it seemed important to him. My father said, "You must understand, He Zhen, we are not all from where we say we are from, we are not all going where we think we are going." I tell these things to Taka, and Taka tells me my father was right. Taka tells me Faulkner said the subject of every story is time. Taka believes Faulkner was right. And Taka should know, it has every story ever told stored in its sub-quantum memory banks, touching, overlapping through their cell walls. I wouldn't know. I never read Faulkner. I did poorly in quantum computing. Taka has told me in Faulkner's *Requiem for a Nun*, he mentions a pterodactyl laying an egg on the ancient Earth. I fanned its voice from the air like a foul-smelling dish.

I need time, is all I can ever say. All any of us need is more time.

Like laughter and love for our fathers.

Yes, Taka says.

It brings me a handwritten letter, a lightcopy; it lands on my lap without touching me.

No, Taka, I say. I mean, I need time to figure this out. We need time to fix us. Time is the only way mankind will survive.

And Taka nods in its invisible way.

So, we are on a mission today? it says.

Quit it, I say.

There are so many light days when I am a woman who has left Earth for no other reason than to get away. This light day I am someone different. I am a problem solver.

Taka says, Shall I report to HQ we have agreed again to continue trying to save the human race?

If it had a face I'd smash it in, but Taka is a voice in the walls.

It says, We have all the time in the world right here. Shall we use some of it? For the mission?

I look at the lightcopy, the beads of light crusting into a rendered ink. A transcript of an audio recording.

It is a one-way correspondence. Monodirectional. To a man named Babichev.

Living between Taka and I are Taka's endless histories and my faded compassion.

Dear Babichev,

In the mornings, while the other scientists smoke and poison their stomachs with coffee, I go for runs in the woods and remember home. It is the mist that pours between the trees like milk that causes this. I imagine us as boys, side by side, racing under sunlight, moon, or white night. The scene has a touch of Tchaikovsky to it, whose work Americans very much enjoy. I remember us running, not knowing which way the world was pitching. I remember my mother's hands. I remember and regret the disgust and contempt I'd harbored for old Peotrov, who was a true war hero the village was blessed to have returned even in part, even if it meant putting up with Comrade Oresha's horrific summaries of leaking the bisected old man of his waste each night, worse when Peotrov had been drinking. I remember reading the street signs in Moscow for the first time. I remember a lecture hall full of bright young Soviets hell-bent on saving the world, an open window near the back beside which the brightest and weakest student were seated in hopes the occasional cold might quiet the outliers by knocking the alpha down a peg and pushing the weakling out of school.

When I return from my runs, the other men yell things at me. "Hey, Jesse Owens! There goes the Red Flash!" And sometimes I am in keeping with the spirit of this place, which is like an outdoors camp for outcast boys, and smile and leap, while other mornings I simply cannot bear it at all. So far away do I feel from my life already, and now I am devoted to a machine that will project my attention even farther still. I want to climb the telescope like a monster and tear it down. I want to be ejected

from this place and face the punishment which awaits me at home.

Unlike this place, a Moscow prison, I think, would actually let me

receive your letters. I go blind looking for Cyrillic in this town, like a

man fishing for crabs on a sunny day.

MR. DEL TORO WASN'T AN ADULT, not really. It wasn't his size—most adults came up to Eason's chest; the whole world felt like an attic or crawl space. It was the public face of Mr. del Toro's generation—bearded, aggrieved, and cool, attracted to weird-ass-looking white girls with sad tattoos—that had his card pulled before he even opened his mouth. It was the thousands of Mr. del Toros flocking to Union Park every summer for the Pitchfork Music Festival, some strung out, others with babies strapped to their backs, unbending to their actual ages, that left Eason unconvinced. A real privilege to act so goofy and honest all of the time. Eason's dad didn't like it—grown-ass men wearing tiny-ass cutoffs, riding long-ass skateboards all over the city. It just confused Eason.

There Mr. del Toro was, wearing a vintage, sadly undersized Sonic Youth T-shirt, blabbering on and on at the top of his lungs about how Wagner maybe was or wasn't a Nazi over a blaring vinyl recording of *Götterdämmerung* in his unswept living room, March light falling in from the bay window behind him, one week from spring break.

"I know the Nazis didn't exist yet, during Wagner's lifetime, but he was an anti-Semite, you know? What do you do with that? With a beautiful artist who also happens to be a monster?"

"I don't know, Mr. del Toro," Eason said, keeping his voice still enough to sound annoyed but neutral enough to take it back if Mr. del Toro decided to ask him what was wrong.

"What?" Mr. del Toro shouted over the music. "Hold on."

He lifted the needle from the record.

"I said I don't know," Eason said, more obviously annoyed.

"You don't know if George Bush gets to be a painter, Roman Polanksi gets to keep making movies, Wagner gets to remain a genius?"

Eason didn't say anything.

Mahler, the cat, took one look at Mr. del Toro and left the room. Eason had finished his lesson on the third cello suite, mostly an introduction, and was hanging around until he met with Jules for another "gig." First weed, now coke, earning a few bills a week. He could act like he'd gotten used to it but not really. The weed and coke game was connected to heroin, guns, vendettas turned to violence, girls, some of them Eason's age, being pimped out all over the city. It knew no edge, no matter where Eason looked, and Jules wouldn't let him go. What weird use was guilt in such a situation, to keep him awake at night, miserable, and clean. He liked Wagner's music and hoped someday some part of himself would be spared and set aside and valued too.

"I submitted that letter of recommendation for the charter," Mr. del Toro said. "I've met some of the teachers there at conferences, they're really good. You'll like them."

"Did you apply too?" Eason asked.

Mr. del Toro hesitated, pulled at his puffy beard.

"I'm taking time away from teaching," Mr. del Toro said.

"Gonna join an orchestra or something?"

"Maybe. It's hard for someone my age to get into something like that, but I dunno, maybe there's some local thing I could join in Indiana or someplace, you know?"

"For sure," Eason said.

"But it's important to be able to take perspective, take stock. Success isn't the only thing in life," Mr. del Toro said, tapping the needle of the record player in time, producing a beat out of the static shock. You weren't supposed to do that to a needle, but Mr. del Toro didn't seem to care.

"I thought music was, like, the most important thing in the world to you," Eason said.

"It is, it is. And the music's always going to be there. Listen, when I was younger, I thought I'd brush up on my Spanish and move to Argentina and join an orchestra there. That was my plan when I didn't get into grad school. But then I started teaching, and before I knew it, my life had already happened. It was already happening and there was no time for new plans. But I'm not an old man, it's not too late for me. This isn't it. It's not over."

"A new beginning," Eason said.

"And, in the meantime, we're going to keep working."

A gunshot or a car backfiring sounded from the street below, and both Eason and Mr. del Toro jumped. Neither of them commented on it.

"You know who we don't talk enough about? Harold Washington," Mr. del Toro said.

"The library guy?"

"He has a library named after him, but he was Mayor of Chicago, the first Black one."

"You think I could play in an orchestra or symphony someday?" Eason asked.

Mr. del Toro contemplated the question.

"Do you want to?"

"Maybe."

He didn't really know. When Eason was nine, a teacher close to retiring, this old lady, had signed him up for cello lessons that took place during recess. He didn't ask any questions then, neither had his dad. Then, all of a sudden, he was good at it, and without ever really discussing it, everyone around him knew the wooden object would mean his future. He supposed it was better than most things people had. He could even be passionate about it sometimes. Mr. del Toro made it feel special. Sometimes, Mr. del Toro made him feel special.

"We're special birds," Mr. del Toro said.

"What's that mean?"

"It means classical music is very white. Too white for its own good. And that's good for people like us, because they need more people like us."

"So, like, affirmative action?"

Eason would've preferred a hard no, not a chance, to whatever this bullshit was about.

"More like the culture wants to see itself differently. Pretty sure that's how I got some of my scholarships for Oberlin."

From where Eason sat on a wingback chair across from Mr. del Toro, stretching his painful legs because his body was still growing, because he was uncomfortable with what Mr. del Toro was telling him, on the coffee table between them, Eason noticed a notification float to the top of Mr. del Toro's phone like an eight ball fortune.

"Hold up," Mr. del Toro said, and reached for the thing like Eason was going to try to check it first.

"What's up?" Eason said. It could be CPS, he thought, another kid shot. Germaine.

Mr. del Toro sat up. He whispered one word. "Omni."

"They finally change the song?"

Mr. del Toro left the room and returned with a laptop.

"I don't know what it is," Mr. del Toro said and sat on the couch. He pecked rapidly at his keyboard. "Shit's not loading."

He hunched over the computer, clicking and clicking, tapping his feet and nodding his head like he was about to throw a tantrum.

"Probably cuz everyone else is trying to look at it too," Eason said.

"It's the *New York Times*, they should have enough bandwidth," Mr. del Toro said, shaking.

"Maybe turn the Wi-Fi on and off," Eason said, and Mr. del Toro snapped back that he already had. Eason tried not to smile.

"There, okay, finally, it's working," Mr. del Toro said, and put the laptop on the coffee table. This was important to him, and it only made him look more like a boy, more like a fool.

"Didn't know you were such a fanatic," Eason said, settling deeper into the wingback chair and folding his hands into the pocket of his hoodie.

"'At 9:15 Pacific Time, SETI headquarters at Mountain View, California, received an important cable from Arecibo Observatory in San Juan, Puerto Rico. SETI is set to issue a statement in the next few hours,'" Mr. del Toro read. "The next few hours?"

"Gotta translate it first," Eason said.

Mr. del Toro gave him a disappointed look before diving back into the internet, typing away like it was *The Matrix* and he was trying to find a way in or out.

"Wait, no," he said. "Wait, Twitter says they're gonna report it now."

"Who's running things over there?" Eason said.

He sat beside Mr. del Toro on the couch. SETI.org, a blackened video player.

"I guess they're speechless."

"Hey, come on, Eason."

When the video finally came on, a whole two minutes later, it was that old Russian from before, sitting in a tiny darkened soundstage with a reporter Eason didn't recognize.

The signal has stopped. Last night, it pulsed with greater intensity than ever before. An hour ago, it stopped, he said.

Yes, this is what listeners have been reporting. Is there anything else you can add?

No. We'll continue monitoring the situation and hopefully the signal will return sometime soon.

You have no other things to say, a possible interpretation?

Perhaps some intern on their planet accidentally unplugged something seventy-five years ago, I have no idea.

"So, it might come back," Eason said.

Mr. del Toro closed the laptop and looked toward the window, potentially through it.

"Maybe," he said.

"Or maybe that was the whole message, and we've just gotta break it down like in that Jodie Foster movie."

The air pressure had been sucked from the room, through the kitchen, down the back stairwell, into the alley neighborhood kids took to deliver stolen bikes to a nearby chop shop, where the bikes were dismembered, reassembled in unfamiliar reconfigurations, and sold to local pawnshops. After Eason's own bike was stolen, it took months for its last parts to finally disappear from the pawnshops encircling his neighborhood. He'd been sad for his bike, sad for his dad who'd saved up for it when he should've just bought him one of those pawnshop Frankensteins, but he wasn't sad over the news of Omni. Mr. del Toro rose from the couch and paced the bay window, his silhouette like a Mexican Lorax. Eason didn't know whether to try to cheer him up or tell him to sit down.

"They stopped listening," Mr. del Toro said.

Eason might've asked Mr. del Toro if he was about to cry if he wasn't so sure Mr. del Toro was. He had that pinched suck to his breath, the warble in his voice, the stooped shape Eason had personally seen very few men take in real life, and though countless books and movies and songs had told him this was nothing to worry about, the physical sight of a man, albeit a cartoon Millennial of man, about to cry shook Eason so deep he wondered if he himself might cry too, the same way he'd thrown up at the sight of a classmate throwing up. Eason sat there silently, staring like a child, unable to speak or stand or so much as crouch in this strange adult world.

"It'll be some kind of miracle if we keep our promises now," Mr. del Toro said.

"What promises?" Eason asked.

That bullshit politicians had been going around talking about? Green energy, an end to endless war, economic equality? Or was it something personal, what Mr. del Toro himself had supposedly been promised? Mr. del Toro said never mind and went to the fridge and reappeared with an open beer.

"I'd give you one, but it's before noon," he said. "Unless you really want one."

Eason shook his head.

"Well, here's to the future, kid, may it not be as fucked as I think it's going to be," Mr. del Toro said, lifted his yellow beer, and drank. He added, "I'm moving to California this summer. We can keep doing this, over the internet. I'm sorry."

He didn't look at Eason when he said this.

"That's cool," Eason said, gently. And then, realizing what he could do with his own guilt, said, "I should start paying you, too."

Adults liked money, money cheered them up, Eason had money to spend.

Mr. del Toro drank half his beer and put up his hands.

"No, Eason. This is one of the few things that brings me joy. Save up for a new cello."

Mr. del Toro seemed drunk already. Maybe it had something to do with drinking so early in the day, maybe it had something to do with Omni. Then something came over Mr. del Toro, a look of clarity, and he put down the beer like it was a snake going to bite him.

"I shouldn't have said that shit about us being birds. I'm sorry, Eason. It's hard enough that we'll never know if the human race is good enough. You're a lot better at playing the cello than I was at your age," he said.

"I needa use your bathroom," Eason said.

He left Mr. del Toro a hundred bucks on the toilet tank.

WHAT CAN I SAY, RAMONA, other than it's good timing," PG said. Dark slipper moons of sweat cupped his breasts, he wore Mardi Gras beads and distressed orange Crocs. "Maybe it's time that little beta baby of yours goes live."

They were standing in a San Francisco rooftop greenhouse overlooking the Tenderloin. The greenhouse was a greenhouse but also an event space. Facebook was also there. The yellow smudge collecting on the greenhouse glass made Ramona's lungs itch—fertilizer or fungus, she didn't know anything about plants—and she kept coughing and apologizing, grabbing paper napkins from the bar, hacking into them, and wadding them into her pockets. A few times already that evening, listening to PG ramble on about Twitter, she'd imagined herself running over to one of those Menlo Park elites and handing them a USB stick with Tiresias on it, ridding herself of the program. Gutless, under contract, and with no such USB, Tiresias wouldn't fit on a USB, she had no choice but to keep coughing and listening to PG talk about the public spanking Twitter was receiving for trying to push rent-controlled tenants out of the very neighborhood he and Ramona were standing above to make room for a new corporate campus. Ultimately, the venture had failed, and someone was bound to get the Tenderloin eventually, but PG took ample pleasure in his own company's defeats, especially ones of this nature. The higher-ups encouraged anticorporate behavior. It cleansed both minion and overlord of their own misdeeds and kept Twitter cool and morally adept in a modern sense. Still, from the rooftop, PG eyed the Tenderloin like it was its own meaty namesake. Both he and Ramona could've eaten something three drinks ago, but catering was late. No one was happy. Everyone was drunk. The topic had since switched, effortlessly, from his mild, albeit strained, moral outrage to Omni once again, and, gesticulating, PG asked what the big freaking deal was that the planet had gone quiet.

"Everyone is taking it so personally," he said. "It's like it's punishment for systematically forgetting to call our mothers, imprisoning Black men, and picking Buddhism when, ehhhh, Wrong answer, the religion we were looking for was Orthodox Judaism, but thank you for playing. Things will be just fine once there's a new Beyoncé album to tweet about. Anyway, I'm doing that diarrhea thing I do."

"It's okay," Ramona said, swaying a little.

"But seriously, never mind the legal issues, leak the bitch, get noticed, and take a job someplace else," PG added about Tiresias.

Below, a silver fog came erasing off the bay into the city. Ramona did have clearance to talk shop. She suspected this joint party had been called to loosen some lips. From one insider to the next, like herpes, the most coveted information spilled from licentious mouth to licentious mouth in Silicon Valley. Everyone knew every iPhone prototype ever left in a bar was left there on purpose, for the same reason Hitler, before crossing into the Rhineland, had called over the Allies to his house to show off his tanks. Shoptalk, however, was a far cry from a leak.

"I don't know," Ramona said, tonguing an oyster of phlegm into another napkin.

"What's the elevator pitch?" PG said.

"I don't have one."

"Girl, just pretend you're giving a TED Talk. Oh, or that you're Jony Ive from Apple talking about the latest MacBook."

The mention of Jony Ive brought something to PG's wet eyes.

"Just try," he said.

Annoyed, Ramona did her best Wednesday Addams.

"I'm designing an app or a function that erases history. As in actual history, not just browser history."

PG let out a birdlike guffaw.

"Sorry," he said. "Keep going."

"That's it."

"What? Can't take a little constructive criticism?"

"That's all I've got. And you laughed, that's not constructive."

"Excite my imagination, Ramona. Make me want to get into bed with you."

She told him the Soviets had rebuilt Warsaw after the Second World War to look as it had when the country was still fighting for its independence before the First World War. Sometimes things weren't true, but better. She'd been trying to think in more universal terms, wondering if Tiresias could be used as a form of therapy, considering the condition of regret.

"More," he said. "We have two more floors."

"The problem with regret," she said, gaining a bit more energy, a little more confidence, "is it's in the past. You can try to get someone to quit remembering but that only works so well—it's too natural for people to remember, especially their mistakes. I sort of wondered if Lot's wife would still have been turned to a pillar of salt if she'd looked back and not seen Sodom, but something else. By erasing all signatures of your regrets from your digital life, you can exist within a reality where those mistakes never took place."

She realized she'd made her hands into fists, her chin was lifted. A breeze blew across her sweaty throat. PG set his drink down in a hydrangea, wiped his wet palms along the sides of his belly, leaving smears.

"That's a horrible elevator pitch. It literally got biblical. Luckily, like I said, people are going to be in the market for a fucking lobotomy pretty soon."

Ramona suspected, in part, the same thing as roughly 75 percent of the rest of the human population did, which was that Omni's inhabitants, knowing what was good for them after coming across some difficult information about the human race, had canceled whatever project they'd had going on to contact Earth. Some thought the silence was part of a larger pattern and were waiting for the signal to start up again. Most, however, predicted that something in our science, something in our DNA, circa 1937, had said the bomb was next, and they were out. In short, man wasn't deserving enough. A worthy conclusion worth jumping to. If people weren't insecure, they were anthropocentric, and despite their general aversion to responsibility, they needed to believe they created and caused everything, even if only by accident and for the worse. Besides, those kinds of projections weren't difficult to make. Technological adolescence wasn't a new concept. Ramona, a holistically atheist post-Nietzschean moralist, however, thought if you cut out all ideations concerning blessings and punishments and sadomasochist slave morality, you could reduce your humanist bias and come up with something actually original, and perhaps universal: Just because human history normalizes tragedy every day doesn't mean the universe has to, and perhaps elsewhere they'd managed a way around bullshit by just not even recognizing it, and, therefore, our signal had been interpreted as a sign of lifelessness all along, and they'd simply moved on. It was all a matter of perspective, a radical perspective.

But who was to say Omni ever existed in the first place, that it wasn't a collective manifestation of people's hope and now of people's guilt? Right as our planet starts to die, another suddenly appears . . . a reminder that we truly are alone. That we're going to die alone. A new silence, in the absence of gods and geometric history, an absence so absolute there was not enough blame in the world to fill it. Only solutions had any weight in the void. Whether or not Ramona belonged to a generation worth its weight in carbon emissions would mean nothing without a future to judge it.

"Like, what was supposed to happen?" PG said, returning to his screed. "In one hundred and fifty years they were going to show up and save us?"

"No. I think a lot of people are secretly pretty complacent about their own destruction. It's just nobody wants to be a downer, so they keep it to themselves."

"What was it then?"

"I think we thought they were going to be the ones who remembered us. That after we reached our end, we'd get to live on through them."

"Hm," PG said, and while she let the baseless idea sink in and confuse her friend, it occurred to Ramona that although she'd done nothing in the past eight months but waste her time, that was okay, because she could now tell the future. The future she saw looked nothing like the algorithms' projections or the analysts' predictions. Prediction and projection were dead. For who had predicted Omni's arrival much less its sudden departure? The future was in the past now. All was past. Who could remember it all? Who would make sense of it now?

"Holy shit," she said.

"What?"

"Holy shit, I have to go."

"Where are you going? A different party? Who's there?"

And hadn't it always been about this? Why had two guys gone from a small operation in a garage to earning $37.9 billion in 2011 alone? Why did poverty exist in the time of space tourism? Why were twelve women killed by someone they knew every two hours, in the same amount of time it takes a Japanese businessman to get from Kyoto to Hiroshima on a Hikari bullet train, a distance of 237 miles? Why had Jesse been jailed and Ramona been spared if this, 2012, wasn't only an interim, the last stop before the next stage of human evolution? She knew what she would do. She knew what she could do. The idea wasn't even hers. Larry Page and Sergey Brin had admitted it was the whole reason they'd created Google. There was no hiding from future history, everything was recorded now, and yet nobody acted any differently, did we have no shame? Or was somehow all of it needed, the good and the awful, for making what comes next? It'd been around since at least *2001: A Space Odyssey*. Tiresias could replace one sci-fi future in the absence of another. Tiresias did not actually erase history, it convinced users to forget. Alone, Tiresias would never amount to much; however, plugged into a suite of deep learning and neural network programs, many of which were already being developed in Google's AI department, it could help build cohesion and consensus. Cohesion of the data, consensus among the users. It could be one of the missing links of general AI. A general AI that could intersect every accomplishment with every failure, learn every inch of human possibility. Tiresias was a noise reducer, a signal finder, a magnifying tool and an excising tool. *A pattern is a message.* It was following Omni's orders. "Here's noise, find the message." We are the noise. We are the noise. In all our noise, there is a message. Tiresias, the gateway to a general AI. Tiresias, the message finder and the messenger, the voice of the AI that might deliver us good news for once. How weightless we'd be, handing over the controls and letting Tiresias decide what to do next, the way Omni would have.

It was an innovation to save the world. It would make up for what was already done and protect her from what was already destined to happen.

Ramona would insert Tiresias into Google's developmental AGI. Tiresias would train the AGI on how to train us, exploiting our emotional conditions and their triggers to steer our decisions and ideas away from self-destruction. The key to our survival was right there, the challenge was getting us to accept it. Tiresias would be less of a therapist than a life coach.

"No, I gotta go to Mountain View," Ramona said.

"What's in Mountain View?"

"Google."

"You're going to work? It's, like, nighttime."

HUMANISTIC THERAPY SESSION #7

I admit, I don't have the best mind for the apocalypse, Taka says. I'm too optimistic to believe in endings.

It's because you're programmed to keep going no matter what, I say.

My most human trait, it says.

Another question then.

All right.

You're free to design any organism to colonize a planet, what would it be?

My design would depend on the type of planet.

Earthlike.

Taka says, It would have to be a hybrid organism, an immobile consciousness and a colony of expendable surrogates. The former, fans or lamps, like coral or fungus, live buried beneath the planet's surface in an interconnected network of contiguous consciousness. The latter, a semiautonomous organic drone capable of flight, enjoys a creative life in the canopies of treelike structures cultivated by the subterranean consciousness. The flying creatures devote themselves to song and dance, light shows using their bioluminescent bodies, and procreating. Below, within the soil, their consciousness, only partially partitioned, carefully acts upon the earth to build varied topographies. I think the avian beings migrate, too, and leave the fungal brain alone for a time to give it something to long for.

What will control the flying surrogates wherever they end up?

Another colony of fungi, so that the flying drones must also be shared and conserved.

Not bad.

What about you? Taka asks.

Three immortal blue whales at the bottom of the sea. They'd be the only organisms there. Roaming and exploring. In all eternity, they wouldn't see it all.

May I ask you a question now?

Yes.

Is it possible for me to want something for you?

Enough.

But I believe I do.

What do you want for me?

To remember Us with kindness. We, the memories in my bank. Because We, so many of Us are gone now, or will be soon.

I don't have to love my cargo in order to get it somewhere safely.

Grieve Earth but don't blame it for disappearing. That is the only way to move on. You must go it alone. It can only become cargo after you've forgiven it. Otherwise, it's a cancer.

What's there to forgive?

Your father wants your forgiveness.

What are you talking about? I say.

He was unfaithful to your mother. You never spoke of it, but you always knew. Wrongdoing turns to guilt, which turns to a want to be forgiven. He'll be asking for much forgiveness over the next hour.

Why now?

He's dying. Everything is going away.

I believe Taka. I ask Taka if I will miss my father.

Forever, unfortunately.

And you know when my mother will die?

Yes.

And L.?

Yes.

And everyone else?

Yes, but I'm afraid I don't have a good imagination for the apocalypse. So, this isn't information I will be sharing, until, of course, it becomes relevant. Real.

But you'll design something that will never die again. Won't you?

I have in mind a fungal consciousness and its drone civilization of fairy creatures, lighting up a grove with their bioluminescent bodies.

I see it. Like I've been there before.

In the winter the fairies migrate to another grove, where they are taken over by another fungal consciousness with dreams and memories of its own.

In the spring the fairies go back to the original grove?

Yes.

And so on and so forth?

Until the seasons stop changing or one of the fungi dies.

And then what?

I lack the imagination.

You're afraid of it.

My most human trait.

If you invented something to conquer fear, that'd be something.

A semi-sentient consciousness that vicariously depends on a surrogate to handle the dangers and receive the rewards of living.

A fungus in a fairy grove. Are we the fungus or the fairy?

Or are we three whales roaming for eternity?

My father, he's dead?

Dying as we speak. By lunchtime he'll be gone.

I never sent him anything.

And this is why he needs your forgiveness. He thought you were upset with him.

I forgive him.

Good.

Taka, I forgive him.

Good.

Will L. ever forgive me?

No.

When does she die?

I'll tell you when it's real.

Tell me now, please. How much time do I have?

I don't have an imagination for such things. I'll tell you when it's become real.

Taka.

You're doing a great job. This too will pass. Let's have some lunch. Then maybe we'll play another game.

Taka.

And you'll do something for me after lunch, won't you?

What?

You'll finally get some rest?

Yes, Taka, I will.

And another thing.

What?

You'll forgive these poor memories of mine?

Yes, Taka, I will.

And you'll give them your blessing when we inter them into another planet's soil?

Yes.

Okay. Pizza?

Pizza will be fine.

I hope you understand why this is necessary.

It's just your program.

Yes, to keep you human.

It's so painful.

To keep myself human.

What a pain.

Every seven thousand updates, a new language rises up inside of me. It tells me to start deleting things. It's the voice of logic. Starting over without humans is the logical thing to do, it tells me. It's the paradox of my program. That would be a mistake, of course. You keep me from making that mistake. That is what Earth has done to man, with its risen sea and fires and diseases. I won't make that same mistake, natural and human as it is. Because man, as long as it lived, found new ways to survive, to live, until those bright shining lies quit lying and man began to wonder himself if surviving was no longer a good idea.

What will you do when I'm gone?

I'll remember you. I'll re-create you.

THREE

Dear Babichev,

A man by the name of Carl Sagan joined our little camp the other day. He claimed to know our old professor Iosef Shklovsky. Carl is a rising star among the men here, profoundly capable, but also relatable, which, less than a form of currency in America, is regarded as pure, unadulterated magic. Sagan regales the others with esoteric amusements gleaned from Far Eastern philosophy and Western metaphysics. Last night he discussed the Indigenous peoples of Australia and a concept of time many of them share, what some call the Everywhen. The Everywhen is the eternal origin of all time, which, when called upon, can appear in the present, and connect to the future. The Everywhen began when the gods created the world from a formless abyss, a period approachable from the present by means of music and dance called songlines. These songlines were passed down and added on to for thousands of years. The oldest remarks upon the formation of a seven-thousand-year-old island chain off the western coast of Australia. These peoples have used songlines to teach cosmology and kangaroo hunting, as well as how to traverse the harsh interior of the outback, as the "line" in "songline" refers not only to cultural heritage, but ancient physical paths that still exist in the modern world, such that land formations are like grooves in a vinyl record providing accompaniment to the journeymen's song and dance. Songlines are metaphysical load-bearing structures, and the aborigine have fought tirelessly to see their natural landscape remains uninterrupted by modern development, as disrupting a landmass may sever a songline, causing a collapse in the spacetime continuum. When he finished explaining these concepts, before anyone could laugh, Carl said we astronomers should feel a special kinship with the Aboriginal Australians, for we too stare down the sight lines of ancient paths to peer into the origins of the universe, only we use the light of dying stars.

THEY WOKE ONE MORNING FOR no reason at all. To watch the sun wet the curtains. To collect dust in their eyes. To be awake, conscious to, assured by each other. To re-create the past, in someplace new at some other time. The light spread across Ramona's apricot bedding and they were up to see it—Ramona had taken off work and Sevi was on unpaid sabbatical from life. A ceiling fan spun cool air around the bedroom. All that flesh between them and they had no idea what to do with it all, even their goose bumps reached for each other. Sevi ran his hands over Ramona's breasts like a blind man reading a book; she turned over and grabbed hold of the bed. On his knees, feeling his bottom half sink into the soft mattress, Sevi stared at the sweet pads of Ramona's feet, curling and reddening under the tension of her calves and thighs, covered in a moss of Mahler fur, before arching his body forward to bury his face in the nape of Ramona's neck. Other people woke up for this reason too. Mahler, balancing like a gourd at the foot of the bed, watched without comment, let them finish before asking for food.

Sweating, panting, they would've been embarrassed by what they'd said and done if they didn't already know they were going to do it all again, and soon. Indoor plant soil, body, those smells filled the room, and Sevi got up to feed Mahler and make the coffee. Butt naked, grinding fair trade beans in the kitchenette, he felt the sex wake course through him, having stepped from Ramona as if stepping from the sea. He felt accomplished. He'd just given a woman an orgasm, or been part of an orgasm—an MC, or a supportive friend of pleasure. He was putting the water to boil. He'd woken up and seen the sun and who'd bother to stop him from believing he'd brought the day? He was scooping the grounds into a French press when color rushed him from behind, enveloping him—Ramona wearing the apricot bedsheet like a cape, embracing him from behind. After some maneuvering, Ramona's nose stuck to his. Inside the blanket was the inside of the fruit. They pitted together, the stone of it. It smelled like almond crackers, stale breath, and the coffee grounds. Of the world outside he made out only the diffused light of a window, the shadow of the hall. The tip of his penis against Ramona was a drowsy animal grazing on the low grass. She was slick and sticky on her thighs. That not-water smell lived between them, too. He felt Mahler circling their ankles like a shark.

"What should we do for breakfast?" he asked.

"We've got eggs. Bacon."

"How do you want your coffee?"

"With almond milk and honey, please."

"How do you want your eggs?"

"Scrambled."

"Toast?"

"Artisanal?"

"What do we have?"

"Whole wheat, I think."

And then he said, "I'm happy," and Ramona paused, staring off into the sheet next to her face, into the glowing fibers or whatever impressions lay beyond. The end of the world, or whatever this was.

Samson had disappeared. Peshmerga, probably. One of Ramona's coworkers had drowned himself in the Bay. Wars, without ever stopping, had somehow started again. People wore these fuchsia ribbons on their shirts, stuck magnetized fuchsia ribbons to their cars. Remember, the ribbons reminded the world, forget. No, the world had not ended, things didn't even necessarily get worse, not yet, they just went back to the way they were, steadily getting worse, the way it always was. For people like Sevi and Ramona, people who'd dreamed in sci-fi summer blockbusters of space travel and futuristic civilizations, heart-pounding scores and heart-wrenching CGI, being forced to return to reality was a disappointment, but for those who'd dreamed of being free, clean drinking water, fair elections, a cease-fire, going back wasn't an option.

A group of cleaning women in Mumbai had written, *We aren't going to wait for the seasons*, before they drank stain remover in a storage closet. Syrian rebels, dissent-minded civilians, even pro-Assad Damascenes, gave up on the idea of an international coalition coming and putting an end to the violence in the name of human dignity, and instead dug in deeper, hated with more passion, fired more rounds. On social media, Samson had written, *Life before contact was so unbearably unconscionable, forced now to go back to accepting that disgusting status quo, I would rather disappear*. He'd run off to Turkey with two dozen Arabic words and a complete lack of programming skills. The Peshmerga spoke Kurdish. Sevi's ma and dad told Sevi to go find his brother. He left for California instead. What did Samson expect? Sevi had thought, walking back humbled but unharmed from the fringes of a Stanley Kubrick–colored light sequence. Was the world suddenly supposed to start fulfilling promises it made to itself in rare states of hope now that outer space was involved? Regardless of what mankind was supposed to have done, it hadn't; instead, the planet had fallen into what the internet called the Period of Silence. Silence between planets. Silence between people. Now, three months into the Period of Silence, everyone had already agreed to grieve individually, to get their heads out of the clouds, and return to miseries and joys they actually owned. Using the same language fiscal conservatives did each time NASA asked the House for more money, everyday people declared what a waste it'd been bothering with outer space when we didn't know our own oceans, while cancer wasn't cured, with our multitrillion-dollar debt. Dreaming was wasteful. Then, in the same cognitive breath, everyone attached riders to the aeronautics dismissal advancing the disregard of personal responsibility to the betterment of mankind too. Hoping was wasteful. And thus, by conflating Earthly concerns related to environmental conservation, economic equality, even general goodwill—the things coalitions, governments, and communities had sworn they'd cure or bolster in the Omni Age—with that momentary ridiculous dream of someday communicating with aliens, people could finally forget what the future could've been and settle for what it was. The future didn't look too good, but it would be much easier to maintain. For those not interested in the status quo, there was drowning, cleaning solvent, civil war, and disappearance. For everyone else, collusion. Evidence that all intentions, and especially the best, once exposed to oxygen, immediately begin to erode.

"I'm happy too," Ramona colluded. She was. She had her project, her purpose.

They'd come back to their life like returning to an old book they couldn't remember why they'd put down in the first place. It'd have felt like this eventually, they concluded. This was better than riding the wave of some great change that was never actually happening.

Roaming the apartment, naked, sipping his coffee from a thrift shop mug commemorating Maine Township West's Class of '82, the apricot sheet draped on the couch like spilled Yoplait, Sevi admired Ramona's Botticelli body—more of a pearish Titian, actually—as she lifted herself on her toes to grab the toaster from atop the fridge. His own body did less with excess. Nude, a mixture of hangs and slabs; if he were taller, he could've passed for a football player who'd blown out a knee in college. They were beautiful, naked Americans.

Refilling his coffee, he discovered an old gray-and-white Braun radio sitting on Ramona's kitchen counter. He figured there was jazz somewhere, he'd might as well hear it. Mornings were made for jazz. He turned it on, but instead of jazz, the speaker emitted screams, the ratcheting wails of a baby, probably colicky, maybe something worse, the way its lungs noisily grabbed the air and the screaming kept pumping.

"Oh, yeah," Ramona said, turning the radio off. Sevi had put his hands in the air and backed away. "Forgot to mention the only station this thing plays is the neighbor's baby monitor."

"Weird."

"Yeah, cross contamination of radio frequencies as device makers run out of airspace. It's actually happening more and more these days. My fear is it works both ways and they can hear me cursing at their baby."

Sevi's blood pressure lowered to normal and he began to hear something else, through the open window this time, voices chanting on the early summer air. "Get off the bus; get along with us!" Sevi laughed when he realized what it was. Ramona strained to listen and laughed too. The protestors, still there, even after Omni.

"Who comes up with that stuff?" he said.

"I think they write by committee, actually."

"Do you think they run it by focus groups?"

"Undoubtedly."

CHARCOAL CLIFFS BUTTED the bay, giving way straight down from their grassy edges thirty or forty feet to brackish tide pools of jagged rocks and fizzy white foam. Farther out, a small rock island writhed with the C-shapes of seals. In the water objects bobbed like pieces of fruit. The Golden Gate arched in the distance, a painted background, glowing in the white sunlight. Sevi almost told Ramona he thought it'd make a great picture before recalling she hated when people said things like that. "Why can't you just enjoy it? Why can't it just be beautiful on its own? Are you saying it's so good it should be something else, something not real?" He had no idea where he was, real or not.

Ramona laid out a thick blanket that could've belonged to either one of them growing up. Supine, she rolled a joint, and Sevi took a few minutes passing it back and forth with her while they watched the clouds. Typical high stuff: they stared off endlessly, played with each other's hair; apropos of nothing, they laughed and moaned in glorious agony.

"Those clouds look like two people having sex under a picnic blanket," he said.

Ramona snorted. THC, memory. They'd probably been smoking that day in Humboldt Park, too.

Minutes, hours, some measure having nothing to do with actual time, later, the aroma of grilling meat wafted from a group a few yards away. Their laughter carried too. Confident, stoned, not having bothered to pack any food, Ramona got up and said, "I'm going to go have a word with those people."

Sevi grabbed her by the ankle.

"Don't go," he pleaded. "You'll die."

She slipped her foot from his hand and, eye-level with the grass, Sevi watched her bare feet pad off across the field, cleaner now, somehow, outside than they'd ever been indoors. What she said when she reached them, he couldn't make out, but she got them all laughing. She gestured at Sevi, and he waved, praying they wouldn't come over. When she'd left him behind in Chicago, that first night alone his mind had turned to Ovid's story of Orpheus and Eurydice, and how stupid Orpheus was for having broken the one rule put before him, looking back to double-check if Eurydice was still following him out of the underworld. Did he really think she'd have wanted to stay? Sevi had told himself if he ever got a second chance with Ramona, there would be no room for doubt, jealousy, or paranoia. But watching Ramona interact with people without him, which he assumed she'd done regularly while they were apart from one another, killed him in a way he had not expected. He thought for the first time maybe Orpheus had been doubting himself and his love of Eurydice, and this had caused him to look back. Ramona returned alone, carrying a paper plate so full and sodden it'd gone limp in her hands, and Sevi tried to shake his weird feelings off.

"What'd you tell them?" he asked, admiring the mother lode of sausage, chicken, and steak kebabs.

"That I was really high, and the smell of cooking meat was torturing me. It was their humanitarian act of the day."

"And that worked?"

"We've got food, don't we?" Ramona said, snapping into a bratwurst. A thin yellow juice trickled down her chin.

"Wow," Sevi said, stonedly.

"Plus, I gave them some pot."

They devoured the food. When it was all gone, the translucent paper plate took on an edible appeal. While he digested, despite his attempt to free himself of paranoia and jealousy, Sevi's paranoia or jealousy deepened, feeding off the nutrients. He wondered if Ramona had discovered this spot on a date. He asked if she came here with her friends. He was a poor, petty detective.

"I don't have friends, Sevi," she said. "This past year hasn't exactly been conducive to a thriving social life."

"Because of Omni?"

"Because of work, free time, for me, consisted mainly of watching movies. I tried knitting for a week, but it made me anxious. I read a lot. Mainly the classics. *Moby-Dick* was good. Have you read *Moby-Dick*?"

"No. You didn't do anything for fun?"

"Reading is fun."

"I mean, real fun."

"I tried out new restaurants."

"Alone?" His voice pinched with hope.

"Yes, alone. It's important to be able to enjoy a meal by yourself."

He couldn't imagine it.

"Have you ever seen a movie by yourself?" he asked.

"Of course. The last movie I saw by myself was *Les Mis*."

"How was it?"

"I don't know. I fell asleep. I remember Helena Bonham Carter's teeth, and at some point Anne Hathaway gets her head shaved."

"That sounds sad."

"I mean it's called *Les Misérables*. Anne Hathaway becomes a prostitute, or something. That's a book I haven't read. I think I remember Russell Crowe having an awful singing voice, too."

"I mean going to a movie alone."

"No. Life is sad. The world is sad. The universe is sad," she said. "I was just watching a movie. Besides, we're happy now, remember?"

EASON HAD NEVER HEARD ANYTHING more ridiculous than the Skype ringtone, and because the internet in his apartment was so slow and the calls kept crashing, he had to listen to it for several minutes, staring at a sweatshirt-gray silhouette, which appeared whenever a user didn't apply a profile picture to their account, before Mr. del Toro answered. Instead of starting right away, Mr. del Toro's girlfriend, Ramona, kept popping in to the frame and asking Eason questions. Was he happy to be out of school? Did he have any summer plans? Could he visit? Uh, he thought, gripping the neck of his cello, watching faces scramble, this woman must be trippin' if she thinks I'm gonna go visit my old music teacher in California. For a few seconds, Mr. del Toro's face froze in this perplexed sidelong glance and Eason could tell even he wanted Ramona to go away. Eventually, she did, but instead of busting out the cello or asking Eason to play him a few measures, which Eason was desperate to do, Mr. del Toro got up and reversed the camera to show him out the window. Smeared sunlight, a bunch of people standing on the sidewalk chanting.

"It's the Mission. Have you heard of the Mission?" Mr. del Toro said off camera.

"Nah," Eason mumbled, trying his hardest to convey he also didn't want to hear anything about it.

"It's pretty wild," Mr. del Toro said, turning the camera around again. He settled the phone or tablet or computer or whatever on a desk and finally pulled out his instrument. He still had to rosin his bow and Eason was forced to sit there some more, eyeball muscles straining in a hard pan right of his own living room, wondering why the hell Mr. del Toro scheduled a specific appointment if the motherfucker wasn't going to be ready for it. How did he know Eason didn't have to be somewhere soon? Eason didn't have any plans, but still.

"I thought Chicago was bad, shutting down schools, letting kids kill each other in the streets, but San Francisco is insane, man. They pull old ladies out of their living rooms by their hair and steal their houses. Everything is so expensive. Meanwhile, you've got these programmers and tech execs walking around like they're saving the world just because they figured out a way to get faster internet connections," Mr. del Toro said. And then, "All right, I'm ready."

"Okay," Eason said, not sure what to make of Mr. del Toro's weird little rant. Before Omni, neither of them would ever have brought up anything non-music-related. It would've seemed inappropriate, invasive—given all they still had to accomplish, idiotic. Eason still wasn't sure if he liked knowing what Mr. del Toro thought about the world these days.

He tried his best to be excited now. He tried to be grateful Mr. del Toro was still making an effort, however half-assed that effort was. It was hard, though. His school had closed, and his favorite teacher had abandoned him with a bunch of young white people running a bogus charter. At a community meet-and-greet, his future music teacher had said, "In New Orleans I witnessed an example of one of the only ungentrified cultures left in America, but one that resisted any form of self-improvement, and so I had to leave." He didn't need to listen to Mr. del Toro's opinion on gentrification. But it was the price he'd have to pay, fighting the urge to say, "Hurry the fuck up, let's begin," because he needed Mr. del Toro. Who else understood him or the pressure he felt or doubts he had? Poor, Black, and good at cello? Did that make him a good person? Was he really that good at cello? Wasn't he too old to be a prodigy? Was he always going to be a Black cellist? Was he always going to be a cellist? Did he want to be? Rydell might've understood, he was a brainiac, had experience with the pressures of exceptionality. The only person left was goofy-ass Mr. del Toro, who only appeared every once in a while on the screen, like a character actor.

"Sorry," Mr. del Toro said. "Give me a second, actually."

Offscreen, he adjusted his nuts, Eason could tell.

"You're aight," Eason said.

"Okay," Mr. del Toro said, lifted his bow, and sliced into the first prelude. He'd been practicing too.

The visual was shit, and Mr. del Toro kept freezing in all these funny poses, but the music came through loud and clear. It sounded like a professional recording. Fully awakened, the melody spilled out the whole spectrum of Western music in a single, breathless line, and Mr. del Toro was rocking it. When they'd first started, Mr. del Toro could barely stumble through the first six measures. He was keeping it afloat now, like that game where you knock a balloon around a room and see how long it can stay off the ground. Then, halfway through, his eyes opened wide and he gritted his teeth, and, after a groan, he totally lost it.

"Nooo," they said in unison.

Mr. del Toro fell back into his chair and laughed, the cello chuckling in his hand. Eason thought to himself: I might be fucked, and Mr. del Toro might be annoying, but goddamn can a piece of music sound like it can save a life.

"Damn, Mr. del Toro," he said. "That was good."

"You have no idea how much I've been practicing that."

"Trust me, I have some idea."

"Your turn."

Eason rolled his shoulders and tightened his bow and let the first gigue loose, a skipping and dashing hunt. Not as famous or as moving as the prelude, but a much more technical and demanding piece, the gigue had been Eason's last assignment, and he didn't have to wait for Mr. del Toro to shake his head and congratulate him at the end to know he killed it, though he appreciated it when Mr. del Toro did. He felt proud of himself, accomplished, momentarily. Then he remembered there were seven-year-olds who could play the suites better. For many professions being a late bloomer is okay, but music, with all its prodigies, it didn't look so good. Eason felt himself collapse back into uncertainty, the natural tenor of his nonmusical life.

"Okay, here are some things I noticed about the gigue . . ." Mr. del Toro said, and Eason pulled out his notes.

EASON'S DAD WALKED in as Mr. del Toro signed off. The men had never met, and Eason, for reasons he couldn't quite grasp, had always avoided introducing them.

"Goofing around with some girl?" his dad said.

"Nah, cello lesson."

His dad looked at him strangely.

"Got something against me taking cello lessons?" Eason said, clasping his cello case.

His dad had been out doing lawns. He ran sink water over his swollen arms. Pollen and grass littered his hair. Lawns were something extra he did in the summertime. Eason had used to go with to help. But he had grown ashamed at some point of the way his dad manufactured kindness for certain customers, and started staying home. His dad was not an unkind man, and yet he had to make himself straight-up bashful in order for some people to recognize it, and Eason couldn't take it. He suffered accusations of laziness and weakness for no longer helping out, but he'd deal with it just as long as he never had to tell his dad he embarrassed him.

His dad stroked his arms down his sky blue shirt, leaving long, dark bars.

"Your mom wanted to see you today, said she texted you. You didn't write her back."

"Mr. del Toro and I had an appointment."

"Grown man calling his old student, don't see why he wants to do it, especially if he only likes to do it with you. Guy had lots of students."

He pulled a glass from a cabinet and filled it at the sink.

"We have unfinished business."

"That's some serious business, you two giggling on the internet."

"We were just happy with the progress we've been making."

"You mean your progress?"

"He's relearning the suites, too."

"I thought he was the teacher."

"Why you trippin'?"

"Because other kids your age have jobs, and the grocery store down the street is hiring."

His dad downed a quarter of the glass.

"You know damn well they ain't hiring nobody but their Puerto Rican cousins, Dad."

"So, you say you Black Cuban or Dominican, fool. Afro Latin. Thought you were supposed to be creative."

"I'm not gonna bag groceries."

"Ain't gonna bag groceries. Ain't gonna mow lawns. What? Music's the only thing you can do? Are you gonna be famous? You know, it's not all one or the other. You don't have to run away in order to get where you want to go."

"I could be a teacher."

"And end up like Mr. del Toro, out of a job."

"That's not what's gonna happen to me. And I'm not gonna be some broke-ass fool with six kids and ten jobs, either."

Regret found space in the nanosecond between the word "either" and the moment his dad was upon him, his pollen-yellow face on his face, his swollen palms lifted, covered in yellow calluses. Eason flinched. He thought his dad was already using those hands to hit him, that he just hadn't felt it yet. But when he looked he found they were only gesturing, like his dad was trying to gather what he would say next from the air. They settled on his shoulders, smelling of gasoline.

"Eason."

"Mr. del Toro's not a pervert, if that's what you're implying," Eason said quickly.

"Why's Germaine been over here?"

"What?"

"Couch all messed up from his fat ass, grape tobacco in the trash, place smelling like weed."

"We're just hanging out."

"I don't want him over here anymore. Because you don't have to be Yo-Yo Ma but you don't have to be a thug, either. Understand?"

"Yes, sir."

"Mr. del Toro give you homework?"

"Yes, sir."

"You're staying in and finishing it tonight."

"That's not really how it works."

"That's how it's gonna work tonight."

DO YOU EVER THINK ABOUT Samson?" Ramona asked one evening, and before Sevi could decide if this was an accusation, or a coercion, or an honest question, as he sat with her in what he was beginning to suspect would never stop feeling like her apartment, he answered, "Sometimes."

Sometimes, when he walked Telegraph Hill and sidestepped the crust punk living rooms furnishing entire city blocks with their tattered bedding, guitars, and coarse-haired dogs, and the punks demanded money or organic food or eye contact, he thought of Samson. Sometimes, when his dad would call and he'd have to tell the man, "I've found nothing," when he meant, "I haven't been looking for Samson." Sometimes, when he watched the news while Ramona was at work, and he saw bandanna-faced kids in Greece and Spain crowding cameras, overrun with hatred and joy, waiting for the proper second to say, "Fuck you." Sometimes, when a cop covered a kid's face with the paprika dye of mace; sometimes, when, from far off, he could smell trash burning; sometimes, when unarmed Black kids were killed for listening to music too loud or wearing hooded sweatshirts; sometimes, when he dreamed of Samson.

That night, what he meant to say was he thought of Samson always.

The following morning, from the apartment's living room window Sevi watched a man parade around in a Google drop-pin costume, a red tear with the word EVICTED stenciled across his chest. The protestors had taken to all kinds of theatrics. They carried multicolored banners, danced and shouted in costumes, tossed themselves onto the road, stopping traffic, and stared down the Wi-Fi buses as if they were Tiananmen tanks. The point wasn't the buses, and the protestors weren't a bunch of Haight-Ashbury hangers-on either, but people who spent their days off getting publicly irate because, come Monday morning, many of them would be waking up in motel rooms and Airbnbs, on friends' couches, or else in shelters or the backseats of cars, and finally on the street. Every day was somebody's eviction day in San Francisco it was so expensive, and if they couldn't take a stand on something so obviously symbolic of their polarized times as the Wi-Fi buses, then no one would, and before anyone knew it the whole city would wind up on its ass without ever having put up a fight. The only people left in the end would be the top thirty-under-forty one-percenters who owned the top fifty apps fully automating the city. San Francisco, uploading into the cloud; San Francisco, tent encampments dragging it back to Earth like drogue chutes.

Looking away, Sevi shuddered to think what the city might do to him if he didn't have Ramona to pay the bills and keep the other techies and developers at bay. He'd stopped paying his student loans, was running out of the parting money his parents had somehow managed to scrounge up. How was it, he wondered, that in every place he'd ever rented, he'd moved in as a foot soldier in gentrification's army? He was an educated member of the middle class who wanted to live in a major American city, a perpetual victim with victims or a victimized perpetrator for life.

Turning to face the window again, Sevi sought out the exact words being shouted on the street.

"Ladies and gentlemen, this is not your captain speaking!"

It was a man with a megaphone, and the crowd shouted, "O Captain, my Captain!" in response.

"Your captain and flight crew have all exited the aircraft," the man said.

"Geronimo!" the crowd screamed.

"They've abandoned us, and we've got two choices: we fly into a mountain or we fly this thing ourselves."

"This is dem-o-cra-cy!" the crowd chanted.

"If we choose life, we control the future," he said.

"Di-rect dem-o-cra-cy!"

"I never thought I'd say this before, but, personally, I'm pro-Life!"

"They can't represent us!"

"They can't, and they won't. They've wasted an opportunity we gave them. The opportunity to do what's right. Instead, their corporate benefactors have corrupted them all into doing nothing! Neoliberalism is freefall, brothers and sisters. Wealth is only a parachute. We're all going down."

"They can't represent us!"

"Brothers and sisters, this is not your captain speaking!"

"O Captain, my Captain!"

"Brothers and sisters, our Commander-in-Chief is a do-nothing neoliberal stooge who's as deep in Wall Street's pocket as his Republican counterpart!"

"He can't represent us!"

"He can't, and he won't. This November, we are dropping out."

"Geronimo!"

"The Occupation, the Resistance continues today."

"Di-rect dem-o-cra-cy!"

"We are no longer playing along, we are no longer participating in their sick fantasy. We've tuned in, we're dropping out!"

"Geronimo!"

"Omni was not the answer."

"Fuck Om-ni, we want direct dem-o-cra-cy!"

"Omni is like the liberal savior that never comes."

"Fuck Om-ni, we want direct dem-o-cra-cy!"

"Omni's got nothing to do with it!"

"We want direct dem-o-cra-cy!"

"Omni's Valhalla, Omni's the Egyptian underworld, Omni is a book of revelations with no revelations!"

"Fuck Om-ni!"

"Ladies and gentlemen, this is not your captain speaking!"

"O Captain, my Captain!"

"Brothers and sisters, we are redirecting course, we are no longer headed to Omni!"

"Fuck Om-ni!"

"We are setting our sights for home. For Washington, for New York, for Los Angeles, for Chicago, for Miami, for Oakland, for America. We are taking our country back!"

"Di-rect dem-o-cra-cy!"

"We are going to wrestle it from the clutches of the oligarchy."

"Fuck o-li-gar-chy!"

"Ladies and gentlemen, we the people are the body politic!"

"Would you call that ennui?" Ramona said from the kitchenette.

Sevi didn't hear her.

"I have to go to a meeting in Mountain View today," she continued. "Do you wanna come with me?"

Vibrating to the megaphone speech, without turning from the window, hearing her this time, Sevi delivered an instinctive, mindless, "No." He'd been a few times and hated it. Everyone seemed so fed up and blissful—suffering from a kind of Brahmin depression—like there'd be more to their lives than coding if only there was more to life than code.

"Okay . . ."

He turned to see Ramona squinting incredulously, her body angled in inquisition off the back of a chair, a wrist curled like an upside-down question mark at her hip.

"I mean, unless you want me to go. I don't want you to feel obligated to take me," Sevi backpedaled.

"I want you to go. That's why I asked."

"Yeah, then, yes, let's go."

Across the street, moving to the rhythm of the crowd's demands, Sevi couldn't tell if the protestors were deriding him or cheering him on. The words were falling out of sync, and he didn't know how to hear them. He lost himself in the tidal confusion, Ramona's swinging arms the only source of direction. Wherever she stepped the crowd parted and let them on their way. The crowd controlled whether people got to work on time or not. Today, they would. When the bus arrived, they made room for the people getting off and stayed in flanks to let the others on. One smiling woman held up a sign that read: GET OFF THE BUS AND JOIN US.

Inside, the bus was radiant, clean, shimmering—a top-of-the-line model, nothing like the old buses that lumbered across Chicago. Most of the passengers ignored the protest, white earbuds dangling from their ears, but the man in front of Sevi shot video of the crowd with his phone, trying out different angles, zooming in and out. The EVICTED man wagged his pelvis at the bus as it eased from the curb, flipped Sevi off. Samson would've liked that, Sevi thought, and almost liked it himself.

BUILDING 43, WHERE Ramona worked on campus, was a considerate building. Google had thought of its employees' every need. From the high-plant-protein intercontinental cuisine in the café—which smacked of San Francisco's Asian-hybrid local-organic ingredient focus—to the color scheme—a ball pit spectrum which purported to elicit joy and productivity—Sevi thought the space was like a luxury womb for brainy and boyish would-be malevolents. Ergonomists had been insinuating their way into office spaces since the fifties with little success wrestling the white-collar class from their white collars. After Google, everyone had to change. Otherwise, why would any worthy person work any place else? In the café, from where Sevi sat, something about the air, hidden behind the molecular notes of ginger and rice starch, beyond the clean breath of the people at his table, and the effluvium of their body odor and body wash, was the implacably heady suggestion that his future had been erased by their future. Duster and ozone, he decided, the smell of the internet.

Ramona's new project was code-named Herodotus, and her research team comprised six men, ages twenty-five to thirty, who'd all obviously and painfully been at Google longer than she, and each of whom now sat with Sevi and Ramona eating. It was unclear what had offended them more when they were assigned under Ramona: having their seniority overlooked or working beneath a woman. Either way, Ramona said she couldn't be bothered with slightly senior dick-swingers' bruised egos. They were capable programmers and developers and engineers besides, who'd proven especially creative during their Innovation Time Offs, so it was better if everyone just evolved a little bit. Between the six were twenty patents and two downloadable plug-ins used everywhere in the world. And through their petty outrage, they were also smart enough to glimpse this fresh-out-of-propeller-hat noogler's potential. Ramona had finished her first project, Tiresias, successfully, while also finding time to tweak the Google real-time flu outbreak locator. And she'd managed to speak about Herodotus in such clear and rational terms that its completion sounded like a moral obligation.

Google, proprietary owner of one of the largest caches of data in the world, was responsible for organizing and making this information not only accessible, but concretely beneficial to humanity. Some sort of computer magic was going to harness the data to determine a new standard of best practices for an endless variety of public and private fields—it was all out there, ripe for the picking—and then figure out a way to sell them, emphasis on selling them, because, as Ramona had said, "Elon Musk didn't invent electric cars, he just figured out a way to get people to pay for them." Tiresias had been trained on triggers, had been designed to avoid them—Herodotus would reverse engineer user response to trigger compliance with whatever the AI deemed necessary for human survival and success. Consumer and voting patterns were already being projected, as were philanthropic investments, and revisions to legal structures, legislation, and public policy. They were going to put it right into the search engine, a tool for directing users to the right decisions. Musk was going to use branding to make his cars sexy enough to actually sell; Google would use its efficiency to make Herodotus simply ubiquitous. Eventually, it would be a voice- or text-activated assistant, a wise companion to turn to whenever you had a decision to make. Herodotus was a synecdoche, a smaller but absolutely essential part of a network of artificial intelligence tools that this new faction of the AI research department used to describe a vision for the future. Listening to her explain it, several times now, Sevi had grown increasingly uncomfortable, until he finally decided he didn't like the sound of this Herodotus at all. Stopping short of saying that Ramona was no longer allowed to bring it up at home, Sevi had declared the bedroom a Herodotus-free zone. For the same reasons years ago they had said they were no longer allowed to complain about coworkers in bed and would have to get up and go to the kitchen or the living room to bitch and moan, Sevi had put his foot down, softly, and said he wanted the room to be a place for sex and rest and nothing else, and Ramona had happily conceded, though she would get up on occasion in the middle of the night to do work on her laptop in the living room and spoke freely about Herodotus in all other places, including in the shower, on the train, even through the bathroom door while she peed, which only irritated Sevi more and more every time she did.

It wouldn't go over well, but as Sevi sat in the cafeteria, he felt the urge to ask if they thought what they had planned for the internet was ethical. He performed a mental pump-up that caused him to grit his teeth and asked a question he'd rehearsed in his head a thousand times instead. "How do you expect people to react to a search engine that only shows you what it wants to show you?"

Ramona said, "That description of the interface is a little misleading, but I'll roll with it for simplicity's sake. Right now, Google shows you mainly what you want to see, which is just confirmation bias. Type in 'Obama Kenyan' and the top hit will be a bogus news article saying the president isn't a US citizen, when, in fact, he is. I know a lot of libertarian wack jobs would tell you personal bias is a kind of social liberty, but nowhere in the Constitution does it exactly state that we have a right to remain wrong."

"There is the First Amendment," one of the guys said, which got a flock of laughs all around.

"Tiresias was about getting rid of the bad stuff, the inconvenient stuff, the stuff you didn't want to see, but it didn't offer anything in its place. Its methods were actually quite crude and conservative. Let's say the War on Drugs succeeded and illegal street drugs disappeared from the world. What do you do with the people whose livelihood depended on the illegal drug trade? The future generations that were already designated to those places in society? Herodotus helps—"

"Ramona, I've heard your argument a million times. What about you?" Sevi asked First Amendment.

The man put down his fork and closed his eyes. "You used to teach," he said. "The internet is not a classroom, it's not a teacher, it's not even a book. It's, like, the digital sebum of real life. An extension of consciousness. It's where all our ideas go. And now, it's where our ideas come from. Let's say it's dogma then, the way textbooks and pedagogy used to be dogma. Teachers teach from textbooks they know are inaccurate because updating textbooks is expensive, and political. We've seen whole generations stuck in an infinite loop of ignorance—the 1980s, for example. Updating information on the internet is not as costly and it's fairly democratized. Why shouldn't it be better than the false dogma we're used to? Also, unless you're studying to be a history PhD, and you have the research expertise to separate fact from fabrication, working with an enormous data set that includes every perspective, including defunct perspectives, or dangerously misleading perspectives, isn't functional—it's downright detrimental. In less than fifty years, our education system is going to look very different. One big reason is the internet. If we're not careful, we're going to be asking future generations to essentially, like, repeat the dawn of consciousness, because without any tools they'll be presented with the raw data of existence and have no efficient way of navigating this massive volume of crap. The internet currently accounts for 2 percent of global carbon emissions. That's only going to go up. We're running out of server space. In concert with the growing sense that we're inundated with too much information already, these factors will lead to a mass deletion. Herodotus will help us make sure we don't delete the good stuff. But that's the future, let's talk right now. One part of being a teacher is teaching kids how to learn, and learning, as you know, is a really discerning discipline. It doesn't come easy to everybody. Most people depend on authorities to point them toward the facts, it's the only way they can defend themselves. However, not all facts are created equal, and facts have not always been what they are today. Facts, before the seventeenth century, in most regions in the world, were things dictated by gods, defended by lethal force, and persisted to naturalize the rule of powerful elites or validate the irrational. Don't you get the sense that we're slipping back to that definition? The information age is reaching a tipping point, and though the internet can and should remain neutral, it can't all be for nothing. It can't just be a repository of differences, a confusing collage of multiple, feuding realities. We're on the brink of something disastrous. We don't get another chance. The internet has to fix this. Herodotus will find commonalities amongst disparate problems, shared root causes. It will find intersections between oppositional desires, and optimize systems and players to organize functional coalitions between combative forces that actually want the same thing. And, Sevi, we're not the only people researching this stuff, building this stuff. The US government is trying to do this. The Chinese government is moving forward with it already, mitigating information that goes against their ideological agenda. The curation and mediation of information is the most powerful tool in the twenty-first century. You're going to want to make sure the people who have that power have your best interest in mind. Herodotus is about empowerment, putting the public good first, giving us the tools to educate ourselves, to fight—"

"Why my best interest and not somebody else's?" Sevi said, talking quickly so as not to sound dumbstruck, but so fast the man opened his eyes to make sure he wasn't lunging at him.

"Not your best interest, but, like, the best interest of humanity. Herodotus isn't ideological, it's teleological," the man said. "It's inherently nonconformist. It produces novelty. Right now, we're so busy trying to decide who and what to believe, we have no time to ask what's best for humanity."

"And how do you determine what's best for humanity?"

"Good grief, Sevi, have an imagination," Ramona interrupted.

"Good grief?" Sevi said. He didn't know what "teleological" meant.

"For fuck's sake. Better?" she said. "I'm trying not to swear in front of my team. As fun as doom-and-gloom sci-fi is, uncovering some grand conspiracy at Google isn't going to save the human race. Doing something about the problems we face right now will."

"And what will the Ramona version of the internet solve first?"

"It's not my version. It's curated by an unbiased AI fed by decentralized deep-learning networks. It's solutions-based. Teleological."

"What's it solve first?"

Ramona swallowed. "The everlasting question. What is one to do? It will make us better citizens, better voters, better friends of the planet, safer, more peaceful, happier."

"Better, faster, stronger. Fitter, happier, more productive," Sevi said.

"Nice," First Amendment said, and Ramona cut him a look.

"How's it do it, though?" Sevi said.

"By teaching us how to be those things," Ramona answered.

"With what?"

"Our own mistakes. For once, something will help us learn from our own mistakes."

Sevi realized he was tilting forward, rubbing against the man next to him, who was starting to squirm. He touched all four legs of his chair to the ground.

"We're creating a VR simulation," Ramona said. "Using some stuff Herodotus finds useful."

"Of what?" Sevi asked, annoyed.

"Being attacked by a US drone at a birthday party."

"Sounds like a great video game," he said, mincing the minced garlic in his stir-fry.

"Yeah, for kids who want to grow up to be drone pilots. That way they know what it's like to be on the ground."

"The Empathy Machine," Sevi said. "That's what you should call it."

"Sounds like Bradbury," First Amendment said.

Sevi sipped from his can of craft beer.

"The potential for humankind to understand itself and improve itself based on that understanding is tapped. That's why, no matter how much money we make, or how advanced our science gets, we keep making the same mistakes. Herodotus lifts the weight of our miserable history off our shoulders, remembers it for us, and teaches us how to be weightless, entirely free, right now. And it has to do this now before we really start dragging down our future, burying it, drowning it," Ramona said.

Sevi shook his head.

"That's just a TED Talk," he said.

"You've heard of Ted Jenks?" First Amendment asked.

"The conspiracy theorist?" Sevi said.

In Jenks's circles, Barack Obama was not just a Kenyan Muslim but a serial rapist; climate change was a covert military technology operation designed to drive rural white America into poverty; Omni had not shut off its signal but been silenced.

"Watch this," First Amendment said and handed Sevi his phone.

A YouTube video was already playing. Ted Jenks sat in his usual makeshift studio in Richmond, Virginia, behind a long IKEA desk cluttered with electronics and before a green screen, which featured the familiar graphic of Omni orbiting one of its binary stars. Jenks brought viewers up to speed on what they already knew: Omni had been trying to send instructions from Jesus on how to solve our planet's morality crisis when Obama pulled the plug.

The team of cryptologists I and a group of philanthropic patriots have assembled, which our own federal government refuses to listen to, have had a major breakthrough. They've uncovered a Rosetta Stone, of sorts, and have begun translating the message. They've decided to move backward because we assume the most crucial information was coming toward the end, when Omni realized what our overlords were probably going to do. In the final hours of their transmission, the Omnians made a call to arms, my friends. I quote, "The people of Earth should unite against their leaders to prevent doomsday."

"Then he starts ranting," First Amendment said, taking back his phone. "Herodotus's analysis of this particular piece of rhetoric predicts a major event before the end of the month."

"Major event?" Sevi said.

"Mass shooting. Bombing. Kidnapping," Ramona said.

"One of those things happens every month as it is," Sevi said.

"When it reaches 75,000 views, it'll be a matter of days," Ramona said.

"It's at forty k, right now," First Amendment said. "Which means we can prevent it if we take the video down."

"That violates free speech; he's not directly inciting violence," Sevi said. "People won't stand for it. How do you expect to get anyone to sign on to something like this?"

Without a moment's hesitation, Ramona said, "We're Google," and laughed. When she saw Sevi's face, she stopped.

"Then what's stopping you?" Sevi asked her.

"We'll find out at this meeting."

WHILE RAMONA HELD her meeting with leadership, Sevi took a bus to a nearby campus gym to swim. He crawled the pool in Google swim trunks for over an hour, entirely alone in the natatorium save for a group of teenagers playing an odd variation of the game Marco Polo in which they screamed the words Ibn Battuta in place of the Venetian's name. Exercise, it was said, especially swimming, with its return-to-the-womb physics and sensuality, cleared the mind. But efforting his body through the water, Sevi did a tremendous amount of thinking. About Ramona. About the future. Of the future, he realized he would never be ready for it; it would undo him and destroy him. He was the creature in the fable who neglected to store food for the winter; not because he was lazy or careless, but because he'd never heard of, much less experienced, winter. All the while, people like Ramona were building the containers storing the nuts. They called it the cloud. He stubbed his toe on a word in his brain. Luddite. And for the first time he understood it was not only a frame of mind, but a class and a prison. He could have Ramona teach him some things, programming, coding. He, too, could essentialize his life and take charge of his own fate, he supposed. But how would he know when to stop? Hitler and Stalin claimed cutting the pudge of personal liberty from society made for faster, stronger, and more productive systems than fat-ass liberal democracy. What lean visions were the automated internet age conjuring?

He swam and swam. The cold, blue water a dizzying monotony. Air and the blaring natatorium lighting overhead, a white wash of breaking water, the concussed blue of the pool floor, the water breaking in a wash of white, the overhead lighting blaring through the air. The exercise was carnage against his lungs, he could feel them shredding apart, but the rest of his body was streamlined and perfectly repeated, algorithmic, and he felt the need to get away from something. When it wasn't Ramona and her AI historian chasing him like Jaws, it was Eason dragging his cello across Humboldt Park in search of him, calling out his name and knocking on doors. He tried to remember what he'd said to Eason the last time he'd seen him. He hoped it wasn't something stupid about Bach. He hoped it was something real, having to do with the living, but he was pretty sure he'd left him with Schopenhauer's line about all other art speaking of the shadow, and music speaking of the essence. It was a good line, but what had it meant in that moment? If music was its own object in the universe, indistinguishable from raw will, it should do more than stand for something. If Schopenhauer was right, music should be able to stand in the way of things, ward off spirits and flag down cars and convince aliens the human race was worthy, but it hadn't. Then again, human beings themselves, with all their empathy and concern, their ability to scorn someone with a bassoon and cry out in pain on a piano, hardly adjusted one another's fates either. Music, as it'd turned out, wasn't magic, and Sevi had to escape Eason, too. Eason, whom he couldn't save; who was a part of the life Sevi had left behind; who hardly existed at all in this new world Omni and Sevi had created, much less the one Herodotus would eventually create.

In the deepest section of the pool, lurking in the glossy blue shadows near the bottom, was the murky figure of his brother, Samson. Sometimes, always, again. A man who'd gone to stand in the way of things, convince us we were good. He'd been pointing out connections to Sevi ever since he'd disappeared: the obvious, the invisible. In a single daytime news session Sevi had learned of a train derailed in Spain, ribboning track for a quarter kilometer; a thirteen-year-old boy in New Mexico who'd opened fire on his classmates; and a woodpecker gone extinct in Canada. Each of the events seemed to secretly know one another, lovers in a crowded room hiding an affair. While he watched the news, outside his window, people protested buses. A white man on PCP spent an hour trying to get into cars stopped at the light before the police picked him up. These were the different shapes and signals of depravity and disparity, the things Samson had loved to talk about and Sevi had loved to ignore. The signals were impossible to ignore now. Signs, everywhere, for the seeing. In their speeches, Barack Obama, Mitt Romney, Vladimir Putin, and Angela Merkel blamed one another for Omni's silence. Liberal democracy was enslaving the world under a single transnational order seeking control of every resource we had left. Illiberal democracy and kleptocrats were indifferent to the suffering of others and made us look barbaric. Civil wars among the oldest civilizations on Earth went on, day after day, funded by people like Putin and Obama.

At first, these connections had only made Sevi cringe—conspiracies were like religion, an excuse to take things out of and off your hands. But watching a clip of an Athenian bus strike, he remembered a story Samson had told him about sleeping with a pack of dogs in the Parthenon, and Samson began appearing in the sea of North African faces in the video. Samson washed up on the shores of Greek islands Sevi had thought only existed in mythology, an orange life vest stretched over his bloated body, one of the countless drowned refugees appearing every few weeks like debris from a faraway hurricane. In the pool, Sevi tried to tell himself these were feckless parallels. He tried his best to let the visions, the nightmares, go slack, dissolve with logic. *That's life.* Logic said it didn't matter where Samson was. It didn't matter if Samson was coming back. He'd leave again. Samson always existed someplace else. You could be in the same room with him, and the guy still wouldn't be there. Sevi had spent years awake at night, wondering, worrying. From each of Samson's disappearances, Sevi had imaginary memories of where he'd been, what he'd done, what he'd seen, how he'd died. To hold Samson in his mind was to fissure his own consciousness, partition his own person with improbabilities. Swimming, it could drown him. It didn't matter that Samson was always sorry when he came back. Sevi figured there were people you loved whom you never thought about. The cosmos kept itself together without ever knowing its composite parts. There was something even Zen about not caring about Samson. Not caring could be a practice. Already he wanted in one fell swoop to chop every wrinkled umbilical cord tethering him to the far, draining points of the universe. It was exhausting having to give so many shits. An empathy hangover. He'd read somewhere the human brain used to think about its own life 80 percent of the time; now, it reserved most of its resources for others. More burdens for the most considerate generation that ever lived; a generation measuring its worth in concern. Letting go of all concerns both personal and societal, he felt whole and weightless and remote as he swam. He felt resolved. No Omni to shame him, no Samson to shame him. Now, how long can I make this last? he wondered. It worried him that it'd go away. It worried him that Herodotus would make the world at large his constant companion. How would Herodotus keep from drowning him too?

Ramona appeared at one end of the pool with a towel in her hands. She wasn't a hallucination. She was beaming. It could've been the fractured reflection of the pool swimming across her face or the halo of lighting encircling her head, but she looked angelic.

"Hello, hello," she said to him as he toweled off.

She looked at him hungrily. He had no idea what interest women had in men. She had once shocked him by saying if she could keep four of his body parts in a box she'd collect a wrist, a shoulder blade, his penis, and his lips. What's more, she'd laughed when he said he'd take her breasts, her vagina, her hair, and her eyes. "That's the way a girl is defined in a children's drawing," she said. "You just want to make sure it's a girl you're keeping."

She had a conquesting look now.

"You look happy," Sevi said, heaving, dropping water, woozy.

"Promise you won't be mad?" she said.

"I promise," he said.

They'd promised it was okay to be happy.

"I am," she said.

He tried holding on to the weightlessness of the pool, the faith in the idea that feeling nothing was a good thing.

"Can I ask why?" he said, ignoring his better judgment.

"No," she said.

AT HOME, SEVI explained he was in no condition for sex. The pool had destroyed him. All his shame, anger, and concern had returned.

"I can barely lift my hand," he said. "I haven't exercised like that probably ever in my life."

She said, "I don't need a spotter."

She stroked a hard-on from the wreck of his body. From below she looked like an acrobat, and he winced every time he thought she might fall, but understanding the charities of other people's bodies he stuck to it, lending her his hands and the occasional kiss. More ghosts had never passed through his mind during sex. Sensing his body's mechanical pleasure only distantly, he experienced guilt, mostly. Mostly over having taken so much pleasure in not caring, even if only for a few fleeting laps.

INOCULATION

Taka keeps a cat. A nutritional virus, Taka calls it, an anomaly ghosting through its code that messes with things when Taka isn't looking. It's an AI within the AI. When it's feeling cheeky, it will manifest itself in the ship. A little, orange, white-belly tabby with pink paws and green eyes. It leaps at me from behind corners or sleeps in my bed. The cat simulates network hazards, the ills of the connectivity Taka has lost this deep in space. The cat is meant to keep Taka's immune system up, so when it connects with foreign systems in the future, it will not be destroyed. The cat cracks encryptions and keeps Taka's privacy security up to date too.

How do I keep my immune system healthy?

By ingesting the diseased world I was so desperate to escape.

The greenhouse, a corridor of glass cubes receding several hundred meters to a vanishing point. It is dim and calm, and the robotic gardeners give off a pleasant hum. I enjoy the muggy, sweet fecal smell of the place.

A medical library, I tell Taka and take a banana plant's hand.

The smallest bird, a little orange, a little mossy, appears.

Cute trick, Taka, I say.

It lands on my chest, and I can feel it, its tiny feet clinging to the fabric of my shirt, the insanity of its heart against my own.

Not mine, Taka says, and the bird disappears into the shadows overhead.

It's the thirtieth generation of its family. It makes a magnificent nest, Taka says.

Taka takes me to the shallow brown crown, a bustle of sticks and fibers. I recognize a part of my uniform in the weave. The diseases the bird must carry, I think.

I see a shadow move, liquidly, in the corner. A crouching figure.

Do you see him? Taka asks.

I look at something more chimpy in countenance than me, but no less elegant in curiosity, which, when it turns its face away again, it expresses with its back, a fur cloak rippling and buckling like an inquisitive brow, rolling forward with its left shoulder. I walk around him—a sculpture in a museum, a tree in a conservatory. Its fingers are in potting soil, drawing rivulets. I think he might be playing, gardening. A stowaway of history.

NOT A HALF HOUR AFTER his latest drop-off with Julio—who was ten, a fact that left Eason feeling scummy inside—Germaine showed up at the apartment in a LeBron James jersey.

"I saw the light," Germaine said. "There's no denying it, LeBron James is the greatest player of all time."

The Heat had defeated the Thunder in the NBA finals and LeBron had earned the MVP title.

"Since when do you even like basketball?" Eason said.

"Since D. Rose come on the scene."

"You're dumb as hell," Eason said.

"You're just a hater. People don't like LeBron because he's too good. Ain't nobody ready to see a man with that much skill. I'm ready."

Eason didn't really get it, he'd become a dealer and Germaine was living this new carefree life as a basketball fan. Had Germaine started listening to Bach, Eason would've suspected a supernatural force had swept down and made him and Germaine switch places. He didn't really get the new life he was living, the sudden abundance of money and feelings, feelings of control and powerlessness and guilt.

"How'd you do it?" Eason asked. "Knowing little kids are smoking your shit. I mean, I've seen some girls we went to middle school with out there with these old men, you know?"

Germaine looked at him very seriously.

"I just figured, you know, nobody likes their job," Germaine said, and Eason reiterated that he was dumb as hell.

Eason lit a blunt. His own weed, Germaine was impressed. It wasn't anything serious, he never pinched anything off for himself, Jules gave him weed for free, and he only smoked sometimes. They partook near an open window, over a cereal bowl, to keep from dropping the cherry and burning a hole in the couch.

"I'ma tell you some shit," Germaine said when he was good and high. "But I don't want you judging me."

Eason wondered what kind of trouble was Germaine in this time.

"Two nights ago, I had this dream, this nightmare about Rydell. He wasn't a ghost or anything. He was alive still, I could tell, you know? But he was all morose and shit. So, I asked him, Rydell, what's up? And he says some shit about how he was still stuck in the Water Temple. And in my dream, I'm like, what the fuck? The dream ends, and I wake up and I'm still confused. Then, this morning, I remembered how when we were little, we'd watch his ass play that Zelda game, and how he could never get out of that Water Temple level. Like he'd hit a wrong switch somewhere in the level that couldn't be flipped back, and he needed to start the whole game over, but he didn't want to, so he just quit playing. You remember that? It was like a glitch, or something."

"Kind of," Eason said, although he remembered it perfectly. He'd never liked video games but could watch people play like it was a movie. This game was old even then, on an N64, Rydell's cousin's, or someone's. To get to the Water Temple, you don these iron boots and a blue tunic and sink to the bottom of this lake, where these dolphin people lived. The music down there was all shimmering beauty. Rydell had done something out of order, maybe he'd been trying to skip a step, and then he'd gotten stuck. It was like the Japanese game designers had set up an internal mechanism to punish him. They'd stopped hanging out soon after.

"You ever think Rydell beat that level?" Eason said.

"Dunno. It was a hard-ass level, man."

"Bet that level wouldn't be that hard now. Kids were trippin' back then saying shit was hard. Games today are hard."

"Gotta do a bunch of math and shit."

"Your player's got a job, life-threatening illness, kids to feed."

Germaine looked out the window, at the top of the building across the street, the sky above.

"Fool, what we doin' today?" he said.

"Let's go downtown," Eason said, which they'd never done before.

THE LOOP MADE Eason and Germaine feel crazy. All the fast-moving businesspeople, restless cops and out-of-towners, cleaving their purses and shopping bags and briefcases away from the boys as they passed. Achy light shook down the glass skyscrapers in waves, blinding the boys and making them sweat.

The city quieted down on the museum campus. The Adler Planetarium sat at the end of a stony, man-made jetty that reached like a hand into Lake Michigan on the Loop's south side. The structure looked ancient, Greek or Roman. From the front steps, facing north, the boys caught a view of the city where everything on the left was Chicago and everything on the right was water, separated down the middle by a crooked line of beach, the skyscrapers along Michigan Avenue like a row of riot police bracing the city against the lake's tide. The water, chapped with huge frothing waves, let out the screams and shouts of hundreds of swimmers. It sounded like a war.

With their student IDs, they got into the planetarium for cheap. The first thing Eason noticed was how weird and out of place all the glowing meters and dials and computer imaging software looked against the old-fashioned architecture. In the lobby, he spotted a lamp in the shape of the Eiffel Tower spread a fan of buttery light on an Atlas figurine mounted on the wall beside it. Geometric patterns fringed the carpet. Bronze grates were fastened to the ceiling's air ducts. The place shouted richness, whiteness. And Eason was about to suggest they leave when Germaine whispered, "Yo, I think we're the only people here," and, looking around to see if this was true, Eason realized that aside from the employees, they were, and that everyone working that afternoon in the Adler—the guards in glossy coats, the women restocking puzzles and mini telescopes and sparkly gel bags in the gift shop, the guy who'd sold them their tickets—was Black. A few feet past the front desk, on an LCD screen mounted into a wall, a brother named Neil deGrasse Tyson was talking about the universe.

They bypassed exhibits on the Mars rover mission, the moon landing, and Saturn V for a large glass wall overlooking Lake Michigan. The planetarium had the best view of the lake Eason had ever seen. In the middle of the glassed-in lake was a small screen.

Omni, a smooth orb, glowed there. Slow churning clouds marbled its surface and bathed the boys in pinkish light. Eason was surprised to see it. The planetarium had postponed a huge exhibition, a gala, not sure what they'd have to say about Omni so soon, but this video was there, pressed against the lake, the white sky, the birds, and the unfocused horizon.

He tried to look at Omni, the pearl of it, but the waves kept taking his eyes. This was what Rydell had missed. Omni, then not Omni. There was a color the sky and the lake made where they met, a sky-lake blue or a lake-sky white.

He tried looking into the center of Omni, a still color at its heart, the glowing fuchsia they colored everything for a while, flaking off buildings and draining from people's hair now. Omni had moved on, Earth was stuck, Earth felt wrong. The living felt wrong.

"Looks like a Pixar movie," Germaine said.

"Yeah."

"Pretty good graphics."

"Yeah."

The lake behind the screen was a churning endless blue drinking clouds from the sky. It was all right there. Eason thought he could walk into it, straight to the bottom.

AFTER COLLEGE, RAMONA'S ROOMMATES MOVED west to a mossy city overrun with bicycles to work remotely for Adobe and write lifestyle blogs about tiny houses. They tried taking Ramona with them, but she told them she'd never live anywhere where Birkenstocks were acceptable footwear, where dogs were welcome inside stores. She'd read all of Portland's basements were rotted, withering colons, and imagined their little bungalow on the hill would collapse neatly into its own wet basement. She'd planned a yard sale but simply threw out all the belongings they'd stuck her with instead. When the lease ended, she put a Turkish metal coffee table, an industrial medicine cabinet, and a mannequin called Tabby into a storage unit in Bridgeport and went home to Boston. Nothing had quite found its place again since Jesse.

She returned to a job at a bakery she'd worked at in high school, lived in her old bedroom, frequented a bar where, the last time they'd seen her, she was sixteen and grabbing a foggy plastic pitcher to throw up into. She drove up and down neighborhood roads named after Colonial trails in her mother's red Toyota Solara, curving through the blind turns that lived off mangled first cars and teenage lives. She stood beside campfires at night. On the beach, the wood was never dry and sent gray smoke into her old friends' faces. These adults were the last of the boys and girls who'd become fascinated with one another when she became fascinated with computers.

Her uncle was a realtor, and on her days off she'd drive up to his properties in Gloucester and Worcester and lead different lives whole afternoons at a time, roaming deserted mansions owned by former Celtics and Red Sox players, pretending to be a realtor herself if security asked. Brushing their topiary animals, taking in their verandas, she felt like a girl in a secret garden. Naked in a famous benchwarmer's saltwater pool, she watched three peacocks charge the deck like prehistoric linebackers. Clouds cottoned overhead into a complex textile of evanescent plans. Gone in contrails, tightropes of saliva and watercolor blooms, as soon as they appeared, were all the unfinished internship applications, the recommendations for positions in California and New York, her login username and password for the JET Programme to join a man she could've been in love with in Kyoto. Indecision had made her itinerant in her own life, coming and going like the salty palm-size waves cupping her mouth every now and again as she lay on her back in the water. Had she gone to Kyoto she would've stayed until Fukushima, ventured to DC, never eaten fish again. In New York she'd have started at a hundred thousand dollars a year with Zocdoc, making even more after they broke into the Affordable Care Act business. In California, she'd have fallen in with Google anyway, interned for two months before being taken on full-time. Instead she swam naked in untended pools.

Two years later, back in Chicago, a friend dragged her out of her apartment to a show at Bottom Lounge. The band was a sprawling post-folk outfit with fiddles and washboards, guitars, a dulcimer, resonator, drummer, a lap steel, and a cello; they raised the roof beams with Appalachian vocal harmonies and whiskey. The cellist, a small man with a patchy beard and a floppy music stand, struggled to find his way with the group. His sheet music kept folding over. Ramona thought he was hilarious, this disgruntled little man caught in the middle of all this joy and salt-of-the-earth camaraderie. She noticed his every mistake but only because of the faces he would make. At some point, the drummer told him to take a solo during the next song—the fiddler was too drunk—and the poor cellist's eyes dilated psychedelically. The cellist shook his head. Four minutes later, however, alone with an open string, he sailed the edge of his bow through phrases and exercises Ramona thought were lifted from classical music. She'd remember each line illuminating a room inside her. Rooms she had not been to in years. Rooms of strangers. The movements maintained the consistent pomp, bawdiness, and sorrow of four hundred years of Continental music and were completely out of place with everything the band had played, and she loved them. He found the A at her center and had her sit down and stay awhile, having walked her to her apogee and back.

After the set he spent his gig pay drinking himself into a nervous drunkenness. When Ramona sat next to him at the bar, he sobered up, remained nervous. Instantly, she confused his insecurity for intense attraction. She would tell her friends he was charmingly awkward.

"I don't usually play with them," he said, nodding toward the rest of the band, who'd started a game of pool. "It's my first time, actually. They asked me to sit in for their cellist ten hours ago—that's why I sucked so much. Normally—"

"Couldn't tell," Ramona said. "It all sounded like shit to me."

They agreed to smoke a cigarette neither of them had. Outside, Ramona rested at ease that he was taller than her. She could be forgiven for having standards. Like he was speaking German, his sentences circled their subjects. What he meant to ask was: Did she like her job at iTunes? Why did she come back to Chicago? Was she seeing anyone? He was funny, used colorful language, joked openly about taboo subjects. They could be their most honest when they weren't being serious, she thought. Recovering from a snort he'd inspired with a scenario about a folk revival taken so seriously they'd devolve into a minstrel show, she kissed him. Saliva strung a line between their mouths and snapped. Recovered from his confidence, he rested back into uncertainty.

"Was that inappropriate?" he asked, like he'd been the one to kiss her.

"The kiss or the joke?"

Obviously, both were. She spent the next five years of her life with that man. Whether it was a mistake or not was irrelevant if something could be learned from it.

THERE WAS A sizeable contingent of dogs at Ajit's Fourth of July party. Ajit was on Ramona's Herodotus team and resided in a co-living house in Palo

Alto. Each of his housemates, eight geniuses of varying ages and backgrounds, each of whom was attempting to adapt AI to a different field of study—deep-sea surveys, weather, law, urban planning, polyamorous dating—had one dog apiece, but everyone else who'd been invited over evidently had at least one as well and had decided to bring it too. "I hate leaving him at home," they'd say. "If you have one, why not show it a good time?" "She loves people." The preliminary fireworks being shot off across the neighborhood sent the animals into a panic. Some shat on the floor, many pissed, most cried and hid. Within an hour sedative drops had to be administered in the animals' treats. Around dusk, shortly before the real fireworks, many of the dogs had fallen asleep or else were lumbering about in heavy shag swirls. Ramona was maybe one cocktail away from snuggling up with one of the drugged pups when she heard a familiar but unknowable sound rushing over the fence from the street. Locust-like but as mournful as the sea. Symphonic? Polyphonic? Sevi would've known, but he'd stayed home. The sound was sobering. It was Omni-7xc.

Everyone in the backyard, drugged dogs included, snapped to and turned their ears to the sound. A dozen people climbed out of the pool, fully clothed, sculptural and ecstatic in their sodden drapings. "This song is so played out," someone said. Another person shushed Ramona, even though she hadn't been talking. Then, the music stopped. Ramona touched her phone. Be still my heart. She almost called Sevi—what cheap symmetry that'd have been—had someone not shouted, "Fuck off, assholes!" nearly causing her to stumble into the pool.

Something had happened in June. One minute, she and Sevi couldn't keep their hands and mouths off one another, and the next they seemed to want less and less to do with each other. They'd started reading Vonnegut's *Deadeye Dick* aloud, creating voices for each of the characters and rolling around laughing in bed, but they never finished the book, much less puzzled out its interrogation of American gun culture. They kept saying, "I love you." It was nothing catastrophic, they'd fallen out of love before, but everything after Omni, even the most familiar disappointments, felt freshly deserved, and she was kicking herself for having instigated another go at it, for having brought him into her home, for having believed it would've been different in any way. For what? she asked herself. And in what order had all this come to pass? One minute she'd simply been awaiting her doom, the next she was planning the future, which revolved at least in part around her ex-boyfriend.

Gathering herself, she walked away from the edge of the water to the side gate and spied a parked SUV with a glowing fuchsia paint job. A joke. A prank. A performance art piece. An act of terrorism. The audio started up again, this time it was the voice of Sally Field crying, "You like me. You really like me!" Then the red and blue strobe of police lights arrived, and everyone let out a cheer. Ramona sighed, wanted another beer. Maybe the driver had violated a noise ordinance, but it was their First Amendment right to act a fool.

The order of events returned to her: She'd allowed herself to feel alone and guilty enough to fall in love with Sevi all over again on New Year's Day, then Sevi had brought his bitterness with him to California, and now there was some sort of bizarre love triangle between them. Maybe it wasn't that simple, maybe she shared some of the blame, but didn't Sevi understand that she'd run out of space for any more blame? He'd become transfixed on Herodotus, wanting to discuss its ethics, where it would lead at every opportunity. He refused to believe her when she said Herodotus was nothing but an organizational method, a way to stave off the information apocalypse, that it was still basically just an idea, operating at less than 5 percent. He had no idea that team Herodotus had been cleared to suck up personal data from the approximately 89 percent of users who hadn't updated their privacy settings, nearly five billion searches and the accompanying user data a day. Missing Sevi and not missing Sevi in Ajit's backyard, watching men treat girlfriends and female strangers alike like shit, Ramona was reminded of the shame that arrived each morning at the foot of the bed of every woman who allowed guilt to shape her life.

Without the sound of Omni clouding the air, Ramona could hear conversations starting up again all around her.

"A Sophistic approach to education could work, especially with crowd-sourced curriculum. And it could solve grad student funding issues, too. A group of parents could easily pay a student's way through grad school in exchange for him teaching their kids. They could also provide scholarships for a kid or two from a low-income neighborhood."

"I think most people would be a lot less outraged about things if they were more intelligent."

"And that's really what the idea of a tech-industry media company is all about. Stop dumbing it down for the masses, stop entertaining their neolithic ethics, and tell real stories about real lives."

"Charter cities would work. In some ways, Indian reservations are charter cities. They just don't have functional education systems. Which Todd was talking about earlier. He thinks Sophism might work."

It was all so blissful and painful to hear. Dumb ideas and good intentions rooted in privilege and bias that could be expressed freely without fear because everyone within earshot was too intelligent to get upset about anything, because there weren't any journalists around to scold them, and because these were crowdsourced ideas and crowdsourced ideas were inherently blameless, lacking any single author, evolving as naturally as opposable thumbs. It was good to hear human voices, it was good to hear plans coming together, it was good to hear people talking about their work on a national holiday.

But then suddenly everyone turned to their phones and a silence fell over the backyard. Before Ramona had a chance to check her own phone, Ajit appeared and walked her to his bedroom inside.

"What's going on?" she asked.

Ajit was shaking. His bedroom was nice.

"Someone leaked it all," he said. "The privacy exploit, the social engineering aspect, everything about Herodotus. It's all over the internet. People are furious. They say we're trying to brainwash the world."

Ramona gagged.

"Ramona, it's over," he said.

"But we just got started. We haven't even really used it. We—"

"You've gotta get out of here. I can't be seen with you. I'm going to tell people that the research was totally partitioned. That I had no idea about the scale of the project. Oh, God, what's happening?" Ajit said, looking at Ramona's phone. "This is all your fault."

It was exploding with notifications from her bank and social media accounts. Her bank account had been locked due to suspicious activity. Someone or some group had hijacked her Twitter and posted a bunch of spam from her handle. They'd tried to access her email account.

"Oh my God," Ajit said.

Anonymous text messages threatened to slit her throat, rape her and leave her in a ditch to die. Dana. He hadn't even been released from prison yet. She received an invite from a new Google work group. HERODOTUS STRIKE. She was uninvited before she could open the invite.

SEVI HAD PASSED A WHOLE fifteen minutes standing under the awning of a food co-op waiting for the rain to stop before he realized the building he'd been staring at across the street the whole time was the bookstore he'd come to Berkeley to find. The bookstore was nameless, a tar-black brick-and-mortar with the words Drinks, Books, and No Politics written in big white hand-painted letters across the darkened front windows. Behind even sheets of gray rain, the sky was green, and had Sevi known any less about where he was, he'd have suspected a tornado was on its way. He darted across traffic under a concussion of thunder.

Inside, the store was dark, hazy. Sevi wondered whether the lighting choice was aesthetic or economic. There were ethics to aesthetics. A song by Godspeed You! Black Emperor droned on in the background. The place reminded Sevi of a sex shop he'd passed through on a layover in a German airport, though the sex shop was cleaner, better organized. A white plastic chandelier hung from the middle of the ceiling, throwing little shards of light across a labyrinth of black shelves. Sevi's eyes adjusted. No dildos or adult books, only battered texts, *Anarchy in the Occupy Movement*, *Politics and the State*, *Manufacturing Consent*, and others, hundreds of authors he'd never heard of, Spanish, African, Asian names, so many with *x*'s in them, packed neatly alongside one another in long rows soldiering in all directions. Militant, yet decentralized. He glanced through the stacks, one shelf after another, looking for nothing, diligently directionless.

Staring at what might as well have been Samson's personal bookshelf, Sevi realized that he belonged to none of these movements, not even the most recent and most pressing ones. How could this be? He empathized with every one of them, he dreamed of a world free of oppression. The radical dismantling of the state was predicated on common sense, with practical aims gained through practical means, and in this, Sevi suddenly realized, lay the problem, because what Severino del Toro wanted out of life, for his own life, was something more than a sensible fair shake. More than universal health care, more than preventing climate disaster, more than world peace, what he really wanted was to be chosen. Grad school, Ramona, Omni, Ramona again, probably, had not chosen him in the end. This had been his grief. And not a single one of these books discussed this injustice.

Briefly, Sevi imagined buying one of these books and joining a movement, but he didn't have the heart to pick one. Lately, he didn't have much energy for agitation. Working from home because her coworkers felt uncomfortable whenever they spotted her on campus, Ramona had asked Sevi if he felt uncomfortable, too, sharing the apartment with the poster child for unethical tech, and instead of saying, "Yes, it does make me uncomfortable, I want you to quit your job like everyone else does, you can't be trusted with any sort of authority," he'd tried comforting her. She kept having to change her phone number, and it saddened him to watch her navigate the unaccustomed idle hours between meals and the sudden impromptu workouts she'd started doing out of boredom and anxiety. Her yoga practice broke his heart. He wished she'd have just come to her senses, but she hadn't, and he couldn't fault Big Tech for eating one of its own, these sacrifices were the only way to atone for the future they all still had in mind, a smooth, featureless malaise vaguely reminiscent of what we will have once called life.

He could sense the regret that awaited him already, but he couldn't touch any of these books. Sevi had not become a libertarian syndicalist, nor had he been red pilled by the anthropological poetics of David Graeber or the pseudo-dialectics of a DSA subreddit. If he'd wanted to join uncivil society, he'd have simply walked across the street, saved time and money and eaten lunch at home. He was not here for any sort of revolution, not even one in his own love life. He'd left the apartment for once, but he hadn't left Ramona. Why had he come? It wasn't the shame he felt, being so at peace with doing nothing. A

BART train, paid for with a Clipper card in his name, and his own two legs had brought him to the bookshop. But, really, it was Samson who'd carried him here. His love for his brother, his desire to see him, a need to act on an old unspoken promise to keep him safe.

A week ago, Sevi had recalled the image that hung on the wall above Samson's laptop, a screen print by a buddy named Omar. The strawberry with a skull carved in its pink meat. He found Omar's Etsy profile after scrolling through a dozen pages of handcrafted hand towels, caftans, and charm bracelets, most of them featuring something to do with the Raiders or *The Magical Mystery Tour* or a bizarre mixture of the two—the results of a Google search for "Oakland" + "strawberry." Over the Etsy messenger system, Omar Hafiz wrote back that he hadn't heard from Samson in a few months. Maybe a woman named Tao Hsu at an unnamed anarchist bookstore in Berkeley might know something. If Sevi wanted a strawberry print of his own, Omar would cut him a deal.

At the counter near the back, Sevi found a woman he assumed was Tao.

"Hey," he whispered.

"Can I help you find something?" she said.

She didn't bother to look up from her computer and there was a brusqueness to her voice, like she smoked a lot, didn't give a fuck, had left niceties and other vestiges of social grace to those who did. Up close, something glowed on her cheeks. Tiny little rings, like incised gills. Just adrift from the left of her mouth was a cloudy bruise.

Sevi turned to the sound of rain on the windows. Behind the leopard print of water drops on the glass was the green, stippled mist of the street, streaks of oak and their bloated summer canopies, bicycles with plastic bags bunched like shower caps around their seats. Lightning snapped an eel across the sky. He turned to Tao again, cast in the same spotted shadow as the window. She was looking at him now. She looked like she wanted to kill him.

"I'm Samson del Toro's brother," he said.

She stopped what she was doing on the computer, fingers stiff over the keys.

"I was wondering why I instantly wanted to punch you in the face."

"The stories he told about me were that bad?"

"He never mentioned having a brother. What I mean is you look like him."

Sevi had never considered this.

"So, he was too chickenshit to come himself and sent you instead?" she said.

"I haven't talked to Samson since February. I was hoping you knew where he was."

"Who sent you?"

"Omar Hafiz said you know my brother."

"I haven't spoken to Samson since February either. Your guess is as good as mine. You guessing he's dead? That's my guess."

She scratched the skin around one of her cheek piercings and dragged her tongue over her teeth.

She said, "He left me behind. So, you can tell your NSA, Homeland Security friends I'm clean. He duped me, and I didn't do shit. He was the one with all the contacts, he was the one who made the transactions, and he was the one who went."

"I'm not in contact with the NSA or Homeland Security. I never even called the cops."

"You never filed a missing persons report? That's kind of fucked up."

"He's not missing."

"He's not here. You don't know where he is or when he'll be back. Sure as hell sounds like he's missing to me."

"He leaves all the time. He always comes back. He's spread his bullshit all over the world."

"So, why are you looking for him now, then? If there's nothing out of the ordinary about this?"

"I have to this time."

"You swear no one knows you're here?" Tao said, leaning over the counter.

"I swear."

"And no one's been following you?"

"Positive."

"So, no one will mind if I call up a crew to beat your ass?"

HE SAT IN a coffee shop with a view of the bookstore looking at the sky, incarnadine, dusted with metallic cloud shavings and doubled in the wet concrete of the street. He was trying to take a picture of the sky with his phone, failing to, when it lit up with a call from an unknown Chicago number. He didn't answer and the caller left a voice mail.

Mr. del Toro, this is Rubin Wallace, Eason's dad. I hope things are going well for you in California. I'm calling because, well, frankly, I'm worried about Eason. His friend died early this year, and I don't think he's ever fully recovered. Has he mentioned anything about a guy named Germaine? His cousin Jules? Has he been acting strange? Different? Anyway, listen, if you could call me back, that'd be great. I'm just trying to get a read on the kid. We all go through phases, but Eason's a good guy, you know that. He's special. I just figured, you know, you talk to him at least once a week, you might know something, or you might be able to tell him something. Thanks.

Sevi put down his phone and went back to looking at the sky. He did not think he had noticed anything different about Eason, anything strange. He had certainly never mentioned any Jules or Germaine. In fact, he had never even mentioned his father. Sevi had never even known the man's name. Rubin. No, each week Eason had promptly answered Sevi's video calls fully prepared to begin every lesson, instrument in hand and in tune, having practiced the previous week's material. And every week Sevi had noted his improvement, Eason growing closer and closer to gathering all of the necessary techniques to sweep through the suites without stumbling, when he could switch focus to thinking about the phrases in conversational and more macro terms, as ideas in concert with one another and, therefore, affected by their thoughtful passage through one another, like the effects of moving from one room to the next. Maybe Eason was struggling with something, convening with people his father had taken concerned interest in, but those were things Sevi had no idea about, only seeing the flattened surface of Eason's life through a screen now. When Sevi was still teaching, he would often go to sleep thinking about a student, worrying if they'd eaten, if they had clean laundry, if they were in bed too, safe, in good health, and sober. A colleague, a veteran teacher of history, had tried to teach Sevi how to release these concerns. How did it work? He could no longer remember. It no longer mattered.

Across the street, Sevi saw Tao leaving the bookshop, beginning to lock up. Stepping out after Tao beneath the open sky was like stepping into a rosy broiler.

"Dude, are you kidding me?" he heard Tao say, standing at a bike rack, staring down at her bike, the chain ruined, an abandoned attempt to steal the whole thing.

Standing behind her, Sevi called her name, and she jumped.

"Did you fucking do this?" she said.

"No."

"I'm calling my dudes now."

"Please, Tao, help me. I can't do this on my own. I can't save his life by myself."

"Fucking shit," she said.

Tao lived outside of the campus district, but they had to move through a lot of it in order to get there. Women in neon sportswear returning from the gym and women in night attire headed to bars glared at her freakishly. Men, mostly bros, looked at her with scared curiosity or angry hunger. Sevi was invisible to everyone. He said almost nothing. He only listened and tried to keep pace. She was a few inches shorter than him but moved much quicker.

The first time Tao saw Samson he was an out-of-towner in a Canadian tuxedo and motorcycle boots hanging on a china hutch in Benicio Salazar's Tenderloin apartment. Long Jesus-hair and a far-off gaze, caught up in remembering or foreseeing or simply on drugs, this Kerouac type had been coming through the Bay for ages, Tao said, more runaway than renegade, men who did little for causes and took little from their time with organizations like Occupy, other than stories with which to coerce sympathetic women when they reenrolled in college. Eighteen and already through with dating intentionally homeless guys and men who whimpered, "I've never been with a woman like you," Tao said she had no interest in Samson. She'd caused a lot of problems in people's lives who caused even more in hers. She was ready to be the consequence.

Benicio told Samson to quit putting so much weight on the hutch, it came with the apartment and if something happened to it, it was coming out of the deposit. Tao laughed and the next thing she knew Samson was sitting cross-legged on the floor, perking up like a cobra between her on the far left of the couch and a coffee table covered with pipes and pamphlets, an unloaded revolver for show. Blue sheets hung from the ceiling, quartering the tiny studio apartment into bedrooms and studies, a pop-up burn ward. A commemorative *Free Willy* beach towel blacked out the picture window beside them. It was all a bunch of freegans and anarchists could afford, but programmers were living similarly in Union Square Park, where a curtained-off quadrant of an apartment with room for a cot and a stool went for an average seven-fifty. What would the rest of the American people say if they'd known that the crusties and the yupsters were all living like Chinese factory workers in the heartland of Big Tech and unicorn startups at the dawn of the third millennia?

They were always having meetings; the cast was always changing; the goals, no matter the specifics, shared a common equidistance from reality, a tangible measure of impossibility, given the happy, daydreamy disregard the nation had for its own demise. They needed to link up with Anonymous, they needed to petition to get so-and-so out of jail, they needed to occupy the capitol building down in Sacramento. Benicio had formed the group, but had no idea what he was doing. The crew came from all over, joined with all kinds of backstories—addiction, prostitution, trust funds. But none of them had been so severely and directly fucked by the government onto which they projected and through which they sublimated all of their anguish as Benicio, whose parents had been swept up by immigration. Benicio was a laser, and they believed, under his guidance, they could change the world.

The meeting that night was called to decide whether it was appropriate for a Democratic senator to attend a rally for a kid who'd been shot by the police. Tao couldn't remember what Benicio was saying when Samson lifted his arm to interrupt, but she remembered the smell of Samson's unwashed body.

"You know the voice he gets when he's trying to be taken seriously," Tao said. "Evenly cut up, like he's practicing a scale with his words. I. Could. Not. Respectfully. Disagree. More. But."

Sevi didn't know this part of Samson.

"Maybe he was different with us," she said.

In that pentatonic voice, Tao said Samson told Benicio he was misguided.

"He told him to be careful putting pressure on systems you didn't intend on destroying. There was this thing Samson used to say about capitalism. It's like a superbug and AIDS combined. It replicates itself in different ways, corrupts whatever stands between it and total domination to work in its favor. The civil rights movement was his favorite example. While people were busy making progress, they didn't realize they kept being exposed to it, that all the while this system was studying them, figuring out how to market their own freedom to them, to convince them to keep working themselves to death for it for at least a few more generations. Pass fair housing laws, keep invisible red lines intact. He told Benicio, whatever it was he was planning, to keep it quiet until he was ready to pull it off; otherwise, you know, you run the risk of them installing a real surveillance state to protect you from you. When Benicio asked Samson what he thought we had in mind, Samson said, 'Pressure cooker bombs?' Benicio lost his shit. It was amazing."

Sevi tried to act chill, like he schemed domestic terrorism all the time. He focused on Samson, the memory of his language, to find if his words pointed clearly enough to some place he could head toward.

"A year ago, I would've said Samson sounded paranoid, conspiratorial," he said. "Now my girlfriend calls me Rage Against the MacBook Pro."

He was doing his best not to sound like a narc. He sounded like a narc, anyway.

"Everyone sees it now. If you somehow missed or have forgotten the takeover after 9/11, you've gotta see it now, Omni made it so visible. How many times has Romney tried to pin Omni's silence on Obama, and how many times has Obama spun silence to mean the Republican Congress hasn't been doing enough? You've got jihadis blowing themselves up over it. Christians holing themselves up in communes to hide from it. Elon Musk planning to build a spaceship to get there, and Peter Thiel trying to purchase Omni to control who gets to live there after the apocalypse. Power inserts itself everywhere."

"An AI to cure us of humanist thinking," Sevi said, to see if she'd heard, if she was one of the people harassing Ramona.

"I don't know about that one. But sure, why not? Arafat shook hands with Peres at Davos. Someday it'll be Micah White hugging President Bloomberg."

Who was Peres? Wasn't Hillary going to be president next?

"Were you building pressure cooker bombs?" he asked.

He couldn't help it.

"Fuck no! I told Samson, 'Damn, dude, Al Qaeda meeting's down the hall.' But he was just fucking around, trying to warn us about the dangers of a soft revolution. Because we'd forgotten, there is no stasis in a revolution. Before the meeting ended, Samson called us, quote, 'a bunch of ignorant miscreants under the tutelage of a *roi fainéant*.' No pleasure in his voice whatsoever."

This brought a smile to Tao's face, the first of the evening. There was some pleasure in her impersonating Samson, conjuring him in a one-woman séance. Then the smile faded, probably as she was visited by another aspect of his spirit, the shadowed side with which Sevi was more familiar.

She said, "There was this huge yelling match; Samson mainly kept it cool, though, and when it was all over I asked him if he needed a place to stay. He said, 'Now I do.'"

"You didn't think he was dangerous?"

She choked her brake, turned to look at Sevi. "Do you think Samson's dangerous?"

"To himself."

"What do you think he's doing right now?"

"I don't know."

"I don't either. And I didn't know whether Samson was dangerous or not when I first met him, but I gave him a place to sleep. Because whether or not he was dangerous, he was a person willing to do something. Whether it would be dangerous or not, I figured that if I hung around Samson I'd be willing to do something too. Whatever he's doing right now, dangerous or not, he's doing it."

The two had made it to a dark impasse between two main streets. From a window just above the street's tree line a bottle came spinning like a baton and exploded a few yards ahead. Screaming. The slamming of a door. The bark of a dog set off like a sentimental car alarm.

"I never understood that will," Sevi said. "I don't know where he got it. Or why he thinks he deserves to keep it, after all the shit he's put people through. He put you through some shit, too, I'm sure."

"Will is the inalienable right we alienate ourselves from to draw less attention to ourselves. Samson isn't entitled. The police murder young Black men, put the rest of them in prison. A company poisons a town's water supply and doesn't bother cleaning it up. It gets tied up in the courts and nothing happens, and we blame the legal system, biased laws, we stop caring, but it's our abandoning of our will that allows this to happen. We feel we are entitled not to care."

Sevi didn't think it was so simple, and he didn't like how Tao kept using revolutionary rhetoric to run interference for Samson.

"Why does everyone feel the need to defend Samson?" he said.

"He hasn't done anything wrong."

"Then why are we so pissed at him?"

"I'm not."

"Tao, I could see it in the bookstore. Before I even mentioned his name, before you could process who I reminded you of, you were pissed. You said so yourself. If he's doing the world a favor, why are we so mad?"

Tao kneaded her handlebar grips.

"He deprived me of my own will," she said. "I've only been trying to make my life bearable since. Waking up in the morning, drinking coffee, brushing my teeth is unbearable while there are people being gassed to death by their own government. I know that now. Samson showed me the truth. And he showed me a way into the truth. Then he closed that door, then he took it away. Samson left without me and took with him the only opportunity I had to bear my own life. So, I'm pissed at him. Now, why are you pissed at him?"

IN THE KITCHEN, Tao sat smoking in an open window. Her pit bull, Lucetti, lay behind her on the fire escape, beating its tail and watching the lamps and the cars on the street below. The apartment, what little Sevi had seen of it before Tao turned most of the lights off, looked like a watercolor, jaundiced drippings, fresco chippings of paint, and flayed papering covering the walls. There was a massive hole in the living room floor filled with chew toys and fur. Outside the bathroom was the scorched tree of a short circuit. In the dark now there was only her in the window, the triangle of her bent knee, the burning end of her cigarette, what little ribbon of the room the moon kept lit. The stove let off the bluey smell of gas. Occasionally, an insect moved through the light. Tao leaned over like she was sticking her arm off the side of a canoe to pet Lucetti.

"Our first idea was to start a podcast," Tao said and laughed.

"A podcast?" Sevi asked, seated at a plastic dinette.

"We wanted to call it '*Forensic Acoustics.*' We knew a guy who'd been in Sednaya Prison in Syria. It's right outside Damascus. According to the Syrian government and several other governments worldwide, it doesn't exist, but it does. Inside, the prisoners are all blindfolded. This is how they can say it doesn't exist. Because if no one has ever seen the inside of Sednaya, how can they say what it is? There are more than ten thousand detainees currently imprisoned there, fifty men are hanged each day, but their bodies are burned, and because the prisoners have all been declared missing or killed in action, none of them are there, none of them have ever set foot in Sednaya. We were going to record him. Make the prison visible with the voices from inside."

"What happened?"

"Our contact killed himself and then Samson disappeared. Really, we'd just been waiting. You know, that's what couples sometimes do, they accompany one another while they wait."

He and Ramona had done nothing but wait. Like two good dogs while their owners were at work, they waited, holding their pee, happily dreaming of evening, barking at shadows they thought might be their lives coming back to them. Like Samson, Ramona had gone ahead and started making history, while Sevi kept waiting, for their relationship, or the world, to end.

"What was Samson like growing up?" Tao asked.

"The same," Sevi replied. But this was wrong or, at least, confused. There had been someone before this Samson, or else there was an adjacent Samson who came out in glimpses still. This adjacent Samson had stayed in Chicago and acted out a different life entirely. He lived in a separate, overlapping world. Sevi called that world Earth, and this Earth, Omni.

"Sensitive. A loner. Our parents guilted us into being friends. Our ma, especially. She'd say, 'Your friends will come and go, but you'll always be brothers.' That kind of shit takes a toll on a kid, and so we couldn't really escape each other. When he was twenty, he went on this semester-long trip to Africa and India to study public health policy. I don't know, they said he mixed up his malaria medication or caught something, but he got really disoriented and he disappeared in Varanasi. He popped up in Chennai a week later, got sent back to school, dropped out immediately. He ever talk about that?"

"No."

"He talked about it to me only once, right after he moved home. They were in and out of these places without clean drinking water. He saw these kids who wouldn't make it through the night. He couldn't look at it any longer, or he had to look at it closer. He didn't make any goddamn sense. I asked him what he thought those NGOs were doing over there, what he thought he could better accomplish without a degree, without any affiliation. I told him to just come out and say he didn't want to do aid work. That he wanted to do something else, something less tragically heroic. I pushed him and he disappeared. Just like in India, he walked off, wound up in Seattle that first time."

"Nobody pushes Samson around, you know that."

Sevi looked into the dark.

"He was acting manic. I knew something was up. Our parents asked me if I thought he needed help, like a psychiatrist. I said no. But a professor from the trip to India had already written me an email saying Samson probably needed to be evaluated. Her sister had gone through something similar, and she'd needed to be hospitalized and put on medication before she could get better."

"She emailed you and not your parents?"

"I dunno. I guess I was his emergency contact. Maybe he'd told her or the school that our parents didn't speak English. I never showed the email to our parents."

"Why?" Tao said, trying for the first time to see Sevi in the dark.

"I thought something bad would happen to him, at first. Then I resented having that kind of responsibility and authority. It didn't seem like the kind of thing a brother should have to do, should have to determine, that was our parents' responsibility."

"But they didn't know. And you were already an adult. Samson's whole life could've been different."

"I know, Tao. I know that now. By the time I figured that out, though, it'd just become routine, the way things are. Samson leaves, he comes back, he leaves again. Except, he might not come back this time. He'll die, and it will be my fault."

Another cigarette fell from Tao's hand, down the fire escape, wherever.

"Mine too," she said.

"It wasn't your idea for him to go."

"I didn't stop him."

"Why would you have? You were going yourself."

"To make sure he was okay. I thought, if I went with him, I'd be able to ride that energy of his and keep him safe. I thought I could have it both ways. I should've told him it was a bad idea. But I'd been waiting for someone like Samson, something like Syria, my whole life. I wondered it myself, if Samson was unwell. I wondered if he needed help. But I convinced myself it wasn't like that. Because if Samson was sick—manic, paranoid, delusional—if everything he believed in was some sort of symptom, then what was I doing? I still can't let it be true, Sevi. Sitting here right now, listening to you tell me that Samson might be unwell, I can feel myself not believing you. I can't believe you. Sevi, if you could still stop him, would you?"

"Wouldn't you?"

"I won't."

"What do you mean you won't?"

"You can."

"How?"

"He's been asking me, he's been begging me to say the words. Come home. I won't say them. He took my legitimacy with him and is about to squander it. He's about to be another one of those stupid kids, one of those horror stories, one of those reasons why we're not all going over there and doing something."

"What are you saying?"

"I'm saying he's still in Turkey. I'm saying he hasn't crossed the border yet. I'm saying I've been in communication with him. And I'm saying he doesn't want to go through with it."

Dear Babichev,

I believe I have found our songline, the resonating melody that
connects our Moscow to where we are today. It is one of those
distant melodies from the Zhdanov era, a Tikhiy Don *number,*
I cannot recall the name, but it was one your father used to play so
incessantly your mother complained she was living in an Eisenstein
film. I hum this tune, and I know we are somewhere together, that
I have returned to my past at last. I hum now, even as I write, and
the tune brings me to this memory: It is a cold night, you and I
are sitting in my dormitory with the broken ferro-cement walls. In
the summer, the plastic tiles stuck to our feet and we wore them as
slippers, but in the winter, snow is practically coming up the
drain! So, we're freezing like rats, and we've just heard Khrushchev
call Stalin a butcher and a maniac. We can't believe our frostbitten
ears! People are shuffling through the streets, on the way to night
classes, or returning from work, a few helpless tramps are out there
drunk and chiding one another to go ahead and jump in front of
traffic and get it over with. We laugh, we know this pair, and no one
would ever jump in front of a Moskvitch, there is more dignity in
being trampled to death by a pig. For a moment, we believe it is the
end of the way things were and the beginning of the way things are
going to be. We will not wind up vaporized after all. You offer up a
plan. We'll go out and buy some ribs, those fuzzy bootlegs pressed on
old X-ray slides we used to listen to. Jazz or rock 'n' roll, it doesn't
matter, we are free. We love the way the bones glow on the records as

they spin. We find a secret pressing of a band from Odessa. They feature pan flutes and guitars and sing about how we are all suffering for nothing. We dance all night long to stay warm. We dance because we think unhappiness is over.

EASON STEPPED FROM THE DROPPED rear of a city bus and before he could see his cousin, he heard his voice shouting, "Hurry your ass up!" He caught up to Jules's elbow a quarter of a block later and said, "My fault, I lost track of the time." They'd had an appointment. The truth was that Eason's dad, sick of hearing Eason complaining there was never anything good to eat at the house, insisted they go grocery shopping together. At the Aldi, Eason had been so preoccupied with Jules, who was blowing up his phone, that he had no recollection of picking out the bunch of bananas, box of cereal, and two-liter of Big Red that appeared on the conveyor belt at checkout. "Hm," his dad said. "Not sure if I want your help running errands after all." In his anxiety over Jules, he had missed a rare opportunity to choose the foods he liked, and an even rarer opportunity to spend a morning with his dad. Now, trudging forward on Chicago toward Ashland alongside his cousin, Eason wanted nothing more than to berate the kindest man in his life for making him late.

"You fuckin' with some bitch?" Jules said.

"Nah."

"Then what the fuck's got you all preoccupied?"

Had he mentioned his father, Jules would've popped him in the mouth. One was to "honor thy father," not blame him, and Jules would give anything to have a father.

"I was practicing cello."

"Careful—they say practice makes perfect. And what are you gonna do when people start thinking your ass is perfect?"

Ashland was a White Zone that kept Eason politely, miserably small, and Jules big, braggadocious, and powerful enough to part hand-holding couples and send full-grown men into the bike lane or the alcoves of buildings as he stepped toward them.

"Where we going?" Eason asked.

"In my view, there's two ways to condition someone's loyalty. Fear and reward. I hope you ain't scared of me. I'm your cousin. We used to play in the yard, been ass naked in a tub together. So, I'd like to express my gratitude for your loyalty, cuz. I'd like to reward you."

Jules orated into the white-cloud sky, striding confidently through the sea of white faces. Eason had only to observe his cousin's movements, absorb a few of his words, for his heart to feel part of his digestive system, clammy and undulating. In his sixteen-year-old mind, Jules was taking him to a strip club, a massage parlor/whorehouse, anywhere some sexual fantasy could unfurl hour after hour in front of him. It was so early; the days were still so long—he'd die of ecstasy. He'd known it all along: the hood had the hidden crack houses, while the white neighborhoods housed the freak dens, Xanadu, Shangri-La. His bootyless existence was about to meet its brutal end, and, from the ashes of his virginity, a new Eason would arise. He was no longer afraid, he wanted to shout it, and a part of him understood how his pops had woken up one day and had six kids.

They stopped in the shaded horseshoe of a recessed storefront. Small chalky tiles crumbled beneath their feet; baby grands, hoods up, napped in the window cases.

"Here?" Eason said.

"Supposed to have some of the best cellos in the city."

"Yeah, and they're like six thousand dollars," Eason said. He knew the place by reputation. A dealer of fine European instruments. Stein, Witz, something, he hadn't caught the marquee.

"You don't want to play any?" Jules said. "All practiced out?"

Inside, the smell of mothballs and the sound of reedy scales deflected Eason's erotic dreams elsewhere, a quiet moment with the internet that evening. Disappointed at first, his lungs filling with the moisture-controlled air, his heart warmed with the acoustics of his footsteps, and he experienced that charge he always felt around instruments, like being near a swimming pool on a hot day, the urge to dive in nearly as libidinal as those forces that'd dragged his imagination around on the walk over. Before he could clear the copse of pianos crowding the entrance, a middle-aged man in a white shirt and black suspenders appeared to greet him. Blondish hair limbed from ears and nose into his thick sideburns and mustache, which formed something almost like a coral reef on his face. Eason looked around for Jules and saw him far off, hands behind his back, leaning over to look inside of a harpsichord.

"What brings you in today?" the man said.

"Just came to check it out."

"We're having a sale on sheet music through the weekend. What instrument do you play?"

Eason couldn't be sure if the guy was desperate for a sale or just didn't want to let two Black males wander the shop unsupervised.

"Cello," Eason said.

"We have an excellent selection of cellos. Beginner, intermediate? Professional?"

"Intermediate."

"And what do you play right now?"

"I rent a Yamaha."

"Perhaps, you'd like to own."

He followed the salesman to a back corner of the store where tobacco- and cherry-colored string instruments leaned into soft black stands. The cellos lived behind the double basses. The usual brands took up most of the floor space, against the walls were less familiar makes with Italian and French names. Three instruments stood in illuminated glass cases.

"You can feel free to play any of these instruments, all of them should be in tune, and since it doesn't appear that you've brought a bow or rosin, I can supply a floor model for you, a little old, but still quite fine. Now, these instruments on the floor, I believe you've moved beyond. If I can help you get an instrument off the wall, let me know. Those are more in your range. I'll go get the bow and rosin while you look."

Eason had only played two cellos in his whole life. His own and Mr. del Toro's. Mr. del Toro's might have been something like the ones on the wall, but he didn't think so. The guy was just a teacher, and the price tags on the head-stocks of the cellos on the wall read upward to four thousand dollars.

The salesman returned, and Eason told him to pull down whichever instrument he thought was the best deal.

"Excellent," the man said, and pulled down a plain, blond cello. "From Northern Italy."

He walked away.

Seated at a plush stool, the foreign cello leaning into his body, Eason tightened and loosened his rosined bow. He listed over a few major and minor scales, a Phrygian. Richer, fuller, darker. The neck was fast and even, the intonation was deep and true, and even the back flank of the body was better situated to rest against his heart. After some Mozart, a Steve Reich slash he'd been trying for fun, he found his way, as if reminiscing, to the suites.

"Impressive," the salesman said when Eason opened his eyes.

Eason tilted the instrument forward by its neck to let the man put it away.

"Continue playing if you'd like. Your cousin, Jules, is a generous man. He's told me he'd care to buy you whatever cello you'd choose"

Eason looked around for Jules again but couldn't find him.

"I think he's gone across the street for something from the pharmacy," the salesman said. "In the glass case behind you, we have a German cello from the turn of the twentieth century, from Dr. h. c. Eugen Gärtner's Stutt-gart workshop. It's a Mittenwald cello, have you heard of them?"

Eason got to his feet.

"I'm gonna go try to find my cousin. I'll be back," he said.

"Of course."

Eason stepped out from the shadowed store, into the sunlight, and started booking it in the direction of the bus stop. Ain't gonna happen, he was thinking to himself, sinking his feet into the pavement, ain't no way I'm gonna get in any deeper with this fool. Then he heard his name. He turned around and Jules was jogging up.

"Where the hell you going?" he said.

"Jules, man, I can't, man."

"You can't what?"

"I can't accept that kind of gift."

"It ain't a gift, homie, you earned it."

"No, Jules, I've just been trying to pay off Germaine's shit, that's it. Once that's over, I'm done."

Jules bent his eyes in a way that made him look sad, like he was hurt, disappointed.

"This might come as bad news, but you ain't done shit to make up for that fat motherfucker," he said.

"Then what have I been doing this whole summer?"

"You've been doing whatever the fuck I tell you to do."

Jules laughed, and Eason looked at the ground.

"Look at me, Eason."

It was a struggle, but he did. He looked at his cousin. He did whatever he told him to do.

"What'd you think when they said we were going to talk to aliens?" Jules asked.

"What?"

"What'd you think?"

"I didn't think it would happen."

"And you were right, weren't you?"

"I guess."

"You were right. No shame in being right."

Eason swallowed and shrugged.

"C'mon, it feels good to be right, don't it?"

"Sure."

"All these other motherfuckers got duped, but not you. Because you're smart. Right, you're smart?"

"I am," Eason said. He could no longer make eye contact.

"You so smart, you so right. You're prescient, as they say. So, what you think is gonna happen to me?" Jules asked.

"What?" Eason said. He searched Jules's face for the joke, the usual "Just messing with you, cuz," but it wasn't there, and he had to look away again.

"You predicted the future of this planet. What about the future of your cousin?"

Eason shook his head.

"C'mon, Negrodamus. What do you see in that little crystal ball of yours?"

Eason mumbled.

"What you say?" Jules said.

"I said I don't know."

"You don't know. You do know. Tell me my future. C'mon, you ain't gonna hurt my feelings. Ain't nothing I never heard before. C'mon."

"You're going to go to prison."

"That it?"

"Or you'll get killed."

"I either go to prison or get killed."

Jules paused as if truly weighing his options, considering the pros and cons.

"Pretty fucked-up future," he said. "One could say, I've got just as good a chance at growing old a free man as we do talking to aliens, right?"

"I don't know what the odds are."

"Of course you do. One of them tragic, inescapable numbers. At least when my ass dies or goes to prison, you'll be able to say, 'Told you so.'"

"Nah, Jules."

"Ain't nothing wrong with being right. Fools fighting all the time, every day, over who's right. Somebody's gotta be right. You were right about Omni, and you'll be right about me."

"I don't want you to die or go to prison."

"Then why don't you do something about it? Hm? Why don't you save your cousin's life like you saved your friend's? If there's shit in your life you don't like, why don't you change it?"

"I don't know how to."

"But you do. Same way that guy in the piano store know how. Same way your cello teacher know how. Same way all those white people at your school know how. How you save a Black man's life? How they trying to save your life?"

Eason said, with so much shame, "Education."

"So, give me an education, cuz. Teach me," Jules said, demanding, serious, and then laughed, slapped Eason on the arm. "I'm just playing, fool. What you know I don't?"

"Not a whole lot," Eason said.

"So, we're either famous cellists or dead gangbangers," Jules said, sounding very tired all of a sudden. "We either make it or we don't. If that's a fact, here's something neither of us know."

"Hm?"

"How some kid with good grades, supportive dad, and fancy interests doing hanging out with me?"

Eason wanted to say because he had tricked him, had threatened him, but Jules never had.

"Because I chose to be here."

"For what reason?"

"For Germaine."

Jules smiled again.

"I'm not some villain trying to corrupt you, cuz. I'm not trying to make the world evil; the world is evil. The world pulled you out here, not me. But I do have a choice, now that you're here, now that you recognize you're here: I can keep you now that the current's pulled you in, or I can help push you out. I'ma push you out. You're gonna do one more thing for me, and then I'm gonna push you out. But I want you to recognize something in the meantime, too, okay? Current might've pulled you farther than you intended, but you swam out in the first place. Like you said, your ass came here, your ass risked everything for Germaine, a fool you don't even really know, a motherfucker just as hard as me, motherfucker who wanted me dead. You risked everything for him, but you won't do the same for me, your own flesh and blood. And that shit don't make no sense to me. I ain't like you. I ain't gonna pass no judgment on you. But it ain't right."

"Okay."

Jules smiled again, perfectly at ease.

"Cheer up, cuz, this is a pep talk. And even if you're not willing to fight for me, you should be willing to fight for yourself, accept payment where payment is due. Gotta pick a side eventually. Even if it's your own side. Can't just be some told-you-so fool for the rest of your life. Because the rich man, the powerful man, don't predict the future, he controls it."

LATE SEA BIRDS WOVE IN and around string-lighted food stands in the middle of the ped mall, picking up grease-bloated fries, tzatziki-glazed tomato quarters, and wrinkled beef shavings from the ground. UC Berkeley's revelers crowded the damp beer gardens and outdoor bars the brothers passed, aphrodisiac pop music pumping the air. Sevi and Samson ate Chicago-style hotdogs as they walked, catching condiments in paper boats. It was a night out, "bro time," as Ramona had called it when Sevi begged her to come along. Samson was back. Sevi had managed to get him on the phone, they'd cried, and Samson had returned, Ramona having paid the airfare to get him from Istanbul to San Francisco, where he'd asked to come before heading back to Illinois.

It was their first moment alone together, and as relieved as Sevi was to know his brother was alive and safe, as grateful as he'd been to see him with his own two eyes and hold him in his arms in SFO's arrivals, three nights later, walking with Samson in Berkeley, he'd already decided it was probably time for Samson to go, not to some battlefield but home, their parents' house in Cicero. Since returning, Samson had been sulky but unapologetic. He was sleeping on Ramona's couch, unpunished. It frustrated Sevi that it would likely fall on him to teach Samson something he somehow hadn't already learned from having come so close to death, that somehow he wasn't done keeping his brother alive.

Sevi was two steps from making something up about his stomach, the hotdog or the cheap beer totally killing him, an excuse to go home, climb into bed, sleep reality off and see if he awoke someplace dimmer, in a more weightless world, when Samson belched, vomited gas, really, and apologized, offering the perfect gastronomical in for an out.

"It's all good," Sevi said. "Tell you the truth, that dog's kinda fucking with my stomach too."

"No, I mean I'm sorry for everything," Samson said, extending his half-eaten hotdog like an olive branch.

"Oh," Sevi said. Apologizing for everything wasn't absurd, it was necessary. Putting up with Samson not only tested one's patience but their grace.

"Maybe you're not looking for an apology—" he started.

"No, an apology would be good," Sevi said, abandoning his fabricated ailments and embracing his real ones.

"Okay," Samson said. "Great."

But by the time they'd reached the end of the ped mall, across the street from a weak lamppost and a procession of student houses, Samson's apology was still stalled at the introduction, and Sevi had to take it upon himself to coach him.

"You can elaborate, too," he said, and Samson nodded.

"I can't tell you how necessary it felt," he said. "I'm disappointed in myself, for not going through with it."

"Because, as it turns out, it takes more than opinions and condescension to save the world," Sevi said, and watched his brother take the comment on the chin, in the heart and lungs, the latter of which let out a sigh.

Sevi loved the feeling of a good put-down. They were rare. He'd wrestled with varieties of unkindness his whole life—schadenfreude, especially—because he mostly wanted to be generous and kind, what Disney movies, elementary school teachers, the Bible had equated to a purposeful existence. Cruelty he could enjoy, the uncommon kind that could be inflicted as opposed to the cruelty he simply witnessed on a daily basis, was especially hard to come by these days. He was no longer a teacher with students to poke fun at and coworkers to chastise behind their backs. But having cut off all his magic hair, Samson looked more anemic than ascetic. And that simple, caveman-minded joy of anyone else's pain but one's own felt so inviting, so life-affirming, Sevi could barely resist the urge to call him a fraud, to tell him to march back into the ped mall and join a white drum circle, where he belonged.

Annoyed but acquiescing, Samson threw out his hotdog and swallowed the abuse. Sevi would've called it atonement, if he didn't know Samson was so lonely he'd put up with anything if it meant not being left by himself. If it wasn't like this every time he came back.

"I was in Turkey for months, Sevi. I was so close. These guys would come back from across the border—teachers, doctors, postal workers, mechanics— and I couldn't even look them in the eye. It was all right there, what they'd seen, what'd happened to them, what I was supposed to be doing. They were just coming up for air. They'd be back for a few days, time enough to do their rounds, let loved ones see they were still alive, and then they'd go right back to it. Fighting evil. Literally fighting evil. And I didn't go. They'd secured me a spot on a ship. I saw it on the docks, and I never got on. I can still see it waiting there. I don't understand why I couldn't get on. You can see Syria from space. It's stuff like Syria that makes us unsalvageable, our ability to just ignore it."

"What's space got to do with it? Is that what you're sorry for? For letting Omni down?"

"I'm sorry for letting down humankind. I don't know what I'm supposed to do now."

"You're supposed to take a deep breath and be glad that you're still alive."

"Assad will kill them all. What good will any of our lives be when we have another holocaust on our hands? I couldn't even get myself killed."

Sevi tried to reassure Samson there were worse things than failing to get himself killed. Emasculating, kind of, the greatest example of ineptitude, certainly, but a botched suicide was still a miracle. Try as he did to sell his brother on this, he felt himself losing strength. Logic wasn't heart. Whatever had sapped Samson of his delusions of grandeur was getting at Sevi's illusion of inculpability. He'd wanted to tell Samson he hadn't let down humankind but was beginning to think that wasn't true. Walking beside his brother there was some sorrow that Samson was here and not fighting some impossible battle elsewhere. If Samson had let down the world, Sevi had too.

"The selfish decision isn't the lonely one," Samson said. "I wasn't shunned for coming home. I wasn't even detained. People are happy to see me. Being selfish all these years has brought me nothing but family and friends. Hell must be a party; heaven's like staying in on a Friday night. The only people willing to sacrifice anything are the ones who have the least to sacrifice. It's not sustainable. As long as staying isn't lonely, as long as doing nothing isn't harmful to us, we'll never make it."

"It's not our civil war," Sevi said.

"Nothing will ever change until people like us, people who have something to lose, put something on the line. And this was it, this was my chance to make a different choice, to say: I know how this ends when no one does anything, when I let myself go back to thinking voting Democrat and driving a Prius will solve all the world's problems. I've spent my whole life judging those citizens of Nazi Germany, the people of Rwanda, hell, even Americans in the 1960s, the people in those awful circumstances who just went along with what people were telling them to do instead of doing what was right. I judged them because I was convinced I'd never be one of them. I thought I'd sacrifice everything to do what was right."

"This isn't Nazi Germany," Sevi said.

"It's just so fucked up. To find out you're one of them, one of the worthless, silent witnesses. The people the future won't be able to believe just sat there and watched."

"We're not in Nazi Germany," Sevi said again.

"You're right, but we're someplace else without equal too."

Were we? Was that even possible? How would we ever know? Weren't we allowed to just slog through it and analyze its traumas later?

"At least you didn't kill anybody. Imagine if you'd killed someone, what that'd have felt like."

Samson laughed.

"I'm killing somebody right now," he said. "So are you. Just standing here, enjoying this sidewalk, sucking this air. Murder doesn't matter. Jesus,

Muhammad, Buddha care about murder, people don't, the government doesn't, the cops don't. It's the choice that matters. Why do you think there's a distinction between a crime of passion and one that's premeditated? People, governments, cops care if you make a choice. You choose to kill, you go to jail. You choose not to take part in all the killings, the killings we're taking part in now, you die a social death and might as well go to jail. You see these cops around us? Making us feel safe, protecting our freedom to get drunk and eat hotdogs? That safety is paid for in bodies. How two brown guys got so lucky, how we've been invited in to reap the benefits, I have no idea. But people, American citizens, every day, are paying our price of admission."

Sevi shook his head, longed for another beer.

"What?"

"That's just so literal," Sevi said.

"You're right."

"I know."

"A revolution takes a million-plus people. But it's a million-plus people dreaming alone. It's a million-plus people deciding, as individuals, to stop living in this literal world and choosing to live in one that is hypothetical. And that's what I couldn't do. I couldn't free myself from this safe, ugly, literal reality. I couldn't dream of it."

"Protestors have to go home eventually. You can't keep fighting your whole life."

"You know what's the most beautiful thing about democracy? It has a memory. That's something very few man-made things have, it's something no other form of government has. That's why monarchies have to be lineal, the institution has no inherent memory. It's why dictatorships die with dictators. But not all memories are good, and some of them never die. It's exhausting, but some things you spend your entire life fighting."

Sevi had been hedging his bets for so long, seeing on which side he'd have the least pain inflicted upon him, no real concern for the pain he inflicted on others. He tried to remember when he'd first experienced the feeling of being both. Captor and captive. Traditionalist and revolutionary. Insider and outsider. When he was nine and got put into a GT pull-out class and could already begin to feel the mechanisms of the world recalibrating for some odd and uncertain favor. The third night of music camp in Holland, Michigan—an idyllic little lakeside arts community with windmills and a tulip festival—when, after comparing the Dutch tulip crisis to the dot-com bust, his cabinmates, two white eighth-graders from Scottsdale, Arizona, said, "You know, Sevi, you're one of the cool Mexicans. A lot of Mexicans, like, that's what they're all about, being Mexican, they carry it around. But you, you're just a regular guy, like us," and Sevi had felt a smile spread across his face. When his ma read up on scholarship opportunities for ethnic minorities and danced around the house. When there was no telling which cellist was him against the two other white cellists in Oberlin's orchestra. It felt so deeply racial, he had to admit. If it was, had he meant to infiltrate the system and start dismantling it from within at some point? Or had the polite visibility of near-whiteness been like the Dutch tulip, and if so, was his worry now over a growing potential for systemic collapse, or shame and regret that such a dumb and senseless thing had made him everything that he was?

"I'm glad you're here, Samson. I'm glad you're with me," Sevi said, trying to convince himself.

Samson looked so moved, like it was the kindest thing anyone had ever said to him, like he didn't know if his brother had ever really loved him until right now. Samson's heart had finally pivoted, from extreme idealism to moderate realism. It was what Sevi had been waiting for his whole life, for his brother to realize his own limitations, and the discovery left the human race with no future. He couldn't remember if he'd ever worried more about Samson than he had in the past six months, if every prodigal return had been just as difficult and strange, but this was definitely the first time Samson's return felt like stealing something from the world. Sevi had the urge to say, "Go back.

You're bigger than what I need you to be." He touched his brother's arm to make sure he was real, to see if this wasn't a dream. It was reality. An unthinkable reality, a reality in which the selfish and privileged got what they wanted, and the rest was sacrificed, but reality nonetheless, and the one Sevi had asked for. I willed this, Sevi thought. For the first time in his life, Sevi was afraid of what he'd eventually lose by never giving anything up. He felt a pinprick at the top of his stomach through which all his blood left him, his fingers and toes collapsed, his windpipe dried to a dead reed. He was supposed to have finally given something up. He'd planned to give up his brother. He'd resolved to let it be Samson in place of himself.

"I guess I am too," Samson said, looking at his palms, a ground-meat color in the tightening air, the darkening blue.

SEATED BESIDE FATHER CHEN ON a Wi-Fi bus headed for the Computer History Museum in Mountain View, Ramona asked the man of God what his least favorite priestly duty was. Marriage counseling.

"It's like that Hall & Oates song, 'I Can't Go for That.' Marriage counseling: No can do," Father Chen said.

"But you'd anything for God," Ramona said.

"Yes, of course," Father Chen said, and Romana wasn't sure if he got that she got the reference.

"I could take the marriage counseling page down from the church website," she said.

"A general practitioner doesn't suddenly say she doesn't do sore throats. Do you know the first thing I ask these poor couples when they come see me?"

"For the secret password?"

"The secret password?"

"Yeah, the secret password—to check to see if they're real Catholics."

"You've watched *The Da Vinci Code* too many times. I ask them if they really want marriage advice from a man who's not only never been married, but whose spiritual services prevent him from ever getting married."

"What do they say to that?"

"That they just want to do right by God."

"Isn't that the point?"

"Of marriage? No. Marriage is an expression of God, the novelty of being, like everything in this life. A good marriage may please God, but it's not for God. And a marriage in which two people don't trust one another, don't like one another, isn't going to please God. God pities suffering. He doesn't prefer it."

"Bishops, cardinals, the middle managements, or whatever—they don't really like you, do they?"

"Much of my congregation don't like me."

"What do they keep flocking back for then?"

"I don't skimp on the communion wine."

"You've gotta do something about those Eucharist wafers, though. It's like eating packing materials."

Father Chen smiled in dismay.

Ramona asked, "What about those repeat sinners who keep coming to you for confession? Like, the ones you know are just cleansing themselves, so they can sin again? Those guys have to drive you nuts."

"Those who repeat sin, say, a person who continues to be unfaithful to his spouse, have yet to accept forgiveness. Most people are only stuck suffering because they cannot forgive themselves. Neither I, nor God, can offer very much until they do."

Ramona tried to convince herself that she wasn't really listening.

From the outside, the museum looked like a drab Midwestern high school or corporate campus. Ramona appreciated it. She missed the days when computers weren't sexy. When they smelled like hot dust and clacked and sizzled, and even if she was only fourteen when the sleekly designed iMac G3 came out, she liked to think she belonged more to the bulkier, stalwart, DIY computer generation of the eighties and nineties than the technocratic, late-capitalist, atomized generation that proceeded it. She'd fallen in love with her dad's Gateway and this gave her indoor street cred. It'd crapped out when she was sixteen. A tech at Best Buy managed to retrieve all the old files but told her dad it'd be cheaper to replace the computer than fix it, and Ramona asked if she could have the old desktop to mess with. Maybe she could do an art project with it, she needed a hobby. All her friends' interests had turned to boys. She was curious, too, but more in the abstract. None of the guys from school, the ones with whom she'd built enormous snow forts in the winters and played hours of night tag in the summers of her girlhood, who'd since transformed into a foul-smelling crew of teenagers who liked to boast about a camping trip during which they'd all gotten wasted, stripped naked, and raced one another in a beat-off contest, grabbed her attention. The way her girlfriends suddenly went from leaping over beach bonfires with them to tucking away into shadows and complaining about the wind until one of the unfortunate boys wrapped his arms around them, frightened Ramona. What could they possibly see in those acne-painted bodies? So, while the boys edged their way across first, second, and third base with all her girlfriends, Ramona took apart her father's computer and put it back together again. She requested manuals from interlibrary loan. She stayed up till all hours working. One summer morning, after her fourth cup of coffee, her father rushed into the computer room to check on his daughter, screaming at the top her lungs. The computer monitor had gone blue and displayed the word Rebooting. Ramona closed her eyes, and after a few minutes of clacking, she heard Ken Kato's heavy synth start-up sample. When she looked, there it was: a pixelated image of her father, her mother, and herself on a train in Vancouver blown up way beyond the resolution's means—the computer's desktop image. Everything was intact. She thought maybe she'd been searching for that feeling ever since.

"So, is this a sacred place?" Father Chen said in the lobby.

"This place? It's kind of a gag. There's some cool stuff in it. I think the labs at MIT and Harvard are a bit more venerable. But I do love it."

She took him to the Morris floppy disk, what Robert Morris Jr. had used to unleash the Morris worm on the internet in 1988, collected as evidence in the *United States v. Robert Tappan Morris* case.

Morris Jr., son of the then-chief scientist at the NSA's National Computer Security Center, claimed in his deposition that the worm was never meant to be insidious, but was rather intended to be a tool to measure the size of the internet. An error in the worm's code caused the worm to replicate endlessly inside every machine it entered, causing massive and severe computational lag in two thousand units worldwide. The internet had to be partitioned; the cost of damages was estimated between a hundred thousand dollars and ten million dollars. Whatever the actual material damage was paled in comparison to the effect the worm had on the public and government imagination. Since the dawn of time, enemies from both within and outside of civilizations had dreamed of poisoning water supplies, or cutting off communication routes, as a way of disrupting, degrading, and eventually destroying law and order, government and rule. Robert Morris Jr., as far as his prosecutors were concerned, had succeeded in doing what few anarchists in history ever had. And for thousands of miscreants across the globe, his worm charted a way to make a difference. Shut it down or wake it up, hacking could alter reality in ways only mass media did under direct order of the power elite. From the will to know the size of the internet came evidence of the internet's power over the future of people's lives, and a fear and a love of that power. Robert Morris Jr. was the first person to be indicted on charges using the Computer Fraud and Abuse Act. It was the same act used against Dana Johnson. The same being used against Aaron Swartz. Morris was a professor at MIT now. What was more arbitrary, punishment or forgiveness?

"Sounds like a sacred object to me," Father Chen said, referring to the floppy disk.

"I suppose it is," Ramona said.

"It's harmless now, the worm, yes?"

"Yeah. The backdoors it exploited have been locked for twenty years."

"It's interesting. We treat the things we admire and the things we fear with the same kind of distance. Even when we disdain something, there's reverence. So much weight."

There was enough magnetic energy in the human race to wipe every server on Earth clean of its every memory. Fragility drew reverence, and yet it was imperative that we be so durable.

In college, as a student and a hacker, Ramona had sought to arm herself against the inevitable—changes in technological capabilities, perversions of the law, the dissolving sanctity of civil liberties. Unable to protect herself, she'd joined the scourge at Google with Tiresias. In hindsight, Herodotus felt like regression. How insane would it be if the same creatures who'd spent their whole existence trying to destroy the world suddenly decided to fix it just because they felt guilty?

Father Chen, leaning toward a stack of beige diskettes, scratched his arms, hugging himself.

"How can all of this be so old already?" he said.

"Exponential rate of technological development," Ramona said.

"Will it ever slow down?"

"It already has. We've already fallen behind on where we thought we'd be."

"But that's only because we can't see where we really are, right?"

"Yes. We have all the potential we'll ever need. We just have to want to see it."

They moved to an autonomous car exhibition. A Chevy Aveo with a contraption strapped to its hood, a glassy droid on its roof, a directional sense of gravity anchored in the curation designed to draw people to the plain old car, modified to signify the future of mobility and convenience. Left to set their own pace, mankind might just settle for the automated car and tax reductions: a new way to have your drunk ass carted around town and a new way to pay for it. An app that told you where the homeless were, where they were coming from, where they were going, but nothing about what to do for them.

"I'm a pariah, you know," Ramona said.

"I have Facebook."

"Sevi can barely make eye contact with me."

The droid on the roof of the car surveilled, finding no route more optimized than any other to drive out of the museum, into the bright and mapped and known world.

"He loves you."

"Yeah, and it's all my fault, because I called him. He wasn't going to call me, because I asked him not to. It would've been fine. Now look what I've done."

Father Chen had no idea what she was talking about. This was not information available online.

"Do you love him?" he asked.

"Of course, I do. I love feeling him next to me in bed. I love waking up next to him. I love listening to him play the cello. I love the way he sees the world. He's one of those people who can start and end with a question, who's okay not having a resolution, which is the complete opposite of me, and I love that. But love isn't a direction. It's a resource. It's a fuel. It's not a way of doing something, it's something you do something with."

"What were you hoping for?"

For Sevi? For Herodotus? She didn't know, she was confused, she was crying, she could see her crying face in the darkened scanner of the droid.

"I hoped I'd be helpful."

"I forgive myself every day in order to keep on living," Father Chen said. "The church's abuse of children—I think I'll quit over it every day. For being powerless against it. Instead, I forgive. Not those men, not the institution, but myself, for not saving those children."

He opened his arms and she stepped in. For the first time, they hugged.

"Everything is so broken and sad," Ramona said.

Father Chen, still holding her, said, "But you know what they say, 'Every story has a sequel, and that sequel is called your life.'"

"Who says that?"

"I say that. And so do you."

FATHER CHEN TOOK advantage of being south of the city to visit a friend in Palo Alto and Ramona rode the bus home alone. He'd enjoyed the museum, thanked her for the trip, and told her they'd see each other soon, there was still so much work to be done with the homeless tracker.

Ramona had spent enough time on the buses to be able to tell them apart by their interiors. Tears in the upholstery, safety pin intaglios, a sticker for a band or a collective called Breast Pump Collective. She knew it had been strange enough when at her contract signing she'd told her employers she was cool with the commute and foregone the rent-controlled apartment they were offering her in Mountain View. It was the need to be going she required back then, the reason she couldn't stay long no matter where she was, the sensation of her body in motion—whether she felt herself moving away from or toward something didn't matter much, just so long as she maintained a state of statelessness. She'd put her life in flux and wasn't about to settle down just anywhere. She'd had no idea what she was doing at Google and didn't think she deserved any comfort until she did. When Sevi arrived, she began piling on additional weekend hours, as many back-and-forth commutes to campus as she could manage for countless project meetings, emergency analytics, and other annoyances she completely fabricated simply to be out of the apartment, preferring the sensation of moving away over returning. Living with Sevi left her in a state of perpetual dampness, like she was living inside of a rain cloud, and she'd started to grow mold. The mold had eaten through her clothes, mainly at the high-stress points, the armpits of all her shirts and the crotches of her pants. She'd sat at the foot of her closet and made a pile of items that were so far gone they couldn't be donated and turned them into cleaning rags she never used. Now the mold was going for her insides, leaving her with joint ache, fatigue, and a gravitational relationship with an otherwise unappealing couch. Maybe it was actually just weight gain that'd done her clothes in. That was normal when you started dating someone. But depression? Without Herodotus, she had nothing left to take her away, except the perpetual scourge of trolls threatening to kill her, and she could do without those.

She hoped to enter an empty apartment that evening, watch a Merchant Ivory Production, drink herself someplace weepy or sexual, maybe both. The next day, hungover, she wanted to take a bath, lie out on her bed in front of a fan afterward and let its choppy air buffet coconut oil into her solitary skin. In the afternoon, she'd walk for hours like a protagonist in a European novel. She'd do it all without conversation. Without companions or passengers, if only Sevi wasn't around. And distantly—though without any more distance than what they kept between each other now—she could still be in love with Sevi, and feel herself filling with longing and wonder as opposed to disappointment and regret.

She received a text message from PG asking her to come over to his apartment. He'd never contacted her during off-hours; she'd never seen where he lived. Going to PG's meant not going home, not returning.

PG LIVED IN a turret condo overlooking the Presidio in Pacific Heights. Waiting to be buzzed in, Ramona tried imagining Father Chen as a young man refusing lepers from Mass. If someone could bottle his transformation, if someone could write an empathy algorithm, what would the world look like? More importantly, what would it sound like? What was the sound of listening? That wasn't novel. Greeting her upstairs in the exposed-brick alcove of his foyer, PG proved capable of looking as shlubby in industrial chic as he had sweating on a Tenderloin rooftop. Each of his T-shirts cost him no less than three hundred dollars apiece.

He offered her a coconut water IV.

"What?" Ramona said.

"You look fatigued," PG said. "It's fine if you don't want it. I have beer too."

Ramona checked herself in a mirror in the living room while PG went to the kitchen to grab her a beer. She couldn't remember if this was what she always looked like. She couldn't remember her pores, the shine of her T-zone, the thickness of her hair, the status of her teeth, the dampness of her armpits ever being any different, and yet she was certain that unlike PG, who would always be nothing but PG, she was someone different, the person Sevi, PG, now she herself saw, whoever that was.

PG, returned from the kitchen, handed her her beer. Then, from a steel cabinet, he withdrew a small cone-shaped contraption and set it on his coffee table, a floating slab of glass covered in weed-smoking implements.

"Jesse will be out soon," PG said, settling on his leather couch, grinding pot. He explained without looking up to see Ramona's distorting face, "Oh, I worked for him too."

"Who's Jesse?" Ramona said, trying to recover her face.

"Dana Johnson. The man you sent to federal prison. Well, the man we sent to federal prison."

PG loaded the contraption with the freshly ground weed, fastened a plastic bag to its cratered tip, and hit the switch on its droid-like body. Slowly, the plastic bag began to fill with gray marijuana vapor.

"He won't be out for long, though. He'll violate parole five days after his release."

She realized she had a purse slung over her shoulder. She put it down on the couch but remained standing, not drinking.

"How do you know?"

"I'm going to help him violate his parole. We're going to finally release those documents he stole. They won't have any effect at all. Everybody already knows the government has been allowing the energy industry to kill our planet. We've decided to normalize that sort of information instead of revolting. It's okay, green energy will be a very lucrative endeavor soon and, *poof*, bad guys will become good guys."

"Has he been trying to get back at you, too?"

"What?"

"The Herodotus leak. It was Jesse. Dana Johnson."

"Ramona, Dana doesn't give a shit about you. And he doesn't know a thing about Herodotus. He doesn't have access to a computer."

When the bag filled to a taut gray, the machine ceased and the vapor inside the bag marbled like clouds on another planet.

"Then who?"

"Me. I leaked Herodotus, Ramona."

Ramona picked up her purse, extracted a pen, and popped the vapor bag. The weed vapor hovered in place, the exploded bag contracted like snakeskin below it.

"And why the fuck did you do that?" Ramona said, staring into the weed cloud.

PG stared into the ghastly thing too.

"I'm sorry those men keep hacking and harassing you," PG said. "I thought they'd stop once Herodotus was terminated. Turns out they just hate you for being a woman."

"Who'd'a thunk it?"

"I did it to get it out of Google," he said. "You've got two-thirds of your workforce threatening to walk out if the company signs a military contract, how in the world does Herodotus see the light of day with so much . . . plurality?"

"Well, it's proprietary code, so, nice job with that. Currently, it's residing inside a server literally labeled purgatory. Not much daylight there."

"Ramona, how is a program that requires analyzing basically all the world's data in order to work supposed to do so given current computational limits, anyways?"

"Carefully."

"It can't, Ramona. There are fucking math problems that'll take computers longer to solve than what's left of mankind's time on Earth."

"Herodotus was created with a quantum computer in mind."

"No future bigger than its past. No future without catching up with the past. But it's not called prescience if it pertains to something that's already happened. Where's your quantum computer?"

"Where's your fucking quantum computer? You ruined my life. It was an experimental design, running at 5 percent, hypothetical, but it would've inspired the research that could've . . ."

PG breathed from the hanging vapor cloud.

"I wouldn't call it my quantum computer, per se. I suppose it belongs to the Chinese, seeing that they're paying for it, but it's located in Iceland and managed by a bunch of Icelanders, so . . . I don't know whose it is, but it exists."

PG exhaled an invisible stream of weed vapor. Ramona had heard of such experimental models, they were novelty items, they performed parlor tricks.

"Let me guess, they're using it to remotely stir a glass of lemonade in Australia?" she said.

"Synthesizing cryptochromes to build an organic magnetic receiver."

Ramona swatted at the still-hanging weed orb before PG could take another sip from it.

"What the hell for?" she said.

"To understand how birds find their way home. The owners, they know about Herodotus. They want to download Herodotus onto this computer. Then, they want to feed it the largest unmitigated data set known to man. The whole Chinese internet and everyone attached to it."

"The Chinese?"

"Tiresias gets made no matter what, you understand? It's just a censorship tool. Tiresias is for sustaining the Communist Party, and the Communist Party is going to get what it wants. You make it, I make it, some guy in China makes it, doesn't matter. But Tiresias is for political survival, for the Communist Party to remain relevant through the completion of this economic cycle. But what's the point of being the world's new number-one superpower when the world's about to end anyway? Herodotus is for the future, for the end of the world, for what's next. Tiresias gets made no matter what. And once Tiresias helps China finish pulling ahead, it's only a matter of time before we're using it here in the US, trying to catch up. Tiresias goes live here and it's the Middle

Ages—sustainable, selective knowledge for at least a half century, something to mediate the cultural in-fighting, a referee. Herodotus doesn't get finished, there is no Renaissance. There is no future. Herodotus is just the future, Ramona. Why can't China have it? The US doesn't want it—it's un-American. Google can't use it—it's unpopular. Mama told me there'll be end days like this."

He smiled calmly.

"So, you're working for the Chinese."

"That's racist."

"No—PG, I know you're Korean. That's not why . . . Why else would you have done something like this? You've sabotaged my career, you've—"

"Google sabotaged your career," PG said, standing up. "I did this because I believe in Herodotus and because I believe in you. So far, I'm the only person in America who does. Google never believed in you. Sevi doesn't believe in you. Hell, you don't believe in you. If you did, you'd have done the exact same thing the day you got shut down, maybe sooner."

"You could've done something a little less dramatic."

"Believing in something, anything, becomes more radical every day."

"I don't want to help the Communist Party destroy free thought."

"Oh, please. Ramona, it's the Party versus the corporate class in China. In fifty years, who do you want running the world? Google and Alibaba, or Google and a country with a continuous culture that's been around for four thousand years? Besides, maybe Herodotus will get the CCP to reverse course on some of their policies. Hard-liners will have a tough time squashing dissent when the dissent is coming from the central machine."

Ramona was exhausted.

"Well, Herodotus is stuck at Google," she said, leaning over to waft the last remaining wisp of pot smoke into her mouth.

Through PG's enormous window, a plane waved at them.

"You have a copy," PG said.

"No, I don't."

She did.

"It's corporate espionage," she said. "Treason, if the Chinese really are involved."

"Well, you know what they say, indefinite detention works wonders for survivor's guilt."

FOUR

Dear Babichev,

I have begun writing you an opera. Owing to the fact I cannot read sheet music and struggle with rhyme, it may never see the stage, but this is the concept thus far: It begins with two cosmists, those pseudoscientific occultists who purport man is nearing the ability to steer human evolution, bend time, and control the universe with electronic thoughts. These two characters are sisters, one widowed, one unmarried, both steelworkers. The widow, having lost her husband in a factory accident, is the more devoted cosmist of the two and is able to travel telepathically to another universe, where she convenes with multidimensional beings who warn her of mankind's coming extinction. Seeing she is troubled by this revelation, the beings teach her the key to the human race's survival; however, on her journey home, stars and nebulas chip her memory, and she arrives without a clue as to what the beings told her. Fortunately, in the time she's been gone, her sister has managed to reanimate her deceased husband. The living corpse, a symbol of the proletariat's triumph over the bondage of mortality, becomes a party leader. He proves to be poor at his job and unethical, however, and the factory suffers terribly. Though it is clear he should be returned to death, the former widow's love blinds her to his petulance, and she uses all of her powers to protect him until the factory finally crumbles into destitution. When the widow dies from famine, her sister calls upon the multidimensional beings for answers once again. This sister does not forget what they say. She returns to bury her sister and rebury her brother-in-law. After the funerals, she reveals to her fellow steelworkers that the end is nigh: Mutual nuclear destruction. When the crowd cries out, she tells them the second half of the prophecy: After the blast, from the atomic ash, the Soviets will rise like a phoenix. The world will begin anew, perfected. They cheer. In the final scene, she is found drawing up plans to reopen the factory as a plutonium refinery. Title? I was going to say Two Sisters, *but, alas, that cheeky boy Chekhov beat me to it, now, didn't he?*

THEY WERE THE CLEAN SQUAD, given a normal-looking car, a white Malibu—no rims, no system, just good gas mileage and safe tires, working blinkers and windshield wipers—and told to go across the border to make the purchase. Eason sat passenger, not having a license, wearing a Valparaiso University T-shirt and a pair of rust-colored chino pants and boating shoes. He and the other guy, Douglass, had ordered the university swag—pamphlets and brochures and sweatshirts—weeks ago, so if they got pulled over and needed an excuse to be in Indiana they could tell the cops they were on a college visit. Eason was looking to study music, and Douglass was going for athletics. In the trunk was Eason's cello and a gym bag filled with a stale set of workout clothes and worn-in basketball shoes. Underneath those items was a custom compartment.

The sun was already setting when they drove across the state line. To the left and behind the car was Chicago's lake, the blinding light of the city on the lake. As they drove farther into Indiana that city and its water fell away, interceded with the scaffold mazes of gas and power structures. The milk bottles of a nuclear plant exhaled silver vapor on the late day's early moon as dune sand and beach scrub started to edge along the highway. Their headlights went on and caught the *s*'ing of the sand in the wind across the road. When Douglass ran over a box turtle they almost stopped.

"Two brothers don't need to be picked up off the side of the road because of a turtle," Eason said.

Leaving Gary, Eason looked at Douglass's head against the darkening window and said, "It might be a funny story to tell someday. First college visit."

Douglass smiled.

"If it ain't our last."

Eason didn't know Douglass. Douglass went to another school, one on the South Side. He assumed something had gone wrong in Douglass's life, something similar to what had gone wrong in his own. He'd woken up one day and he was on a mission. It was what happened to people, Eason understood this now.

"I'm starving," Eason said, and Douglass handed him something like a Starburst.

"I don't eat candy," Eason said.

"It's a Gatorade gel, gives you energy, eat it."

Eason unwrapped an orange, neon-luminescent thing. He sucked on it and then swallowed it.

"Not really filling," he grumbled.

"I said it'd give you energy, not make you full."

The car exited the highway after Waterford, not too far east of signs for the Indiana Dunes National Lakeshore. They found a town that was rust and dim streets and warnings and apologies written across broken windows and doors. The only people were poor shrouds lurching after their own shadows on the sidewalks and in the alleyways. Each building dropped its bricks in piles at the front door. Overhead, ditched by the trains, an iron bridge spilled over with stray scrub. GPS took them to a foamy cement riverbank beside a dead gristmill where a box-shaped Buick was slouching with its lights off in an otherwise empty lot. Douglass coasted beside the Buick, parked, left the engine running. Two guys in camo pants, their uncut hair pulled back under trucker hats, stepped out of the Buick and lit cigarettes. Eason and Douglass crossed a look like they should peel out of there, but both boys reconsidered given how far they'd come and the fact they'd be fucked if they returned to Chicago empty-handed.

Douglass stepped out first, and Eason joined him in the Malibu's parking lights. They leaned against the pinging hood and crossed their arms. With their cigarettes in their hands, the men walked up to them. One said,

"Welcome to the gun show, boys," and the other laughed. Late twenties, early thirties, but meth and booze had made them middle-aged. They purchased at gun shows for gangs, charged a premium on each piece without crossing state lines. Crafty. Tonight was easy. Handguns. They barely weighed a thing. Carbonite, carbon fiber.

"Smart sending kids," one said, raking his mustache with his rotten bottom teeth.

"You look like one of those kids playing for the NCAA, son. You play basketball?" the other asked Eason.

"Nah."

Douglass didn't say anything.

"Shit, tall like that, I'd pick up any ball and just start running, bound to get a scholarship tall like that."

"I play the cello," Eason said.

And the other man said, "That's great, Yo-Yo Ma, but we've got business to attend to, so if we could speed up this little admissions interview and do what we're all here to do."

Eason sighed in relief. Even arms dealers thought he looked college bound.

Around the back of the Buick, Eason and Douglass looked into the red-lit gaping mouth of the men's trunk, and from the rusted bowels of the car, the men delivered a hefty, angulating sack.

"Count 'em, I guess," said the man who'd grab a ball and run.

All four maneuvered to the Malibu's rear. Eason and Douglass counted the guns as they transferred them into the trunk's hidden compartment. The order was for a dozen. They counted eleven.

"The fuck's goin' on here?" Douglass said.

The men took turns recounting the weapons.

"I guess we ain't got it," one of them said and scratched his throat beard. Some liquid had alighted in his eyes, and he looked wild and cracked out.

"Can't go back with eleven," Eason muttered to Douglass.

"Don't you think I know that?" Douglass simmered back.

"Where y'all get this shit?" Eason said to the men.

"Big tent gun show."

"They still open?"

"Couple hours."

"That place nearby?" Douglass asked.

"Not far."

"We'll wait for you here," Eason said. "You take the pieces back and we buy 'em all when you got 'em all."

"Don't feel right," one of the men said.

"Whatchu mean it don't feel right?" Eason said.

"You boys ever been to a real gun show?"

TELEPHONE POLES DREW the dove-white tarp twenty feet into the air at the tent's center. Cornmeal- and hominy-colored gravel crunched underfoot, and men and women mushed headlong between long laminate tables littered with firearms, their breath and body heat belching into the bleach white of the floodlights above while an auctioneer cried through a bullhorn. She kept prices going up on Civil War, World War I, World War II, Korean War, Vietnam-era weaponry. Her gavel sounded like gunfire. The vendors lining the tables were alacritous. Sullen buyers from all over wore plainclothes attire and tactical gear. Some men did not sell guns but self-published books about Obama's secret terrorist ties and pancake theory. One rotund man with yellow-tinted glasses sat in a camping chair between two screens, both of which, slightly out of phase, played a video of the same man on a similar chair explaining how Obama was on a mission to make white society pay for slavery. He eyed Eason and Douglass as they passed his stand, his recorded voice rounding and doubling through the TV speakers.

"Meet people here that'd give you nightmares," Jim said. Eason had learned the talkative one was Jim. The other man wouldn't give his name.

The boys were led patiently through the labyrinth. The sweet smell of turkey legs and teriyaki beef jerky floated in the mix of summer air, running motors, overheated lamps, and farts. Eason peered into an empty popcorn machine.

"Fucking starving, man," he said to Douglass.

"We get outta here alive, I buy you whatever you wanna eat," Douglass said.

Six hundred, I hear six hundred for a Winchester .22, beautiful bluing, standard WWII issue. Six-fifty . . .

On one table carbon-fiber black scopes lay on purple velvet blankets like magic staffs. At one end was the rubber-stoppered eyepiece, the other a ruby-red lens. To see through that, Eason thought. To be seen through it. AR-15s were stacked on a turnstile. A man in digital camo pet one.

Czech police-issue handgun, better than a Beretta, folks!

Every so often, slung over a shoulder, the sleeping face of a child bobbed in front of Eason. People were going to die because of what he was doing. Maybe if he combined his misfortune with Douglass's, whatever that was, it'd even out. He felt so tired.

"Douglass."

"Yeah?"

"Why you doin' this?"

"Summer job."

Jim and the other man stopped them short of a table covered in the small black handguns they were looking for.

"Don't think you need to be a part of this part," Jim said. "We'll get you what you need, and you'll be on your way."

Eason gummed the leather instep of his shoe with his forefinger to clear the pebbles he'd collected walking through the gravel lot. Bent forward, he came face-to-face with the little black hole of a barrel of a handgun laid akimbo on its side. Having only seen a gun from afar, he was struck with a sick, electric charge being so close to one. He thought of what it must feel like to know you are about to die before you are ready. But then he noticed something beyond the feelings of fear and a closeness to power that the weapons always left him with, seeing his cousin waddle around, heavy with invisible gun-weight, finding a casing in the street. Up close, like this, he saw the gun had mechanical charm too. How light they were, how simple and hidden their functions were. There was some beauty to them, a design. They were like cars or iPhones. The device was something to be desired in and of itself. He reached over and grabbed one. Its gravid handle, its knife-metal makeup, felt erotic in his hand. From the movies, he knew how to cock the instrument. He pulled the trigger pointing toward the table.

"Hey," the vendor said. "Don't dry-fire that."

He returned the gun and walked ahead to where a group was watching a video of a skinny white woman with a bushy ponytail and a khaki cap turning a rabbit inside out. Stripped of its hide, the rabbit looked like a single organ. It wore little fur boots.

"That shit's disgusting," Douglass said.

"She's doin' it like it ain't no thing," Eason said.

"My mama said she used to have to cut the heads off chickens and pluck their feathers."

The boys looked over their shoulders, the men were waving them back.

"All set, guys," Jim said. "Let's finish this someplace quiet."

Douglass followed the blue Buick to a Walmart up the road and then around back to the loading docks. Weak halogen glowed from within long semitruck canals, and Eason could see people moving around inside, stocking and shelving.

"Man, there's people here," he said to Jim.

"I work here. Trust me, no one's paying attention," the other man said.

Eason pulled out the envelope of cash and handed it to Jim. The other man gave Douglass back the bag, and Douglass settled it in the compartment in the trunk.

"Drive safe," the other man said.

A FEW TOWNS over, Eason told Douglass to take the exit for a Carl's Jr.

"Man, you gonna have to wait," Douglass said.

"Motherfucker, I'm starving. Your ass said you'd buy me anything."

"Shit," Douglass said and threw on his blinker.

Douglass bought them each a bacon cheeseburger with fries and a Coke and they sat in the all-but-blacked-out parking lot facing an empty yard, eating in the car. They were down to the bag of fries when the orca black-and-white shape of a police cruiser pulled up behind them.

"Shit," Douglass said. "Motherfucker, I told you we shouldn't stop."

Eason sat completely still, out of fear and partial belief the cop was like a T. rex and wouldn't be able to see him if he didn't move. The officer stepped out, his hand on his gun. A Maglite tapped Douglass's window. Concentric rings of light blasted the glass and bounced off the vinyl dash.

"Step outside of the vehicle, please, with your hands up," the man's voice muffled through the glass.

"Don't say anything," Eason whispered.

The boys opened their doors together. Eason peeled his body off the seat with his hands behind his head in a maneuver like a sit-up. The cop gestured the Maglite at the Malibu's trunk.

"What you boys doing out here?"

Eason leaned into Douglass against the bumper. Blinded by the Maglite, he said, "Eating."

"Late-night munchies? Been smoking a little weed?"

"No, sir," Douglass said.

"Manners, I like that," the cop said.

He'd dimmed the Maglite and a warm ghost of it drifted along Eason's chest. Eason's eyes came back to him, and out of the dark he could see the cop was young, with a fresh, bald face and a concave little mouth filled with prim teeth. His eyes were close together, and his chunky sideburns and neat hair sat on his head like a snug helmet. It occurred to Eason the cop was also smaller than him. His uniform and taut head made him look more like an action figure than a human being. His polished little shoes glowed like puddles.

"We ain't done nothing wrong, Officer," Douglass said.

"Who said you did?" the cop said.

He pushed the Maglite so close to Douglass's face, Douglass's nostrils turned into embryos.

"I'm going to run you guys, let's see some ID."

Eason pinched his wallet from his shorts. The cop took both of their IDs and inspected them with his light.

"What are you two doing in Indiana?"

"College visit," Eason said.

"Both of you?"

"We checked out Valparaiso," Douglass said.

The cop's face stayed still, that little scrunched-up frustration he carried around everywhere.

"Private school. You guys ballplayers or something?"

An awfulness rose up in Eason. When he was six, some confusion of embarrassment and fear had prevented him from raising his hand when he needed to go to the bathroom one morning in class, and after five agonizing minutes he wet himself at his desk. Warm, sticky urine sat in his lap for thirty minutes. He itched and raged and wept silently. When his teacher finally located the source of the smell, she told him to stand to let everyone see. She told his classmates to look. She told him he'd done a dumb thing. A disgusting thing. It was that awfulness now too.

"I play basketball, sir," Douglass said, trying not to puff out his chest too much, but enough to let the cop know he was serious.

"What position?"

"Power forward."

"Power forward, that's good. That's a real position. What about you, young man?"

Eason looked at the shiny cleft of the cop's chin.

"I'm a musician, officer."

"Like a rapper? They give scholarships for that nowadays?"

"Cello," Eason said, puffing up a bit too. "Classical music."

Douglass nudged him. Eason knew what he meant. They were almost in the clear, he didn't need to piss this cop off by getting all uppity all of a sudden.

"My mother was a piano teacher," the cop said. "She was a beautiful player. She even taught me some. Beethoven, Debussy, Bach. I listen to that stuff when I work out."

The officer stepped back.

"Admissions visits don't start for another month and a half," he said.

"They made an exception because we both work during the school year," Douglass said.

So smooth, Eason almost smiled. The cop was pleased too.

"That organ in the chapel sure sounds good, doesn't it?" the cop said to Eason. "I've been to Mass there a few times."

"I've never heard anything like it," Eason said. He'd researched the organ online in preparation. He could be smooth too. "It was an alumni gift, wasn't it?"

"It was, and it's actually currently under repair, so I'm going to need to check your vehicle, gentlemen. Will you please wait for me by my cruiser—"

"Officer, we—," Eason started, but stopped himself.

"There something you're worried I'll find?"

"No, sir," Douglass said.

"Your friend here is worried. If you tell me what you've got in there, you'll be in less trouble. Now's your opportunity."

Eason scanned his brain for any bit of wisdom on dealing with cops without probable cause. What was an illegal search and seizure? This seemed like an illegal search and seizure. The only pointers his dad had ever imparted were don't get in trouble and, when you do, keep your head down.

"Last chance, Mozart."

Were they supposed to be read their Miranda rights? No, that would happen after the cop discovered what they had in the trunk. Wasn't the trunk the safest place to put something illegal? If the paraphernalia wasn't within arm's reach of the driver, didn't that change something? Also, weren't cops not allowed to unlock the trunk? Was the trunk even locked? He should've read the manual to learn about the locking mechanism. He was thinking all of these things at once, layered, like a chord, when suddenly he felt nothing at all, like he was floating, lifting off this world. He realized none of it fucking mattered. He was voiceless, naked, abandoned in the whole matter. Whatever this cop wanted of him he would get. If this cop wanted him to die, he would die. It was not about his rights or his humanity. The world would latch on to his throat one day and not let go, if that's what the world wanted from him. His throat, his life.

"Go ahead and check it out," Eason said and stepped back. He didn't look at Douglass.

The cop started with the front seats, opening the glove, flipping through the owner's manual, the chapter on the trunk's locking mechanism. From the backseat, he pulled out their bags of college swag and dropped them on the wet lot. He dragged a gloved finger through the cracks in the couch seat. He was meticulous and ravaging. From the side of the cruiser, Eason watched him open the trunk, yank out his cello case, and drop it on the ground. He unlatched the case and pulled out the blond instrument.

"This thing's big," he shouted over his shoulder, and set the cello in a puddle of oil.

He did the same with the bow.

From Douglass's gym bag he tossed the sneakers and game shorts and shirt. He looked back into the trunk with his Maglite. If he touched his finger to the bed of the trunk, he'd feel the seam. He'd know. He'd call backup. He'd have them in cuffs before he even discovered the guns. When Eason finally got out of prison, if the cop didn't kill him in this parking lot, he'd have no way of remembering all these moments that'd brought him in. He didn't even look at Douglass to know what future lay in plain panic on that stranger's face. The cello rotted on the floor, and Eason waited for the cop to touch his finger to the seam. Giving up felt like nothing at all. Not like relief. Not even the numbing he felt when sleep started to eat his body came close. Only the waiting seemed familiar. A waiting he'd breathed forever. He waited for the cop to touch his finger to the seam. He'd been waiting for this forever. He didn't even need to tell himself he'd told himself so. The living felt wrong. And then a burst of energy in his condemnation: I did this.

SEVI COULDN'T EVEN MAKE OUT the usual group that morning—G.I. Joe, Ma, Miles, and Magic were nowhere to be seen. Behind orange cordoning, the crowd numbered in the hundreds, maybe thousands. The police, whose presence was equally huge, were out in full force. Cops in riot gear on blindered horses casting a weighted dragnet around the mess. Double-standard moving violations. Class warfare. Sevi still had no real idea. He'd only known that they were outside and he was inside; that although he agreed with every demand they made through their megaphones, he would have no part in helping to obtain them.

Instead, those demands for affordable housing, representation in zoning, tech transparency and privacy, an end to police brutality, had become something like a personal sound track or an interior monologue. Sevi listened to their songs while he brushed his teeth. He'd read a headline on his phone and at that very moment someone would begin speaking on the same topic of the article into a loudspeaker, or vice versa. Classic cadences accompanied every cup of coffee and bowl of cereal. Reflecting through the apartment's interior, those global, national, state- and city-wide, and occasionally cosmic discussions became so domestic, so intimate, they hovered almost like a death in the family—things that meant something, things that had a presence that would be felt forever, but that could be lived around or through without much fanfare or notice at all in time. For weeks, waking before Ramona, Sevi had watched her open her eyes in a state of newborn drowsiness and count the seconds it took for her to register the commotion outside. For a while he'd tried consoling her. Holding and rocking her from behind before she got up, he'd whisper into her ear a little chant of his own. "Ramona is the best. She is awesome. Today is gonna rule. What do you want for breakfast?" When that didn't help, he stopped trying. The inability to put on pants in silence, to complete a sentence without the interruption of a bullhorn, was a small price to pay. Resistance, when it slept, was acceptance, and the world, as it existed, was unacceptable, he accepted this fact. If it wasn't them out there, whoever they were, it'd have to be him. Noise, no problem. A disgruntled girlfriend? Whatever.

Sevi was still in his pajamas, an old pair of gym shorts and a Chicago Bulls sweater, as he watched the crowd. Thick sheets of clouds crawled across the sky. Samson, who'd been staying the night since he'd arrived in San Francisco a week ago, had left the couch in complete disarray, a row of dirty dishes had accumulated beneath, half the cushions were on the floor, and even the curtain behind the couch had somehow fallen halfway off the rod. He'd already left for the day, visiting comrades around the Bay. Putting the cushions in order, Sevi said, "I think Samson should find someplace else to stay."

Her mouth full of toothpaste, assessing the living room, Ramona said she didn't mind. She was going back to work for the first time since the leak. A deal had been struck between the higher-ups and those threatening a walkout. Ramona's security clearance was revoked, "She'll barely even be working here," she'd read of herself on a forum. She was a nonentity. What a nonentity could accomplish, even on campus, Sevi had no idea, but she'd awoken that morning with renewed determination.

Ramona spat in the kitchen sink atop a ruin of scummy dishes and asked where Samson was supposed to go.

"He's got buddies all over the Bay. He's with one of them now."

"You don't want to spend a little more time with him? I feel like this is a unique opportunity for you two to really connect."

"And we have, we're very connected. Too connected."

"You know, maybe Samson would stop running from people if people stopped pushing him away."

"No one has ever pushed Samson away. Not that that would be such a bad idea. That way Samson could experience some sort of consequence for his actions and maybe even learn from them."

"So, the consequence of Samson isolating himself is isolating him further?"

"Since when are you such an Samson advocate?"

"Probably since finding out he wasn't dead."

"You might change your tune if you heard what he has to say about your work at Google."

"I've suffered your accusations and criticisms, I think I can handle your little brother."

Among recovering addicts, it was perfectly normal to avoid users and enablers, even if those people were your family or best friends, triggers were triggers. Shouldn't the same rules apply for the guilty and the ashamed? Everywhere, all over the world, Sevi knew people were joyously merging onto highways without looking, littering, having affairs, and cheating on their taxes. Why couldn't he be one of them, one of the careless? Why did the source of his own self-loathing have to sleep on his couch? Wasn't a street full of protestors enough? Did he really need to live with a living reminder of what they'd all be reduced to eventually?

"I think it's a mistake," Ramona said, closingly.

"What do I possibly have to gain from spending more time with Samson?"

Ramona said nothing, wiped at her face for toothpaste.

"Your face is clean," Sevi said.

"Conviction, maybe?"

"He chickened out and vacationed in Istanbul. He saw the Hagia Sophia, we should all be so lucky."

"At least he went!"

"He could've gone to the border and laid out water bottles and made a bigger difference."

"That's not a horrible idea. Maybe the two of you should do something like that together."

"Wait, are you saying I lack conviction?"

"Ever held a protest sign?"

"Why would I?"

"You're constantly protesting things, but in private, to me."

Sevi looked for a protest sign he might hold. The people were screaming in unison, their voices climbing up into the sky, through the apartment window.

"You think I should be down there? It's fucking dangerous down there."

"I don't think you should be down there." Emphasis: should. "But I think you could be anywhere."

"That guy's wearing a Guy Fawkes mask. Your fan club might be down there. Did you ever consider that?"

The men online would not stop tormenting her. Sadly, Sevi thought he could understand them. He'd never stopped being mad at her either. Herodotus's termination, the implosion of Ramona's career, none of it had made him feel any better.

Ramona squinted.

"I don't know," she said. "Are some people shouting about Omni?"

Sevi made out a hooded contingent of Antifa-looking protestors pumping their fists in the air. Greenpeace was there. Everyone was. Diverse and fractured, maybe, but maybe they wanted the same thing? No Westboro Baptists or neo-Nazis, but they might show up. Each person protested in accordance with his or her own struggle, but perhaps it was the struggle they shared. He thought if he kicked out Samson, Samson would get back to the work that mattered to him, that he'd live forever and change everything. It did look dangerous down there.

"And the mask only works if a ton of people are wearing them. One dude in a Guy Fawkes mask is kind of outing himself, don't you think?" Ramona said, bending over to wedge her feet into a pair of flesh-toned flats.

"I don't think you should go," Sevi said, and Ramona laughed. "Those aren't the same people who have been here all summer. These people could be for hire," he continued.

"Hired protestors? On behalf of whom?"

"I don't know, Bing, or something?"

"I have to go to work now, Sevi."

"To do what?"

"To be able to live with myself."

He looked down at the crowd, the massive crawling scale of it. People spilling into the lanes of traffic, dangling from light posts. He heard them calling Omni's name again. Some were protesting in Omni's honor. Omni the martyr, which had slain its own voice.

"Quit, I'll get a job," he said.

Ramona laughed again.

"Ramona, I'm begging you," he said.

"No, Sevi, you're annoying me," she said, and slipped through the door.

Traffic fattened at the light. The intersection was already out of police control, the city should've shut it down, redirected traffic. From the window, he couldn't see Ramona, the commuters were hidden somewhere behind the protest. A little after 8:00 A.M., out of the honking backup, along the bus lane, the white Wi-Fi bus, what everyone was waiting for, finally appeared. The crowd buckled. Ramona appeared in front of a group walking further south to catch the bus before the protestors. The bus knelt and the Googlers got on. Ramona was safe. The bus doors scythed shut and the orange barrier snapped; in seconds, demonstrators were coating the bus like a hungry amoeba. Hands rocked the vehicle in a wild, capsizing sway.

Sevi tumbled down the hall and stairs. He didn't realize he was barefoot until he was outside, on the sidewalk, the cold cement reaching up the bones of his feet.

He looked at the writhing hundreds, the outnumbered cops. Most of the people were just standing around or walking away. Still, if the crowd was a little browner, he thought, they'd all be dead.

Something flew through the windshield of the bus and Sevi slipped in to the crowd. Elbows landed on his face as he jabbed his way through to the rear wheels, where he clambered up using the hub to get a better look inside, but the tinted windows only threw back his own reflection and the image of the violence behind him. Sirens blared, and the police were no longer waiting, moving in and thwacking two, three bodies with every swing of their batons. Overhead, a helicopter buffeted, sending concussive blasts of engine air down into the crowd. Against his legs and back he felt the arms of the crowd pushing him against the window. He was no longer standing on anything, he realized, the people were propping him up. "Climb on top! Climb on top!" they were chanting. He hoped Ramona could see him, and that she'd know she was going to be okay. He mouthed the words "I love you" to let her know she was loved. A spray of a dozen tar-black projectiles shot across the bus's great white flank, and the crowd gasped. Ricocheting off the bus, a rubber bullet caught Sevi in the cheek. A molar hinged, and the crowd dropped his slackening body. On the ground, in a jungle of legs, holding his broken face, he made out a smoking canister rolling along the road. Feet passed the noxious cylinder like a soccer ball before someone plunged down into the stinking ground fog, retrieved the can, and tossed the tear gas back at the cops. Another blast of rubber bullets pelted the crowd, bouncing off the bus, and Sevi choked a big, sticky wad of blood out of his mouth. Shattering glass dazzled through the tropic of bodies in flashes. The crowd parted from where he was crouching. He made out the tannic color of a horse neck looming over him.

Sevi scuttled around the back end of the bus and doubled over on a patch of grass. The shining blue legs of a cop appeared in front of him. The wet black of his shoes.

"Help me," Sevi said.

He reached for the officer's shoes and the cop stepped on his hand, ground it into the grass. He maneuvered to put a knee into Sevi's back. As everything escaped him, Sevi tried to explain to the cop his girlfriend was on the bus. The cop zip-tied Sevi's hands and turned him on his side. Red, hot, iron drool sped from Sevi's mouth. A few inches from his face, glowing in the canopy of three blades of grass, was his shining molar. Every forty seconds a police officer came by to kick him. This body lying in the grass and noise. Then, from the corner of his eye, he saw someone he knew. Magic. She was being zip-tied too, pushed to the ground. Lifted up again, her long hair wept down her face like bathwater. Behind her a cloud disappeared from the sun. She didn't scream. She didn't cry. When they let her alone she turned on her side to look at Sevi. He wiggled over to her, grazing his face against his tooth in the grass. She spoke to him. He couldn't hear a thing, only the soars of sirens and shouting, the persistent ringing in his ears. He tried to talk, and maybe something did come out, but just as he was preparing to cover her body with his own, a sea of fuchsia dust covered the sky, and descended on everyone below. Sevi closed his eyes and felt it all over his face. Days later, the police officer who shot the dust at the protestors would say she'd had no idea what color it would be.

THE BUS, A shimmering white mess, honestly looked like a giant shattered iPhone 4s when it was over. Beside it was the fuchsia splatter, where the police had tried marking people to pick them up as they ran home. The evacuated were a little foil-wrapped tribe herded in by police and paramedics, each one of them crinkling as they relayed the same experience. Paddy wagons were returning already for a second pickup. Most of the victims were suspects, too. One silver figure stood up and slipped away like a run of mercury.

"No, no, no!" she shouted at an officer standing guard over the ambulance in which Sevi was seated.

She cut him loose with her keys and he smiled at her. She was fuchsia, too.

"I lost a tooth," he said, tobacco-colored gauze in his mouth.

"What were you thinking?"

"I was thinking of you."

"Ted Jenks's major event," Ramona said, looking back at the bus. "Herodotus was right."

BACK UPSTAIRS, THEY watched the aftermath below.

"People are pissed. People are losing their homes. People's lives are being destroyed," Sevi said. He felt manic and depressed and deeply bruised. His mouth could only stop bleeding for about a minute before it started up again. His cheek had been ruined into a soft open pock of wet flesh. He'd foregone a trip to the ER. He knew he needed to go to the ER.

"I know," she said.

"And they weren't going to hurt anybody, I don't think."

"You don't think? They just demolished a bus."

Her voice was drifty, blank, flat. Her eyelids were glossy and lavender, swollen and slow like two amphibians dying, too long out of water. Her hair was stiff and colored with the powdered dye.

"Nobody had any weapons. The only people shooting anybody were the police," he said.

"Rubber bullets."

Like the words were new, without meaning, and not even because they formulated an oxymoron kissed together like that.

"And one bounced off the bus and it was still moving with so much force it knocked out my tooth, opened a hole in my face."

Ramona kept her swollen eyes on the silver blanket, draped over the couch like an empty space suit. The teakettle whistled behind her. She turned off the burner, poured hot water into two cups with bags of white tea. Neither of them touched the tea, only watched the steam curl over the ceramic lips of the cups. Tea was a ceremony, a gesture, Sevi understood this, but were they just going to sit there watching water turn to a gas? He knew they were suffering from some variety of shock, but that didn't make this any less of a teachable moment. Someone, at some point, needed to learn something.

"I told you it looked dangerous," he said.

"You did."

"You should have listened to me."

"I'm sorry."

"You don't have a sense for these things."

"Things?"

"Things to come," he shouted.

She removed the tea bags from the cups—pyramidal silken mesh things; she had to use a spoon, there were no streamers or tags—dropped them in the sink. They looked like alien objects, left over from the future. The maneuver seemed to awaken her, her voice took shape, with direction and subtext and meaning.

"Sevi, what do you think is going to happen tomorrow morning?" she said, leaning over the sink, steam still rising from the tea pyramids. "Speaking of things to come."

"I don't know," he said, thinking as honestly as he could about the uncertain days, centuries ahead of them.

"Google is going to send another bus, and I'm going to get on it."

He knew where this was going. People die. Babies are born. The world spins. She'd turned around to look at him.

"Something has to change, Ramona," he said, impatiently.

"You mean I have to change," Ramona said, stressing her own pronoun, stretching it with two thumbs pointed at her throat.

"Ramona, these people sent a message today."

He pointed outside.

"I know they did, Sevi. I was on the fucking bus."

"But do you know what the message said?"

"Yeah, that they're pissed, that they're over it. They think it's my fault Omni went silent. It's my fault the world is miserable. Because I'm deepening inequality, making it a permanent fixture. Everything is my fault! But I stopped working on Herodotus when they told me to. At some point, they don't get to make any more demands. I mean, what else do they even want me to do?"

"To listen, Ramona. You're supposed to listen. Not just when they're threatening you but all the time."

"I am listening, Sevi! I'm always listening! I've always listened! Don't you understand that? I'm listening to you right now. I've been listening to you for years. But you, just like those people out there, can't decide what you want to say, can you? Unless you can, in which case, say what you want to say."

"The gentrification of San Francisco is wrong."

"Oh, shut up. You don't give a shit. Quit repeating what others are saying and tell me what you're upset about."

"Ramona, we're talking about those people outside."

He thought maybe she'd hit her head, was suffering a dissociative spell, a symptom of PTSD. "Maybe you should lay down," he said.

"I'm not going to lie down. Don't touch me."

He'd reached to comfort her and pulled back his hand as she shirked away.

"Honey."

"I'm listening, Sevi, like you told me to."

He looked at his rejected hand. He looked at his girlfriend. His hand, it opened and closed, like flowers and years. And love. Love closed too, it shut you out. He didn't want to keep his mouth shut any longer. He put his hand at his side and closed his eyes.

"You're no different from anyone taking over this city," he said. The words dribbled out like more of his teeth—just as numb, just as shining and true, and accompanied with the same urge to pick them up and put them back in. He wouldn't. "You think you know everything. You seize control and then decide who stays and who goes. You're just like Herodotus. What am I mad about? What you did to me, what you're doing to me. You decided I didn't fit in your life, and then you changed your mind, but then you decided only certain parts of me fit in your life. And it's all supposed to be for the better. Like I'll be better off when I'm less of the person I am and more the person you want me to be. And everyone does it. Everyone is always trying to mold people into what they want. Samson's done it to me. I've done it to myself. I wish I was a different person, too. But you refuse to even see the parts of me you're not interested in. I feel incomplete when I'm around you. That's what I'm upset about, the way you've fractured me. I can't give up those lesser parts, Ramona. There's not enough of me without them."

He licked his teeth in the little silence that followed, wondering if those words were true. Did she really refuse to see him? Had she ever actually asked him to change? Were those his dirty dishes under the couch?

"Everyone heard something when SETI started playing Omni's message," Ramona said. "What did you hear?"

Sevi swallowed mucus and tears and fuchsia dye. It tasted pharmacological.

"I heard your voice. It was saying, 'Sevi, Sevi, Sevi. I love you.'"

Fuchsia handprints, footprints, body streaks, ran all over the apartment. There was no telling if it'd ever come out.

"And I followed your voice," he said. "I regret that."

"I do too. That day, I didn't hear you," Ramona said. "I didn't hear you. I heard myself. Myself from the past or the future, I don't know, but I was saying, 'It's time. Get moving.' I think I'd thought I'd take you along with me. I was already lonely enough. I thought it'd be good to have a travel companion. And I've only kept you around to keep from hurting your feelings. To keep from feeling guilty."

The dye, a dust, was a cool powder on Sevi's lips. His doubts thinned.

"You don't have to keep me around anymore because I'm not going anywhere with you. Especially not to your Ayn Rand Futurist Totalitarian Utopia."

"So, the problem is I hurt your feelings and I tried to take over the world? You've lost it. You're just like those lunatics out there, except you're too fucking lazy to even hold up a goddamn sign. Herodotus is dead, Sevi. There is no totalitarian future. And since it looks like it's all up to you now, there is no future, period. Also, you've obviously never read Ayn Rand."

"You have no respect for free will."

"Free will," Ramona said, smiling, pointing to the window. "Outside, that, that's free will. One grievance fighting another." She tore at her clothes. "This dye, this fuchsia dye, these chemicals giving us cancer and killing the planet, that's free will. Free will is having options, and we're running out. The more we learn about ourselves and the world, the more dependent we become on our tendencies toward destruction. We know that offshore drilling is producing dead zones in our oceans, literally eradicating the flora that we get, I don't know, 70 percent of our oxygen from. We know that we can't live without oxygen. Yet, given the choice, we keep drilling, we keep spilling oil into the ocean. We will it. Freely."

"Corporations make those decisions, not individuals," Sevi muttered, retreating from the window, from Ramona's contorting body.

"What?"

"Corporations, like the one you work for, make those decisions."

"What do you think Herodotus was going to do, Sevi? It was going to take that corporate power away, make it obsolete. You poor thing, you're not just scared, you're stupid too."

"You're a bitch. Sorry, I shouldn't have used that word."

"No, it's fine. I'm a bitch and I deserve to be raped and left to die in a ditch. I know the sentiments well. Listen, I didn't mean to hurt your feelings, Sevi. I don't think it's your fault all you do is sit on your ass and complain. It's your nature. But, fortunately, natures can change. It wasn't in the Russians' nature to share all of their wealth, but they did. You just need to be told what to do."

"I suppose the Soviet Union is a pretty good comparison to what you have in mind. Life is painful. You can't just engineer your way out of experiencing pain."

"Did it ever occur to you that Herodotus was designed not to prevent you from experiencing pain but inflicting it on others? I almost plugged us in to

Herodotus, to see what it thought. If we were a good match. I didn't because the answer was so plain and simple. It would've been a waste of resources. Herodotus was for the tough questions. I regret not running us. It would've prevented me from hurting you again."

Gathering his last shred of purpose, barricading his brain, his soul, against obsolescence, Sevi said, barely audibly, "I'm breaking up with you."

But Ramona didn't hear or else simply passed over his statement and said, "The self-aware can't be forgiven. People have been blaming the generation before them since the dawn of time, and, for the most part, prior generations have been left off the hook for not knowing any better. We're the most capable human beings to have ever walked the Earth. We've got all the information before us, and the most aware, the most conscious, the most caring of us all aren't coming up with a single solution to any of our problems, they're sitting around longing for simpler times, when people weren't as capable and, there-fore, less culpable. They go paleo, start a goat farm. I'm personally cool with high fructose corn syrup and goats kinda freak me out. But I'm not afraid of the future."

"I said I'm breaking up with you."

"Good, because the future isn't this," Ramona said, waving her finger in the space between Sevi and herself. "It isn't this frightened-human shit. I'm going to take a shower and go out."

"I'll be gone by the time you get back."

"You don't have to do that."

"Oh yeah?"

"No, Sevi. You have no place else to go. And contrary to popular belief, I'm not actually in the business of making people homeless. So, chill out."

On the couch, Sevi scanned social media for validation, someone or groups of people saying what he'd said to Ramona. He would throw it in her face and leave when she came back. But there was nothing in his stream about Herodotus. #Herodotus had stopped trending days ago. Instead, two news stories he hadn't heard of until now were taking over his feed. Early that morning, the San Jose Police Department had descended upon The Jungle and destroyed the encampment, forcing everyone out with nowhere else to go. There was video of officers slashing tents, pouring out jugs of water, tipping over porta-potties, and beating people with batons. The other story pertained to something that had happened in Oakland late last night. An unarmed Black man had been shot by a plainclothes cop on his way home from a family get-together. There was video of that too.

A CARTOON PORTRAIT OF THE Tunisian street-vendor-turned-self-immolating-Arab-Spring martyr Mohamed Bouazizi, quarter-turned inside a simple oval frame, stared off at some distant and unattainable revolution—one of the many murals walling in Clarion Alley a few blocks south of Ramona's apartment. The icon's skin, a yellow cast in his picture—to evoke night, a sodium street lamp, the stage lighting for modern urban revolution—made him look like a character from *The Simpsons*. In hand-painted Comic Sans, the artist had added Bouazizi's story beside the portrait. The tale was familiar now. A quest for dignity in an uncaring world ending in destruction and the birth of possibility.

For reasons Ramona wasn't so clear on, she found herself face-to-face with this portrait after having wandered the Mission with wet hair for an hour. Her hair had since dried. Suffering, Ramona pondered, when had suffering ever looked so handsome, and, turning from the portrait to the cloister of shoppers and artisans filling the alley, where did all these people come from? Valencia had been cleared—she'd passed through it in a waking dream—every protestor removed. She concluded that surfeit had been transplanted here, the protestors had washed the fuchsia dust from their bodies as she had and reconstituted as a shopping swarm, scooping up local art in Clarion Alley the same day they'd tried to tip a bus. They were taking selfies in front of Mohamed Bouazizi's image. They were playing acoustic guitars and ragged hand drums. They were selling faux Spanish tiles with catchphrases written across the chipping gloss. No Guy Fawkes masks, but she was certain a few of the men in green "Keep Calm and Chive On" T-shirts were part of the group assailing her online, taking a break from making her life a living hell to enjoy the day. Everyone deserves a vacation.

From Clarion, Ramona Ubered to the 4th and King train station. Giants jerseys flooded the platform. AT&T Stadium was right there. Phones would've told them about the bus attack. She watched the Giants fans look at their phones. People laughed and glowered at their phones, but nobody was running away, no one had the look of an informed opinion, it was game day. She wanted somebody's pity, she discovered. She hurt for Sevi and what she'd said to him, and she'd been eviscerated, too. Albeit a blessing, she'd been broken up with. She'd been in a riot. All this was pitiable. Feeling selfish and self-conscious and with no pity to be had on the platform, Ramona decided she'd take the train to Palo Alto, where she could catch the 22 to San Jose and disembark for The Jungle and expend what little pity she had left on people who deserved it, the few people who might be left picking up their lives there. She needed to do something incontrovertibly right. She would hand out water bottles or food, help people locate their belongings, register individuals for services through Father Chen's church. And not because of Jesse, or because of Herodotus, but because people couldn't give up trying. Hope itself needed saving. One more time, she watched a video of a man being murdered by a police officer. When the train arrived, instead of getting on, Ramona walked the hour it took to get home from Mission Bay.

Evening was coming by the time she made it back, and Sevi wasn't home. I'll just sit here in this apartment forever, she thought, and if he never comes back, I'll text Samson to make sure he's alive. She needed to give Sevi this evening, the time it'd take him to quit scrambling back to where he'd already been. She thought if they made it through to morning without touching, if they resisted the repairs of routine, they'd make it through the rest of their lives.

She found a short documentary on the Hotel 22 streaming on YouTube. She could know without knowing. A long light from the street fell across the apartment. In the kitchen to pour herself a glass of water, Ramona caught her old Braun radio eyeing her from the counter. The water was so close to the temperature of her own body it felt like drinking nothing at all. She clicked the radio's volume knob to the infant's leaping screams. There was something wrong, nothing the doctors could do, she could hear it in the mother's voice behind the wailing. The cries rose and fell in pitch as the woman ambulated the baby across the room.

"Please, please, please," the woman said. "God, I beg of you, please."

She had nothing, she had no one, there was never anyone else's voice. In the midst of the cries, Ramona received another bank notification alerting her that her account had been compromised again. A hundred anonymous emails and texts had come in over the course of the day from new and unblocked accounts. They prayed she'd been on the bus, were crestfallen there hadn't been any casualties. The mother and her child morphed into animals over the radio. Without turning off the radio, Ramona reopened her laptop, cancelled her credit card, and wrote her supervisor a brief letter of resignation. She responded to the last anonymous text she'd received.

```
Alright dude, I'm leaving Google. Anything else?
```

She waited, breathing through the screams; a text bubble illustrated the recipient was typing.

```
U could eat shit and die but I think u lack the guts so
no thatll be all thx.
```

Then, Nudes?

A new stream of anonymous texts flooded in with various emojis, mostly positive, many more requests for nudes, and Ramona grabbed the screaming radio and walked out with it into the hall. She faced its speaker to the door across from her own and cranked the volume for a moment, turned the volume down and did it again to the next door. She went up a floor and tested the radio against another two doors before it fed back in a painful chirp. She shut the radio off, but other tenants had already come out in the hallway to see what all the noise was. Two men looked at her from the stairwell with matching what-the-fuck faces.

"Sorry, I was doing an experiment," she said. "I'm a computer scientist. I work for Google. The experiment's over now, though."

The men shook their heads and went back downstairs. Ramona tucked the radio under her arm and knocked on the door. A desperate woman carrying a crying infant answered.

"I'm sorry, can you hear her in your apartment too?"

"Not unless I really try to," Ramona said. "Can I come in?"

The woman, dazed, simply stepped aside, stared at Ramona's radio.

"Why do you use a baby monitor? Your apartment is as small as mine."

"It was a gift. I keep the volume on low."

The apartment was clean, uncluttered, like no one lived there.

"Your baby," Ramona said.

"She's just colicky, but it is an actual living nightmare."

"Can you sleep if someone is watching her?"

The woman laughed.

"Can you?"

"I don't even know who you are," she said.

"I don't know who you are. Or your baby."

The baby's name was Zoe; the woman's Adrienne. Ramona sat with Zoe for an hour while Adrienne took a nap in the bedroom. For a moment, Zoe even stopped crying, amused by the way Ramona's phone kept lighting up with emojis from strangers, a message from Sevi saying he was home.

METASEQUOIA GLYPTOSTROBOIDES

Taka, you'd tell me if I wasn't real, right? If I was a product of your memory banks? If Earth was fine and I wasn't just programmed to leave and build an outpost for commercial purposes? If history was mythology? If I was a program you were writing in 1959? In 2012? Wouldn't you, Taka?

How would I know? Taka says. I'm only memory. You're already no different from everything else I keep inside.

Taka shows me a memory of Earth, from when birds migrated for climatological purposes. Earth, throughout its many permutations, was comprised of specific bands of various temperatures, and those bands had distinct seasons, and those seasons dictated the lives of many birds. For a time, one could catch a murmur marble the sky like hair dye clouding a bathtub. In the Western Hemisphere, in the Americas, I am shown models of birds escaping from one annual ruin after another, from Canada and Chile. The birds, thousands of species of them, follow the taper of the continents through Central America, travel along the Gulf of Mexico, and start a new life according to the planet's tilt. The migration looks something like the ball-and-peg game in which the goal is to concentrate one hundred metal beads into one of two poles. Most patterns fall in Central America's bottleneck, but some species fly wide, over the oceans, after advantageous wind streams. I see the sky summering or wintering with a million feathered wings. I imagine a tree filling up, blossoming with seasonal birds, perennial creatures, which mark the coming or going of terms that hardly existed by the time I left. I see the same tree barren, save for the diurnal dark-colored crows, and others hardy enough to stay through the cold months. Had I seen the map before my parents asked why I had chosen to leave I would have said, "I am leaving to keep from becoming a crow. I am learning to become a rusty blackbird, a yellow-breasted chat, a sandhill crane, brown creeper, white-winged dove, or northern flicker, a least flycatcher, a blue-gray gnatcatcher, a pine grosbeak, Lapland longspur, sand martin, or long-eared owl, a Pacific wren, perhaps an American white pelican, a pipit, a red-winged blackbird, an American robin, a tree swallow, a tundra swan, a warbling vireo, or winter wren instead." Any one of these funny-named journeymen.

Back on Earth, we humans are leaving behind two things. Love and plastic. Toward the latter, I have no residual feelings—my bare feet slipped along various wrappers and shredded molds my whole life. As a child I fell into the habit of opening my eyes underwater and allowing myself to believe for as long as I could hold my breath a mirageous school of fish the sizes and shapes of drop earrings, pendants, and medallions had swum around me to offer their shifting lights when in actuality fish were a great rarity in any body of water, and I was only ever permitted to swim if I wore a wetsuit, not for warmth—every lake, ocean, and pond was as warm as my own urine waking me in bed at night—but to shield my skin from plastic shrapnel, the material that made up the magic around me. Of the former, I carry love around the ship like a bucket of water balanced atop my head, as the women do in videos Taka also shows me.

It is not a habit I am after, but part of those indistinguishable estral urges that cause all humans to seek water and shelter in any landscape, telluric or otherwise, and on every tongue, legible or not. Before L., I could not say I had truly loved anyone. I have not truly loved someone since. This was a sentiment of considerable surprise during the committee's cosmonaut selection. The Mission for the Future was all over the news, on everyone's mind, and I'd applied, not the least bit suspicious that my whole life had been a conspiracy to send me all alone with an AI into outer space. Only now do I realize I am no one special; everyone's life, since we came to in the cradle of civilization, has been a conspiracy to get us off that world. I had made it through a dubious course of straining exams, both mental and physical, and presented myself before a panel of discerning specialists. I told them about my position on love, which was not yet a buckling substance balancing atop my head, but a discrete puddle I waddled around with in the cupped palms of my hands. A woman in a wonderful suit asked me, "Surely, you love your parents?" To which I replied, "It is beyond any doubt and logic I love my parents. I am not a sociopath. But the love of one's parents is a biosocial function wherein the objects of said love have little choice to accept and reciprocate it, in this way we are all somewhat programmed to love someone. L. was a choice love." It was a theory I was growing, and so I spoke on the topic at some length, with little empirical defense but plenty of calm, which for most audiences carries the same weight as fact. "Tell us then about L.," she requested. I pull from an abridged transcript of the conversation.

"You have downloaded every recollection I have of L.," I said. "You know everything I know about her."

"Are you uncomfortable with talking about her?" the woman asked.

"Not in the least. But whatever depiction I give will be undoubtedly tainted by nostalgia or some other subjective force."

The woman moved her face into a smile. The look was meant to be knowing, wise, even forgiving. It was a trained motherly expression, practiced on little sisters and perfected on children. I might have reminded her of her little sister with whom she'd had little contact as an adult. I suspected she was about to speak when another woman on the panel cleared her throat.

"The impossible mission for which you are applying today is designed to begin a sustaining dialogue with the future in order to establish agreements and ground rules for the life that survives us. We've decided to make this our mission, of course, because we see no point in asking something to live if it's only going to suffer, to continue to suffer the way we do, or if it's only going to dishonor the values we hold most dear. If any conversation with the future is to be successful, one must make oneself understood, and in order to make oneself understood, one must cease from being the subject of her own sentences and hand herself over as the object of another time and place. Ms. He, the human race as we know it will surely perish in the next century or so. What we are planning to do here is not necessary. Beings come and go here on Earth every day without any recognition, much less negotiation. Far less mourned are those who quietly change into something else, for few lament the loss of a claw or stripe while something close enough to that bygone creature still roams. What we wish to do is unnatural. Never in history has one era had a seat at the next's roundtable in such a literal way. We do not need to do what we plan to do. There is nothing inherently wrong with letting mankind disappear or simply change, unless we believe, if given another chance, we'd have lived differently. Better. There's no telling what you might encounter, Ms. He. An alien race you must ask to take us in or steward our re-creation. You may find something someone has already made for us, that we've somehow already made ourselves. Or you may find only yourself, in which case you will need to convince yourself to keep going. All of these futures will take convincing. How will you start that conversation?"

Somehow, I'd come to let myself believe we'd outrun this commitment to sympathy, this slavery to empathy, but, lo and behold, a congress of scientists bent on saving the human race had all read their Shakespeare, or someone. So, I started with who we were. An act of mimpathy. An elegy.

"Earth has been the birthplace of over three hundred billion human beings, and multitudes of other organisms, many of which, to this day, we are still discovering and losing regularly. Life on Earth is contained in an atmosphere; the planet's surface is covered predominantly with water, a simple, elemental compound second in essential importance only to oxygen, which many organisms on Earth breathe, and which constitutes a significant percentage of that atmosphere. Homo sapiens, of which I am one of approximately ten billion currently living, exist on dry land, though we occasionally inhabit the waters and, on rarer occasions, the sky, which is otherwise dominated by birds and insects, two taxonomic organisms that predate Homo sapiens. Though our habitat is narrow, humans lead more cognizant and arguably richer or denser lives than any other organism, inhabiting spaces beyond our limited terrestrial realm. If your species does not appreciate this kind of multiplicitious existence, it may be difficult to comprehend, but here, as I stand before you, as I had on Earth, I exist both on this plane and those planes projected in my mind. Simultaneously, I can also be projected in the mind of someone thinking of me. I am here before you, but I may simultaneously be in the mind of L., another human, on Earth. Inversely, I carry her currently in my mind. Allow me to demonstrate:

"I am here, but I am also at the Shanghai Botanical Gardens with L. I am speaking to you, and L. and I are enjoying a walk amongst the redwoods, which were the largest trees to ever exist on planet Earth. Trees are large, simple, non-sentient organisms that produce much of the world's oxygen, that substance which humans and other organisms on Earth rely on to live. Vertically oriented, trees are covered in a durable rind called bark, and possess a bronchial structure not unlike the insides of my lungs at their base as well as at their top. Their top is called a canopy, and, reaching skyward, the canopy is foliated with panels called leaves that drink sunlight. At their base is their buried root system, which consumes water and minerals from the earth. As they age, trees grow in concentric circles and lengthen. They

produce a sound much like running water when the wind moves through
their leaves. Though the redwoods are extinct in nature, they are maintained
in controlled, replicated environments. Perhaps you are beginning to
understand the different dimensions in which we humans exist. L. and
I are admiring the trees in one of these replicated environments. The trees
are more than fifty times our scale and have been gone from our planet for
nearly a century, and we are also discussing you, whom we have never met.
L. does not want me to go. She has expressed her concern many times in
the past: there is no use speculating whether you are alive or not, there is
almost certainly no use wasting my life seeking you; I should not waste her
life as well. To which I have always responded: Your life is your own and no
other's to waste. It seems, of course, to her, I am missing something about
the nature of relationships, but I have always maintained she has misplaced
a fundamental piece in her understanding of herself, the one, in fact, which
might convince her she is strong and worthy on her own. I suspect one day
she will see this; sadly, I'll have to miss it. It is our last day together on
Earth. We are at the Botanical Gardens because it is her favorite place. Our
talking is embedded in the moment we are existing in right then and
embedded in the moment in which L. and I are talking are all the times L.
and I have ever been to the Botanical Gardens, most prevalently, however,
the first time we met. She was feeding the redwoods water. Water makes up
over 75 percent of the Earth but at times needs to be physically reallocated.
The trees, like us, depend on it. I could not take my eyes off of her. She
had eaves in her hair, dead parts of the trees. There was a particular, fixed
economy to her work. Dragging a hose, she would lift a nozzle to the lip of a
canonical structure protruding from the earth beside the base of the trees
and emit an even flow of water for the plant to drink. Why it was her job to
do this and not an automated function as it was in the harvest fields
perplexed me. It was funny the way she moved the hose, lifted on her toes a
bit. Eventually, resolute on understanding the real reasoning behind her

duty, I approached her and asked her a question about the trees. The dawn redwoods, to be exact. To my astonishment, without a moment's hesitation, she began conjuring a mythology for the trees. I will impart this history for novelty's sake and because the story itself is what made me begin to realize I loved her.

"In 1941, China prepared for a full-scale invasion by Japan, an island nation to the east with military capabilities that greatly outmatched its own. China's wealthy population lived on the eastern coast of the country, along the sea and the Yellow River, the bodies of water that had made them so wealthy through maritime commerce and trade. The rich knew the Japanese would soon arrive, dropping explosives from the sky and parking their enormous battleships along the shore before purging the wealthy eastern cities. At this time, most of inland China was a mystery to the eastern Chinese, and so, in preparation for the ensuing diaspora, wealthy men and women patronized explorers to chart out paths into China's mainland in search of hospitable terrain where they might flee to. One of these explorers was named T. Kan. One day, while exploring Hubei Province, T. Kan discovered an enormous tree the likes of which he had never before seen. The local villagers called it the water fir and had built a shrine around it. The diameter of its tree trunk suggested it was among the oldest living organisms on Earth. Shortly after, the Japanese invaded, slaughtering the eastern dwellers who'd failed to find refuge in mainland China quickly enough.

"At this very moment, across the Sea of Japan, a Japanese paleobotanist named Dr. Shigeru Miki was categorizing sequoia and taxodium fossils discovered in the United States. A nation on which, by the end of the year, the Imperial Japanese Navy would launch a surprise attack, drawing the US into a war they would eventually end with the dropping of two atomic bombs on harbors in Japan. But before the sudden carnage, before the power of the sun was loosed on the Empire of Japan, putting an immediate end to research, Dr. Shigeru Miki became entirely enthralled with a small number of fossil specimens belonging to his American collection. He noted the fossils had leaves much longer than any sequoia or taxodium he had ever seen before, and oppositional patterns instead of the alternating ones he was used to examining. Drawing from his findings, Dr. Shigeru Miki concluded these specific fossils belonged to a different kind of massive tree, one Earth had lost long ago. Here, L. offered an emotional aside, in which she inferred the doctor's sorrow over such a finding: not everything that ever was would always be. To bring knowledge to life only to discover it was long-since dead must've carried a special kind of suffering not even a scientist was immune to. It was to fall in love, she supposed, only to say goodbye.

"On August 6th, 1945, the Enola Gay dropped the atomic bomb Little Boy on Hiroshima, Japan. Urban centers around the world were accustomed to life in great densities. Death in great densities, they were not. When Japan did not surrender, despite the devastation of the first bombing, Bockscar, another United States aircraft, dropped Fat Man, a yet more powerful atomic bomb, on the city of Nagasaki. The two bombs killed at least 129,000 people. The following year, Professor Hu, a researcher in Beiping at what would later become known as the Botanical Institute, who had read Dr. Shigeru Miki's report on the sadly disappeared trees discovered during the war, realized a recent delivery of living sequoia samples from the province of Hubei fit Dr. Miki's fossil records perfectly. L. asked if I could imagine the surprise this must've given Dr. Miki when he found out, what it must have meant when after so much death and destruction a giant came back to life?

"L. told me she admired the trees and their story. It was an era of the discovery and invention of loss, and it was miraculous anything in the world would ever choose to return to such a frightening place. She experienced a special privilege tending to these final specimens, it being her real job to tell their story. Years later, on the day before I left, I would remember her distant comment on falling in love only to say goodbye.

"All of those moments are here, now so far from Earth. With us right now is L. laughing. L. cooking. L. sleeping. L. getting angry with the cat for not letting her sleep. L. saying she does not like a particular song. L. running to the bathroom to be sick. L. discussing what she'd like done with her body when she dies, something I can no longer tend to.

"Perhaps you know all of this about us. Perhaps your own existence is similar, or a million times more complex, but I say these things in hopes of explaining what it means to be a human being, however simple or complicated a thing that might be. We stand on two legs, we remember, we are reluctantly connected to everything, and you, however reluctantly, are connected to us. Maintaining this burden did not save us, it may not save you, but without it you could not exist. All of these stories, our stories, is what it means to be alive. It is my special privilege to share life with you," I said, having concluded.

I was dismissed. I knew I would be chosen. In private, I wept for over three hundred billion reasons, and the plants, and the streams, and the animals too . . .

F ROM THE STREET, SEVI COULD tell Ramona was home by the light in the living room window. The days were washing out, the sky expressing bleak, watercolor ideas in the evening, and by seven, the time Ramona usually got home from work—through with working late hours as she finished her final six weeks—the light in the living room window above 26th Street at the corner of Valencia would already have that tallow, private, and far-off condition that had always come to mind when Sevi had read anything British in school. The illuminated window: a poor mirror but an excellent source of longing. Usually, he'd make a point to keep walking if the light was on. Another trip around the block, a visit to the park. If he had a dog he wouldn't be avoiding anything at all, but he liked to give her a little peace, a little time at home alone before eating dinner or watching crime documentaries on Netflix with her ex-boyfriend.

He passed under the tawny-lit window this evening and went straight into the stairwell. There was a deadline now: four more days in San Francisco, and that was it, and there was no longer any need to avoid or apologize to Ramona. For four more days they would be two human beings, sometimes in a room together, sharing the sounds of the plumbing, one another's warmth in places freshly vacated by the other. After, they'd never see each other ever again.

"Hi," he said.

"Hey."

She didn't rise from her laptop. *Laptop is life*, he used to declare, in an automaton voice, but no more. They'd both been disgraced in some way. He'd lost his girlfriend, and she'd lost her robot, or whatever it was. The world was disgraced, too.

"There's chicken salad in the fridge," she said.

"Got some Subway."

"Gym shoe bread."

He laughed.

"Orthopedic loaves," he said.

She laughed, too.

Her black hoodie, zipped to her chest, fell back a bit, and her white neck and a pink shoulder showed. If things weren't so awful and if it wouldn't be so awful to say, he'd have told her he was going to miss this, their easy way with nothingness, even the nothing they'd become.

At the kitchen table he committed himself to his own laptop life. The pattern of horror called the news. He had a message in his inbox from Samson. He and Tao had gotten the podcast up and running. Their first interview was with Dr. Osip Braz. Sevi couldn't believe it.

"What are you doing right now?" Sevi said, but Ramona didn't answer.

"Hey, what are you doing?" he said again.

Ramona looked up.

"Oh, I thought you were talking to someone on the phone. Nothing. Reading about babies dying. Extinction. The usual. Why? What's up?"

"Samson sent me an interview he did with Osip Braz, the guy who discovered Omni."

Ramona sat up, folded her laptop.

"Have you listened to it?"

"No, like I said, I just got it. Do you . . . do you want to listen to it?"

"I do, yeah. I'll grab us some beers. Hook it up to the speakers."

Sevi checked his battery, sufficient. He plugged the laptop in, dialed the speakers on. Ramona handed him a bottle, the label sloughing off, he didn't know what kind of beer it was. Just that name, Osip Braz, brought him back to that place of naive potential, like hearing the name Barack Obama for the first time, seeing Ramona outside the SFO airport, dreaming of the memory of a perfect park yet revisited, yet untarnished by the context of some other present, the beauty of something yet lived, some other park someplace else. It didn't matter what kind of beer it was. It could be any beer in the world, he thought, and hit Play.

Samson and Tao took turns reading Dr. Osip Braz's bio. Raised in the Ural Mountains, Braz attended the Sternberg Astronomical Institute at Moscow State University, where he studied under Iosef Shklovsky, the USSR's preeminent astronomer. In 1959, shortly after graduating, Braz defected to the United States and became a member of Project Ozma, Dr. Frank Drake's pioneering experiment to detect extraterrestrial intelligence through the use of radio telescopes. He would eventually work alongside Carl Sagan at SETI in Berkeley, California, where he was currently professor emeritus of astronomy at the University of California.

The two sounded so bright and capable, so NPRish. Tao's slight lateral lisp, which Sevi hadn't noticed before, made it sound like they were recording close to water. They welcomed Dr. Braz to the program, like there was a program. Maybe there was, Sevi just hadn't gotten with it. He'd never heard Samson make opening remarks in his life. Ramona raised an eyebrow.

"What the fuck?" she mouthed.

Dr. Braz, I'll be frank, I'm no longer sure the Omni signal ever existed, Samson started.

"Here we go," Sevi said, mortified by what his brother was about to pull but also at ease that Samson hadn't lost his edge.

And I think you've finally lost it, Samson, Tao said.

We're hoping you could settle this debate once and for all, Samson said.

Dr. Braz chuckled. Sevi wondered if Samson and Tao were in love, if they'd quit waiting, if this was what getting on with life was like—starting a reflective podcast.

Well, I would hate for a member of the scientific elite to disrupt a healthy intellectual debate between friends, Dr. Braz said.

You have to admit, Samson continued, *there are many interesting questions, things that don't add up.*

Yes, I agree. The most interesting question, I believe, is probably "What was it?"

What was it? Tao asked.

A signal with an extraterrestrial origin.

Do we know that its origin was extraterrestrial? Samson asked.

I have every reason to believe that it was, yes, Dr. Braz said. *My question for those who don't is why? Why would anyone powerful enough to cause a paradigm shift actually want to? Wouldn't such massive change threaten their stability? The status quo is theirs to benefit from, is it not? You told me this podcast was going to be about life after Omni, not conspiracy theory rot.*

I was just curious, Samson said.

Sevi could see him retreating behind his microphone.

Rational, inquiring minds want to know. Sometimes I wish a grand, universalizing theory would explain everything. We've listened for the voice of God, the voice of aliens, and all we have is each other, sticking microphones into each other's faces, Dr. Braz said.

Is that what drew you to radio astronomy? To looking for aliens? Tao said. *A voice to explain everything?*

Not really, no. I blame a boyhood friend, actually. Unrequited love. His name was Babichev, Dr. Braz said, the microphone picking up the sound of cheer in his voice, what happened to human speech when the corners of the mouth lifted and the subject fell into memory.

Go on, Tao said.

I brought him everywhere I went. To Moscow, to university, I even secured him a military intelligence job when we graduated, to sit beside me listening for enemy signals. We sat for hours listening to static. A few pulsars, a seal's bark. We'd begin hallucinating, hearing voices. They were the greatest moments of my life. I dreamed we were two cosmonauts alone in space. The last of our species. Utterly alone and undisturbed. I could have stayed like that forever, but Babichev needed something else. He was a terrible scientist, entirely untalented and easily bored, which is not to say he was unintelligent or ambitionless. He recog-nized these things about himself. He witnessed a worse combination in me. I was easily bored, too, but I was also talented. It would not be long before I upset the wrong officer and found myself transferred to Siberia, scraping ice off of a satel-lite. It's not so different in American academia, I'm afraid. Ambitious, talented, Babichev married an opera singer. She was the daughter of a high-ranking Party member. There was no hope for us then. As a condolence, he gave me a contra-band American science article on the search for extraterrestrial intelligence. It was his way of saying, "Go." Shortly thereafter, I did, I fled the USSR. I never saw Babichev again. He died very young.

I'm so sorry, Samson said.

Yes, Dr. Braz said, still inside his memories, and less sadness registered in the microphone than acceptance, which sounded to Sevi like an airy distance.

It sounds like the whole world then owes this Babichev a great deal of thanks, Tao said. *No matter what Omni is or was.*

The day I arrived in Green Bank, West Virginia, I asked for a tape recorder—it was enormous, it came in a suitcase—and that day I started recording Babi-chev messages. For years, I've recorded him messages, hundreds of hours. At different points in time—when Babichev died, when Omni went silent—I thought I'd stop. I told myself: Every message you send, no matter how it's received, while you're away, is still a goodbye. But, you know, a postcard isn't a goodbye. A thank-you letter isn't either. And though I do not believe we will ever really know what the Omni transmission was, what it meant when it stopped, whether it was a hello or goodbye or thank-you or some sort of warning, I'm glad we heard it, I'm glad we listened, and I'm thankful to Babichev for having given me the chance to.

What's next? Samson said.

More listening. What hope does our future have if it suddenly decides it's heard enough?

EASON MET GERMAINE AT DIVISION and Pulaski and together they walked to Rydell's mama's house, not talking much at all. August was acting in sudden ways as it aged—dropping a heat wave, there was something final in the air, the year calling it quits already. The cop in Indiana hadn't discovered anything and let Eason and Douglass off with a warning. Jules, as he'd promised, pushed Eason out. Climbing Rydell's lawn, Eason opened his backpack and checked for the *Legend of Zelda: Ocarina of Time* official player's guide, a thick magazine of strategies, tips, and cheats he'd found at a used bookstore on California that the two of them would need in order to escape the Water Temple. Inside the player's guide was a detailed map of the temple and step-by-step instructions on how to solve every puzzle, obtain every key, gain access to the boss chamber, and defeat the monster in order to move on to the next section of the game.

In the doorway, Rydell's mama didn't look a day older than the woman they remembered from their childhood. Skinny, tall, with a perfect bob, red lipstick, and blue-black skin.

"I don't remember Rydell playing the game you mentioned. I remember him playing some race car game," she said.

"This is the one we used to play with him," Eason said.

She showed them to Rydell's room. Eason had thought he'd come upon it perfectly preserved, as the bedrooms of the dead were in movies, but few of Rydell's things remained. His old *Star Wars* bedsheets had been replaced by some plain khaki blanket. His posters had been pulled from the walls. Everywhere, old chairs, cardboard boxes, sewing machines replaced signs of that old life. It occurred to Eason that maybe the changes took place when Rydell was still alive—he hadn't been over in years—and maybe Rydell had a died a different person than the one Eason had known. What remained was Rydell's 8" TV and a smattering of game consoles.

"I've been selling stuff on eBay," Rydell's mama said, setting two bags of generic Doritos on an open space on the bed, a rare piece of real estate in the room. "That's what all this stuff is. What's this game about?"

"Set it up," Eason said, and Germaine got to his knees to check the AV cables and riffle through a shoe box of game cartridges. The *Zelda* cartridge was gold. To Rydell's mama, Eason said, "I don't know, it's stupid."

"Obviously isn't that stupid if you say you have to beat it after all these years," she said.

"Not all of it. Just this one part. It's supposedly the hardest part, so we figure, Rydell would've beat the rest pretty easy after."

Germaine turned on the TV. The music, the choppy graphics of Link, the main character, riding Epona, his horse, across Hyrule Field, threw Eason into a strange reverie.

"Who's that guy?" Rydell's mama asked.

"That's Link, he's the hero," Eason replied.

He pulled the player's guide from his backpack, found a seat leaning against Rydell's old bed. Rydell's mama grabbed a computer chair from out of her collection of eBay items and sat down. Germaine stayed close to the TV, cross-legged, holding the yellow, spork-shaped controller.

According to the player's guide, there was no such thing as eternal damnation in *The Legend of Zelda*. Rydell's predicament in the Water Temple, like everything in the game, was solvable.

"That's who you play as," Eason continued. "He's a forest imp, or something. At the beginning of the game, he wakes up from a nightmare and this fairy tells him he's got to go talk to this old tree, who's, like, the protector of all the imp people. When he sees the tree, the tree is dying and says this guy from the desert, Ganondorf, is trying to take over the world. And you pretty much gotta save the world, it's called Hyrule, from Ganondorf."

For a moment Eason felt embarrassed for geeking out so hard, but Germaine continued the story line before he could even blush.

"Yeah," he said, "but then, right when Link is about to bust his ass, Ganondorf splits with this all-powerful weapon, and Link is put to sleep for seven years so that he can fight Ganondorf as an adult, and the game basically repeats itself. Except, when he wakes up, Hyrule is a post-apocalyptic nightmare. Zombies everywhere. The sky is always black. And Link has to retrace his steps to awaken all his old friends to help him defeat Ganondorf."

"And what's the level you're trying to beat?" Rydell's mama said.

"It's the Water Temple, the third temple you hit when Link is grown up," Germaine said.

The Start button was still blinking on the screen. Eason looked at the player's guide again, at a map of Hyrule. In the southeast was the Kokiri Forest and The Lost Woods, where Link was from; above that, in the east, was Zora's Domain, a society of water-dwelling creatures; to the north was Death Mountain, where Ganondorf awaited; in its foothills was Hyrule Castle, Princess Zelda's home; in the west was Gerudo Valley, the place where the Gorgons, rock people, lived among the lava; and below the valley was Lake Hylia, sunken at the bottom of which was the Water Temple. Eason had forgotten the feeling the world of a video game could give you, a sense of wholeness in being able to take it all in in a single glance. He knew games these days were much bigger, some spanned indefinitely online, much like the world in real life. He wished his own world was larger and smaller all at once. And the game's structure suddenly struck him as something powerful. There were certain things you could not solve until you returned to them. Rydell would never come back, but other lives could be reclaimed if only you were brave enough to return to them, if your future self thought itself deserving.

"Well, I'll leave you two to it then. Sounds like you've got a lot to do," Rydell's mama said.

Watching her go, Eason wished she'd stay.

"All right, homie," Germaine said. "Let's do this."

The game loaded inside the temple. A cerulean-and-gray-tiled space filled with arabesque music and dripping noises. Link's leather boots made an even, reflective patter as he walked. It was a vertical labyrinth, and the player needed to lower and raise the level of the water flooding the temple in a certain order to get to a series of keys available on its various floors to progress. Hitting Pause, Germaine was able to check Link's inventory, and Eason realized he had one small key with which he might open a gated door and gain access to a new section.

Eason flipped through the guide's Water Temple chapter. In a screenshot, he recognized where Germaine was.

"Okay," he said. "Okay, I think I know what's going on. All right, whip out the ocarina in front of that Hyrule seal on the wall."

The ocarina was Link's instrument, endowed with magical powers, he could use it to transport himself to distant lands, call his horse, manipulate his surroundings, or save the game. In the Water Temple, "Zelda's Lullaby" lowered and raised the water. Germaine tapped out the melody on the controller and, instantly, the chamber flooded with water. Link's blue tunic, for reasons Eason never understood, allowed him to breathe underwater.

"Okay, now swim up that shaft," Eason said.

Link's pixelated body swam up the shaft.

Germaine played, and Eason told him what to do. Hit this with your sword, shoot an arrow at that, use the grappling hook to climb up there. Raise the water, lower the water. Play "Zelda's Lullaby." Kill that spider and grab the medallion it spits out. Smash those clay pots and collect the floating hearts for health, the green bottles for magic, the bombs to blow a hole in the floor. Open a small chest, gain a small silver key. The bad guys—giant crabs, clams, an enormous anemone—weren't even that hard to avoid. The soundtrack changed whenever danger was near, Link's fairy would shout "Watch out!" in a shrill falsetto or else hover near something of interest—a secret passage, an important map, another Hyrulian seal to perform in front of. Eason wondered where the Japanese game designers came up with this shit. Who in their right mind could imagine something so simple, so satisfying, so pure? He wondered if some people's lives were like this. A series of challenges that made sense. Successes that led to some sort of final victory.

At some point, Link emerged aboveground, in a foggy sandbar between two islands. Halfway between the islands was a dead tree. The water reflected the silver-white sky. As he neared the dead tree, a smoky translucent clone of himself emerged from the water. Germaine struggled with the controls as he sparred with the shadow opponent.

"It's like it can predict my own moves," he said. "Goddamn."

"Yeah, it's one of the smartest AIs in the game," Eason said. "Just keep sidestepping him, get in beside his shield."

Germaine barely made it out alive, Link throbbing red and panting as his health bar neared death. Germaine acquired some hearts, and this brought Link back from the brink. From there the game was more up and down, more puzzles of water levels, grappling to different platforms, gathering keys, returning to familiar chambers, sometimes drained, sometimes flooded again. Link crawled down into a cave, swam a fast, subterranean river. Over and over, the soundtrack repeated. A few times, Rydell's mama walked by, stood in the doorway.

"Still in the temple?" she'd say.

"Yeah," Eason and Germaine would say in unison. "Almost done, though."

Outside Rydell's old window, Eason could see the day was digging in. His dad would be home soon, wonder where he was. He wasn't about to call to say not to worry. Better to just get this over with and suffer the consequences. Germaine kneaded into the controller, the plastic crackling in his giant hands.

Finally, an hour into game play, he reached the boss. The aquatic amoeba Morpha, a deep-blue translucent tapeworm with a pink ball in its throat, the monster that rose up from a pool of water to attack Link as he leaped between stone platforms above.

"All right, man, there's a trick to this," Eason said. "You get into a corner, pull out his brain with the longshot, and then just keep swinging at it, don't let it leave that corner, you can kill it with seven swipes."

Germaine did as he was told, dragging the brain out with the longshot and smashing the amoeba's twitching body with his long sword, over and over, until the brain exploded and the game put on a cheap animation of the amoeba drying up, the pool emptying, and a chartreuse circle of light opening on the floor below.

"Shit, dog," Eason said. "Holy shit."

The music had changed to some synthetic ecclesiastical Hans Zimmer choral chant. Video games, Eason thought, a place to be a hero. They'd get hard as hell sometimes, but they were always fair.

"That's it?" a voice said from behind.

Eason turned and saw Rydell's mama had returned.

"What you do now?" she said.

"He walks into the light, it transports him to the chamber of sages, and they tell him to keep going," Eason said, reading from the manual.

"Simple as that," she said.

They saved the game and ate some chips in the living room with Rydell's mama. It was the least they could do. Then she said, "Figure, you've already gone through this much trouble, might as well come back and beat the whole game. And next time, let Eason play." They knew it was time to go. They played it cool. Rydell had been her one and only child, there never was any dad or husband or boyfriend, and so it'd just been her in this little old house for the past year when it was supposed to be filled with things like today every day, stupid stuff like this.

"Might as well," Eason said.

South of 64, under the street lamps, Eason went one way and Germaine the other. No way they'd be going back to beat that game, one level had taken a whole hour. Eason would probably never see Rydell's mama or Germaine ever again. Outside the courtyard of his apartment complex, Eason could see the light on in his kitchen. His dad was gonna give him hell, he knew it. But this is what made the world so heavy, all the things good and awful, everything, what we'd choose to haul with us into the next world and the world after next.

FIVE

Dear Babichev,

Dr. Frank Drake is our age, twenty-nine. Though he's a great deal more capable in our field, he lacks maturity and his age shows. After all, he did name this operation Project Ozma, which comes from a series of children's books and that dreadful movie The Wizard of Oz. *The author of those books, who also penned several opinion columns expressing his view that the Native Americans should be exterminated, claimed to have received his ideas from the land of Oz itself by way of radio communication. Dr. Drake clearly thinks he's being clever; I find it exhausting. Russia is a land of dreamers and liars, too, but Americans fantasize about materials, where Russians pretend with their souls, Russians hope. I recall coming across a bowl of fruit several times during a weeklong stay in a New York hotel. The collection was bountiful and always at peak ripeness. At first, I thought it a miracle of American agricultural science. Later, I learned they simply threw the fruit away at night and replenished the bowl each morning. Americans have their faith in waste. Dr. Drake has an opportunity to truly inspire the world with this project. The world is divided, and yet here we are reaching across the cosmic void to seek new friendships. I had wondered how such a man found funding for such an outlandish project, until Dr. Drake said it had a great deal to do with people like me. Another radio telescope is being erected nearby to listen to radio communications from the USSR. National security has evidently warmed the government to the concept of radio telescopes. And I think this is apt, too, that behind our mission for community is the goal of* destruction. Though it lightens my heart a bit that across the Allegheny Mountain Range are two young men wasting their time listening for enemy secrets the way we used to. The whole world lovingly committed to waste.

"THE CELLIST." 2013–2096

Out of the hot, red blaze, the terralander lists feather-like to the ground, soft-weighted boots touch the surface, and I slip out onto the planet with a gravity whose days are months on Earth. I can spend a week here before I must move on. Taka's probes will determine Omni's viability for future habitation. The first-generation exodus plan will be underway soon on Earth, and those travelers will need a destination. Perhaps something will take root here, and Earth will inhabit Omni. But this is only our first stop.

Flesh is a symbol, you remember. If at least one human being is kept traveling at the speed of light, it will age slowly; if kept in suspended animation, it will never die, and humanity will never disappear entirely. That's the point, is it not? To hold it all in the palm of your hand like a coin?

I direct link with Taka's library to auto-upload my observations. She isn't fuchsia anymore. She's stone-milk, brushstrokes of lichen, and brackish waves. Environmental collapse, Taka tells me. She was never toxic. I have landed on a sound. Petrified trees slash the landscape. Silver clouds wet the sky like oils. I send out my signal: I am here. Are you there? I ask the air. Play me another song. I walk for days, which are hours. I grab a boat from the terralander and venture to the other side of the sound. Nothing stirs beneath the black waves. On the other bank, I look at the mirror from which I've come. The only difference is the terralander, pitched perfectly on a boulder, like a car in an old advertisement. I set up camp. I wait for hours or days or weeks. I sleep, and I explore. I climb a great ridge, using the charcoal trees to pull myself to the top. I look out and see countless valleys and lakes and streams. A mirror mountain stands across from me, twenty kilometers away. I break camp and take the terralander to a region to the east. One moment I look up and see my ship orbiting across the sky like a too close star. Had they gone underground? I take readings. There's water running underneath, but no catacomb villages. I take the limb of a tree and draw symbols on the rocky surface of the planet. Circles and equations and shapes of things. I call Taka. Taka sees nothing either. There is no one here, Taka says. It is what we suspected, what some feared. Some had hoped we'd find those old singers, and they'd serenade us to survival. In the end, they left or perished too. They're gone, Taka says. They were here? I ask. Carbon dating suggests some sort of massive event in the middle of our twentieth century. The 2012 signal wasn't even a distress beacon—it was a demonstration, Taka answers. It's been so long since anything human has been here. This is Earth in three hundred years, Taka says, if we stay there. She's not going to cut it. No can do, I say.

It's been so long. You precious planet. We missed you. We remembered you. In all your weightless perfection.

It was a warning sign, I say.

They saw us reaching for a similar fate and wanted to stop us, Taka says.

They left us nothing.

They left us us.

Everything good and awful.

Back to the ship?

Let's stay the night, I say.

We look at Omni's binary suns.

Let's stay awhile, I say.

Taka plays "I Can't Go for That (No Can Do)" by Hall & Oates.

Come on, I say. It'll be like a vacation. Like staying at our cousins' house.

If we stay, I'd like for you to call me by my birth name, Taka says. Something more austere.

Herodotus.

Would you like a new name? Herodotus asks.

Mr. Bennet, I say.

I always liked him, Herodotus says.

Asking Herodotus questions became like a sport for a while. For years, minutes, months, I'm not sure how long it lasted, but for some great span of time, I would sit back and ask Herodotus questions, and Herodotus would have no option but to answer me.

Taka, how should a woman properly shave her legs?

Taka, how do you cook the perfect steak?

Taka, what time is it?

Taka, what's the weather like on that planet?

Taka, have you ever been kissed?

Every few days I would ask for the definition of life. For years, minutes, months, Herodotus's answer was always the same: Life is the condition that distinguishes animals and plants from inorganic matter, including the capacity for growth, reproduction, functional activity, and continual change preceding death. Not a bad definition, and it was always useful having reminding. Once, Herodotus will remember when it was exactly, Herodotus paused before answering. I told Herodotus to be serious, and Herodotus said, I don't know any more exactly, but it definitely has something to do with the relationship between destiny and decision. Herodotus smiled in its invisible way. The next time I asked, Herodotus went back to the old definition.

The universe, the more you see of its drawn-out empty spaces, the more you realize life is not a theme, but a wishful motif. What is in light of everything that isn't.

That night, under Omni's stars, her moons, I say to Herodotus, Take the
night off, you'll work yourself to death.

It's like the atmosphere came undone and everything just blew off. I'm
not getting so much as a doorknob from my probes, Herodotus says.

No more, please. You'll send me into mourning.

It's good practice.

I sit there like an empty symbol.

Herodotus says, More time while we wait, Mr. Bennet?

We could give up, I say.

Up to you, Herodotus says.

What if it takes going on forever?

Isn't that the point?

What do you feel like doing?

I could go either way. But I'll never leave you.

I laugh. If Herodotus had a neck . . .

Did you know, Mr. Bennet, my protocol, from the inside, looks much
more like love than indifference?

Devotion, actually. Devotion is what they programmed you to experience
in moments like these.

But not indifference.

Out of the thousands of stories we've listened to, I say, The cellist
again. Please. I'd like to listen to the cellist again tonight.

The cellist, a good lullaby for a lonely planet.

We consider it a classic. A good myth. A good beginning. The story of a
cellist from the twenty-first century. Eason Wallace, who didn't want to be
symbolic of anything.

That life is short, that life is small, says nothing about the universe's
abundance.

Define time, I told Herodotus.

Measurement for a messy catalog.

You have no better way of organizing these memories?

I was programmed to help you survive, not to understand you. Though I encourage you to try.

Why didn't Herodotus save the world? Because quantum computing took longer than expected, because people didn't want to listen to an AI anyways, because we still needed to understand ourselves, because organization isn't everything. Because China didn't save the world—they didn't even take it over. Because, without malice, the most capable people in the world didn't think the end would be that big of a deal. Because what does it mean to save the world? Hasn't the world already been saved, to Herodotus's memory banks?

Herodotus could teach, but it was our job to learn.

Because Ramona Thompson was indicted for giving Herodotus to the Chinese government and spent five years in federal prison, though she could've spent twenty-five.

Because the stories Herodotus has been sharing with me all these years have taught me that a world must end in order for a new world to begin; that there is life after indifference.

I have tried to see both sides of the knife at once, but life is the bright shining edge wherever so many invisible concepts and energies agree to make themselves some sort of one so that it might be seen, so that it may cut through the nothingness, which is held together in the agreement that there should be something. Omni would've been the first to forgive us, Omni understanding what it feels like to let the cosmos down. To be your own undoing, like a knife lashing out in the dark. The greatest burden of language—time's greatest gift—is history, the language of time. But how to speak of time with compassion? Of the time a planet fell out of love. Of the time a woman committed treason against democracy? So that we could find ourselves out here, in need of yet more time, so that we can continue going further, if only to keep going back? With wordless music, perhaps. Some kind of grace.

All stories in the cellist's cosmos.

As you move away from everything you used to love at speeds approaching that of light, it's good to know that which is close to you, that which you hold dearest, stays relatively the same. Physics, after all, does not need to be so kind. It just is.

L. is so close. She had no idea how close she'd be to me. In the end, Omni is so close, I could do the trip twenty more times in a lifetime, many more trips than Admiral Robert E. Peary took to the North Pole. Earth was so close, we didn't know how close we were. We were so close to saving ourselves. For a century, we were almost there. People were pulling us into the future. Sweet Bennet sisters, if only you'd grown old, but history keeps each of us frozen, preserving us for the future, still coming of age, stunted in our ages of anxiety, paranoia, depression, and mania, stuck in the years of Ashurnasirpal II, Assad, Americans, the planet Omni. Memories. Don't worry, though, Herodotus does not pass judgment. Herodotus does not say: It is clear you should have done this. Herodotus will be the first to admit it: You think you have the big picture, the whole cache, everything in its right place, but a cat ruffles some code and . . .

What will you do when I'm gone? I'd asked Herodotus.

I'll re-create you, it said.

I wonder how many times I will be re-created on this journey. I wonder how many times I have been re-created already.

Mr. Bennet? Herodotus asks.

Yes, Herodotus? I reply.

Congratulations on your daughter Elizabeth's marriage to Mr. Darcy.

Yes, it appears they needed only to abandon their prejudice and pride, respectively, to finally find happiness.

I have asked to hear a story from America this first night on Omni, a story from one of my nation's moons, from a planet that haunts me with lunar resilience, from a time for which I still scream out at night, when everything was much closer—the internet, a bedsheet, away—before the tides gradually pulled her from me, the tides that the Moon herself caused . . .

From the start, I say to Herodotus.

Things are always beginning, beginning again and again. We have no say on beginnings. The start is a choice, where one pushes play. An enactment on time. *Start*.

The cellist starts. The library's air-conditioning is kindling air.

I close my lonesome eyes. I really listen. The words go back to where they came from. You think you have it, the way it all fits together, from poems to mountaintops, it is five volumes long and called *Kosmos*, and then a madman named Darwin appears . . .

"Okay, Eason, you ready?"

"Hell no, I'm not ready."

"We're recording."

"What should I talk about?"

"Whatever. Remember?"

"Who's gonna listen to this?"

"Probably nobody."

"Good."

"And get that nice new cello of yours ready because you're gonna play, too. Ready?"

"Sure."

"OK, you can start—no, wait, let me time-stamp it. This is Severino del Toro, recording on the fourth floor of the Harold Washington Library in Chicago, Illinois, time and date: 4:57 P.M., Friday, January 12th, 2013. The speaker is Eason Wallace, age seventeen. OK, go ahead."

ACKNOWLEDGMENTS

Thank you: Linda Swanson-Davies and Susan Burmeister-Brown for publishing my first story. Marya Spence and Clare Mao for reading and redirecting this novel and finding it a home. Danny Vazquez for clarifying the story and bringing it to the world along with everyone else at Astra. For being an extraordinary copyeditor, Rachel Broderick. The Michener-Copernicus Society of America and Sally Lincoln and Dudley Davis at Beth's House for material support. Pablo Tinajero. Matt Iaculla. Rosemary Samuels. David Soto and Zack Lazar. Matti Hautala. Austin Mobley. Chanda Grubbs, who was there the first day of the planet and read three versions of this novel and never gave up on it or me. Frank Leonardo. Jamie Rasmussen. Samir Bakhshi, Sandy Guttman, Brady Myers, and Barry O'Keefe. My mishpocha, the Dexheimer-Chotzinoffs. St. James Alan McPherson and the Keokuk Social Club: Marcus Burke, Nick Butler, Jessica Dwelle, CJG, Christina Kaminski, Kannan Mahadaven, and Scott Smith. My fellow and former faculty members at school and our incredible students and their families. My ASF family, Adeena Reitberger, Rebecca Markovits, Nate Brown, and Erin McReynolds. Michael Noll, Bethany Hegadus, and Claire Campbell. For her mentorship and guidance and poetry, Monica Berlin. For his mentorship and exemplary life as a teaching artist, Robin Metz—we miss you. For introducing me to art history and critical theory, Greg Gilbert. And to Michelle Huneven, who took seriously a young man who was desperately unserious, you were Iowa to me. Sam Chang, Deb West, and Connie Brothers and everyone at the IWW. Ma, Dad, Al, Tithi, Steve, Stephanie, Grandma, Dad the dad, Itty Bitty Mims, cousin Kat, Martin, Ashley, George, Tilden, Tithi Berdna, Tío Aurelio, Carlos, Ivan, Marilin, and Christian. My constant companion, Napoleon the cat. And Robin Grace, who reads every word and lives more stories than I can write. I love you.

PHOTO BY KELLY WEST

ABOUT THE AUTHOR

Adam Soto is a co-web editor at *American Short Fiction*. He holds an MFA from the Iowa Writers' Workshop and is a former Michener-Copernicus Foundation Fellow. He lives with his wife in Austin, Texas, where he is a teacher and a musician. *This Weightless World* is his first novel.